# NOBODY'S PRINCESS

# NOBODY'S PRINCESS

⊰◦➤ ᴄ◎ ◎ᴅ ⊰◦➤

## ESTHER FRIESNER

RANDOM HOUSE 🏠 NEW YORK

Copyright © 2007 by Esther Friesner
Jacket art copyright © 2007 by Larry Rostant

Library of Congress Cataloging-in-Publication Data
Friesner, Esther M.
Nobody's princess / Esther Friesner.
p.   cm.
SUMMARY: Determined to fend for herself in a world where only men have real freedom, headstrong Helen, who will be called queen of Sparta and Helen of Troy one day, learns to fight, hunt, and ride horses while disguised as a boy, and goes on an adventure throughout the Mediterranean world.
ISBN 978-0-375-87528-1 (trade) — ISBN 978-0-375-97528-8 (lib. bdg.) — ISBN 978-0-375-87529-8 (pbk.) — ISBN 978-0-375-87530-4 (mass-market pbk.)
I. Helen of Troy (Greek mythology)—Juvenile fiction. [I. Helen of Troy (Greek mythology)—Fiction. 2. Sex role—Fiction. 3. Adventure and adventurers—Fiction. 4. Mythology, Greek—Fiction. 5. Mediterranean Region—History—To 476—Fiction.] I. Title.
PZ7.F91662Nob 2007
[Fic]—dc22
2006006515

Printed in the United States of America

10  9  8  7  6  5  4  3  2  I
First Edition

*This book is dedicated to the memory of*
*Elissa Nicole Sullivan.*
*Through her life, she gave an eternal gift of love,*
*Through her art, an enduring legacy of beauty.*

# ACKNOWLEDGMENTS

I owe thanks to many people for their part in
helping make this book a reality.
To Tamora Pierce and Josepha Sherman, whose
*Young Warriors* anthology gave Helen her start.
To Elizabeth Moon, whose knowledge of all
things equine gave Helen the reins.
To my editor, Mallory Loehr, and my agent,
Russell Galen, whose ongoing support and
assistance have been invaluable.
Thank you all so much!

# CONTENTS

# PROLOGUE

When I was four years old, my father, King Tyndareus of Sparta, dedicated a shrine to his favorite goddess, Aphrodite. He ordered it built on one of the rooftops of our palace because he said the queen of love and beauty was worshipped best under the beauty of an open sky. You could reach the holy place only by climbing an outside stairway, each step covered with painted tiles that told stories from the life of the goddess.

Most of the gods were born in the usual way, but not Aphrodite. She was never a baby, never a child, and she never had to put up with any of the problems of growing up. The goddess was born full-grown from the waves of the Middle Sea when the god Kronos spilled the blood of his father, Uranus, over the sea foam. I never did understand why *bloodshed* would give birth to a goddess of love and beauty, but that's the way I was told it happened: Aphrodite sprang to life out of the waves, and as soon as the world saw her, every living thing fell in love with her beauty. The winds themselves fought for the honor of carrying her to shore.

Now *that* I could understand. It was the part of the story I liked best. Even as a very young child I thought it would be a wonderful thing to be able to fly over the waves, free as a seabird, seeing new lands and having grand adventures. I didn't care if I grew up to be as beautiful as the goddess, as long as I could be just as free.

The shrine itself was a simple thing: A wooden ark sheltered the painted clay image of the goddess, an image as big as a two-year-old child. I was playing in the shadow of my father's throne on the day he received it from the Cretan artist who also made the tiles to adorn the stairs. At first I thought it was a wonderful doll and that it would be mine. I ran forward, threw my arms around Aphrodite's neck, and gave her such an enthusiastic kiss that my lips marked the paint on her cheek.

I didn't think I was doing anything wrong, and so I was confused when I looked up and saw expressions of shock on the faces of almost every grown-up around me. Some of them were whispering to each other and scowling at me. I began to feel afraid, until I heard my father laugh and say, "The child is wiser than all of us. My little Helen has hit on the perfect tribute for Aphrodite! What better welcome for the goddess of love than a kiss?" And he ordered the servants to make me a new dress for the dedication ceremony in three days' time.

On the dedication day, my nurse, Ione, held me and my twin sister, Clytemnestra, by the hands as we watched our father and mother perform the welcoming rites for the goddess. Our brothers, the twins Castor and Polydeuces, were nine years old, so they were given the honor of holding the garlands of fragrant springtime flowers that the king and queen would place at Aphrodite's feet. The boys didn't seem to be enjoying the privilege. The two of them fidgeted as if they'd caught fleas from one of Father's hunting hounds.

Though my parents and we royal children were the only ones entitled to come before the goddess in her new home, the nearby rooftops were crowded with the nobles of Sparta, all of them eager to have a good view. How splendid the men looked with their long hair curled and oiled, the women in their finest gowns, their blue and scarlet tiered skirts jingling with gold charms! The sunlight was striped with the rising smoke of precious incense brought from across the Middle Sea. The melody of flutes and Egyptian harps over the beat of little hand drums filled the air.

The music made me want to dance, so I did, pulling my hand out of Ione's grasp. She smiled. "What a clever child, wanting to offer the goddess such a lovely dance as a gift! But not just yet, dear one. This isn't the right time; you're interrupting the dedication ceremony. Wait until it's finished, like a good girl."

As Ione gently took my hand again, my parents called out to welcome Aphrodite-of-the-Foam. They were dressed in their finest robes and their best jewels, all to pay reverence to the queen of love and beauty. The image of the goddess was a marvel, but that day I saw something that I thought was even more marvelous.

"Look, Ione!" I cried. "Isn't she beautiful?"

"Hush, child," Ione said. "Everyone knows that the goddess is—"

"*Not* the goddess—*her.*" I pointed at my mother, Leda, with my free hand. "Mama. She's *much* more beautiful than the goddess." My voice carried loud and clear across the rooftop.

I no sooner spoke my mind for all to hear than the air cracked with the sound of Ione slapping my face. I was stunned. She'd never raised her hand to me until that moment. I hadn't known that the same hand that stroked my hair or tenderly touched my brow when I was sick could hurt so much. Before I could cry out, she swept me off my feet and whisked me away from the ceremonies. Poor Clytemnestra was left behind.

Our nurse had been a farmer's wife, but the other servants whispered that ever since she'd been brought to the royal palace, she acted as if she'd been born there. Maybe so, but she didn't act at all regal or haughty as she raced down the tower steps, carrying me over one shoulder like a bundle of old clothes. She didn't slow down until we reached the deserted central courtyard of the palace, where flowers bloomed around a white stone well. Here she set me on my feet and shook me roughly by the shoulders.

"Are you crazy? To say such things where the goddess can hear you!" she hissed in my face. "You'll bring a curse down on all of us."

My cheek hurt, but that didn't bother me as much as the feeling of having the ground yanked out from under me. I was totally bewildered. Ione hadn't acted like this when my dancing interrupted the welcoming rites for Aphrodite. Why had a few words turned everything upside down? One moment she'd been praising me, smiling at me. Now her smile was gone, vanished behind a mask of anger and fear.

*Ione's afraid because of something I said?* I gazed at her, astonished. She looked even more terrified than when Zeus made the sky blaze and roar with wild thunderstorms. I'd never imagined that I had that kind of power over grown-ups. *They* were always the ones who could do whatever they wanted, make all the choices, all the decisions about their lives and mine. Up until that moment, if someone had asked me the difference between gods and grown-ups, I'd have said, *What difference?*

Suddenly, it wasn't so. *Something I said made a grown-up afraid? I can do that?* What a wonderful, terrible, dangerous thing for a little girl to learn!

"No one is more beautiful than a goddess!" Ione told me urgently. Her face was stiff with fear. "No one, man or woman, is the equal of the gods. If they hear anyone even *hinting* that an ordinary person outshines the immortals, dreadful things happen! Do you want your mother to *die* because you said something stupid?"

I stared Ione in the face and stood up tall, the way I'd just seen my mother do when she called on Aphrodite. "Aphrodite wouldn't do anything so mean," I said, very sure of myself. "Mama and Papa just gave the goddess lots and lots of beautiful presents and a nice, new place to stay here with us. *That* means they're her hosts, and you taught me that guests and hosts mustn't hurt each other, not *ever*. Do you think the goddess would do something so *wrong*, Ione?"

"Oh, child, what's going to become of you if you keep saying such things? The gods don't have to worry about what's right and wrong for mortals!" she exclaimed.

"Can't they do *anything* wrong?" I asked.

"I—I don't know—I don't think so." My nurse squirmed as if her own words were giving her a belly-ache.

"Why not?" I asked.

"Because—because they can do anything they like. They're the gods." She acted as if that explained everything.

"Then why should we give them presents if it won't make them nicer to us?" I wanted to know. "They're only going to do whatever they want anyway."

I waited patiently for my nurse's answer, but the poor woman just stood there with her mouth hanging open. At last I said, "I think you're wrong about the gods, Ione. They're *much* nicer than you say, especially Aphrodite. She has to be nice. She's the goddess of love! She'd never hurt Mama, no matter *what* I say, because Mama's the queen and she gives the best presents, and if anything happens to her, no more presents for Aphrodite, right? And the goddess doesn't want *that*. Now do you understand?"

Satisfied, I gave my still-bewildered nurse a big kiss on the cheek and marched straight back up the stairs to the shrine. I heard her come scrambling after me, but I didn't feel the need to turn around to be sure she was there. Even if I was still too young to have explored every part of our big, rambling palace, I knew that I wouldn't get lost, because now Aphrodite was with me. I was convinced that I'd pleased her with my kiss, and my dance, and the way I'd defended her to Ione. I imagined that I could feel her hands on my shoulders, helping me up the stairs. Just believing that she was near, watching over me, lifted up my heart and filled it with happiness.

The sun beat brightly on the tiles when I came back out onto the rooftop, and the wind carried the scent of mountain pine. The musicians were playing something light and joyous, and everyone smiled when I stood in the presence of the goddess and once more began to dance.

# PART 1
# SPARTA

# 1

# A SACRIFICE
# TO ARTEMIS

I grew up with the gods all around me. When the dawn came, it was because the goddess Eos brought it. The sun was Apollo's chariot, and the crescent moon was the hunting bow of his sister, Artemis. Every river had its god, and so did each of the winds that blew from north, south, east, and west.

Ione was the first person to teach me about Zeus, king of all the gods; his queen, Hera, who blessed marriages; his brother Poseidon, who was master of the great ocean; and his other brother, Hades, who lived deep under the earth and ruled the dead. But most of her stories were about Demeter, the goddess who gave us bountiful harvests. That was understandable. Ione was a farmer's wife.

Even though we were supposed to revere all of

the gods equally, most people honored some gods more than others. Why would a fisherman bother making a sacrifice to Hephaestus the armorer, god of the forge, when he could be praying to Poseidon for smooth seas and full nets? Why would a metalworker waste time worshipping Poseidon when he could be asking for Hephaestus's blessing?

Everyone did it, including me. Ever since the dedication of the rooftop shrine, Aphrodite was my favorite. When I was five, I made a little clay image of her and set it on a table in the room I shared with my sister. When Clytemnestra saw it, she sniffed. "What's *that* supposed to be?"

"Aphrodite," I told her.

"It can't be Aphrodite. It's *ugly.*" She sounded pleased with herself. "Throw it away."

"It is *not* ugly!" I cried, reaching out protectively for my little goddess. Unfortunately, I moved too quickly. Instead of cupping the image safely between my palms, I knocked it off the table and sent it tumbling to the floor. The unbaked clay shattered to bits and I burst into tears.

"You're such a baby, Helen," Clytemnestra said. "Why are you crying over *that* ugly thing? If you want a real Aphrodite, just tell Papa. He'll get you a *good* one."

But I still cried, because I didn't want an image of the goddess that someone else had made. I wanted a statue that was *my* goddess. The next day, I made another Aphrodite and hid it in the bottom of my clothes chest, safe from my sister's sneers.

By the time I turned seven, I'd learned that Ione had been partly right about the gods. They weren't all as kind as Aphrodite. Just as some people liked one god more than another, some of us *didn't* like certain gods at all.

My father, Tyndareus, didn't like Artemis, goddess of the moon in heaven, the hunt on earth, and the dark powers of magic from the underworld. I first heard him speak against her during a great banquet that took place ten days before the feast of the huntress. This was a yearly festival when my mother, Queen Leda, led a procession of maidens to the temple of Artemis and offered up the sacrifice while they danced and sang for the goddess. It was the one shrine in all Sparta where the queen worshipped alone and the king never set foot.

The banquet was being given to honor a group of very important guests, envoys from the island kingdom of Ithaka. I sat beside my mother and heard her tell one of our guests about the coming celebration.

"No men? Really?" the guest replied. "Well, if that's what pleases Artemis, I suppose you don't have any choice."

Even I could tell that he was just making polite conversation. He didn't really care about the goddess.

My father *did* care, very much, in his own way. "Oh yes, we must give Artemis exactly what she wants," he said. He was smiling, acting as if he was joking, but there was something serious under the light words. "She'll show us no mercy if we don't. If you ask me, she doesn't know the meaning of forgiveness."

"What makes you say that, Lord Tyndareus?" one of the guests asked.

"Oh, the proof's there, in the stories. Take the tale of the nymph Callisto, for instance. Now, if a goddess chooses to remain a virgin, like Artemis and Athena, I can't complain about that. I have nothing against virgins." He paused and winked at the other grown-ups at the banquet. Most of them laughed, including my mother; I had no idea why. "And if Artemis wants the nymphs who hunt with her to be virgins as well, fine. That's her choice too. But nymphs are beautiful, and the gods love beauty. The gods are also used to taking what they want, even when what they want says *no*. What chance does a nymph have against a god? Artemis adored Callisto until Zeus forced her to be his lover and left her with child. It wasn't Callisto's fault, but did the goddess care? Did she accept the fact that the nymph was Zeus's helpless victim? No, she just punished her by turning her into a bear! And *that* is why I leave other people to make sacrifices to Artemis, because I have kinder goddesses to honor."

"Lord Tyndareus, be careful of what you say!" The icy words rang out through the great hall. The man who dared to admonish my father in his own palace was one of the Ithakan envoys, a terribly serious stick of a man, young in years but old and bitter in spirit. I'd never seen anyone with such a vinegary face. I thought that if he'd ever smile, he'd crack his jaw. I'd seen how his heavy brows drew into a scowl while my father was talking about Artemis, how his mouth became small as an olive pit until at last it burst open with angry words. "The lady Artemis will not be insulted, not even by kings! She demands payment for all offenses, and no one has the power to refuse her."

"You mean that she'll take revenge on me? That would only prove my point." My father chuckled. He made it clear that he was joking, teasing that pompous creature. Everyone else laughed with him.

"Wait," the man said ominously. "Wait and see what comes of your sacrilege. The huntress's arrows never miss their target. Remember Niobe!"

My father stopped laughing. He stood up suddenly, his face dark as a thunderhead, and jabbed one finger at the Ithakan. "You *dare* to talk to me of sacrilege? In my own house, at my own table? You speak Niobe's name in the presence of my *children*? The sacred bond between host and guest is all that's keeping me from snapping your neck right now! Get out of my sight."

The Ithakan opened his mouth, but one look at the king's face was enough for him to seal his lips and rush out of the hall. Even though the road from Sparta to Ithaka was long and dangerous, he didn't wait for his fellow envoys. He was gone by next morning.

The day after the rest of the Ithakan envoys left us, I asked my father why he'd been so angry. He wouldn't tell me, but when I went to my mother's room with the same question, she gave me my answer. "Niobe of Thebes was a great queen but a foolish woman. She mocked Leto, mother of Artemis and Apollo, because the goddess had only two children while she had seven sons and seven daughters." My mother picked me up and held me close, as if I were still a baby. "For her offense, the divine twins slaughtered all her children in a single day. Their arrows cut them down, every one, even when the queen threw herself across the body of her youngest child and begged Artemis and Apollo to take her life instead. There was no mercy, and when Niobe's children all lay dead, there was no end to her weeping. The gods finally took pity on her and turned her to stone, but her tears for her children still stream down the face of the rock."

I began to shake. My mother was shaking too. "Don't be afraid, dear one," she said, giving me a tight squeeze. "I know it's a terrible story, but you mustn't worry. Artemis won't touch you or Clytemnestra or the boys. Even though your father won't worship her, I do. You're safe." With that, she gave me a kiss and told me to go back to my nurse.

I refused. I faced my mother and declared, "That's not fair! Father's right, Artemis *is* cruel. It's bad enough that she and her brother punished Niobe for one mistake, but then they made it worse. They had to turn her into a *lesson.* It's not even a *good* lesson! If they really wanted Niobe to learn from what she'd done, they could have brought her children back to life and said, 'Now do you see what can happen if you're too proud?' I bet she'd never have been proud again after that, because she'd want her children to live."

"And I don't want to risk your life even once," Mother said, laying her fingers to my lips to hush me. "Don't anger the gods, Helen."

"You want me to be afraid of them," I said.

"I want you to *respect* them," Mother corrected me.

"I thought I was supposed to love them."

Mother gave me one of her gentle smiles. "Can't you do both, my darling? You know you're supposed to respect Papa and me, but you love us too, don't you?"

I admitted this was true. "But not because I'm scared of what you'll do to me if I *don't,*" I pointed out. "And that's why I'm never going to love Artemis, *ever.* Just like Papa!"

Mother sighed. "I respect the moon goddess, but I must admit, I don't . . . feel as fond of her as I do of some of the other goddesses. Still, there are some things that we must do, whether we like them or not. That's true for queens as well as other women; remember that, Helen. I don't think Artemis cares if we love her, as long as we worship her in the proper way. I hope that you and Clytemnestra will be good girls when you come with me to the huntress's shrine for the festival."

I made a face. "I don't like Artemis and I'm not going."

"We'll see," said Mother.

I knew what *that* meant.

My mother dragged me to the festival along with Clytemnestra and the other girls. I sulked through the whole thing, unlike my twin.

Clytemnestra and I were born together, but everyone said we didn't look alike—aside from both of us having the same thick, long black hair as our mother—and we certainly didn't act alike. The more I turned my back on the rituals that Mother and the old temple priestess were performing for the goddess, the more Clytemnestra behaved like Artemis's most devoted worshipper. She copied our mother's every gesture at the altar, and when the priestess nodded approvingly and some of the women began to murmur words of praise for her piety, she began to invent worshipful gestures of her own. Pretty soon she was raising and lowering her arms to the image of Artemis so vigorously that Mother finally intervened.

"That's enough, dear," she said. "I know you want to honor Artemis, but you look like a goose trying to fly."

Clytemnestra stuck out her lower lip and glared. "You wouldn't say that to *Helen*," she whined. "*She* does everything *right*."

"Nonsense. She hasn't done anything at all," Mother replied briskly, returning her attention to the altar.

My sister gave me a nasty look and started to stick out her tongue but quickly thought better of it and clamped her mouth shut. She smirked for just an instant, then walked to the altar and tugged at Mother's skirt.

"Mama?" she asked in her sweetest voice. "Mama, can *I* make an offering to Artemis? All by myself, to show the goddess how much I love her? *Please?*"

Once again the other women witnessing the rites began to speak softly about what a *good* girl Clytemnestra was. My sister's gloating smile grew wider and wider with every compliment she overheard until I thought she was going to burst with glee.

But she didn't burst. She was squashed.

"What a wonderful idea, Clytemnestra!" Mother exclaimed. "I think that you *and* Helen should do it together." She meant well, but her words were like a dipper full of cold water flung in my sister's face.

"*Her?* Why her? It was *my* idea!" Clytemnestra objected strenuously.

"Me?" I was just as angry as she was. "Do I *have* to?"

Mother's suddenly stern face was all the answer either one of us received. Without speaking a word, she let us know that we would behave like Spartan princesses or we'd suffer the consequences at the hands of Sparta's queen.

Mother could make me sacrifice a few crumbs of incense to Artemis, but she couldn't make me do it *right*. After my sister dropped her pinch of incense onto the coals and stepped away from the altar, it was my turn. Expressionless, I held my chubby hand over the brazier, opened my clenched fingers, and then . . . I missed. I'd held the pinch of incense very carefully, and then at the last instant I threw it away. The old priestess gave a little gasp as the costly crumb of sweet-smelling tree gum fell to the ground and tumbled down the temple steps, but neither she nor my mother nor the dancing maidens made any move to fetch it back.

"Oh, Helen, you clumsy thing!" Clytemnestra shoved me aside and ran down the steps so fast that she tripped, fell, and scraped her nose. She yelped with pain.

I was down the steps in an instant. "You're bleeding!" I cried, helping her get back onto her feet. "Does it hurt a lot? Do you want some water or—?"

"Leave me alone." Clytemnestra jerked away from me. "I don't want anything from *you*." She swallowed her tears and dashed back up to the altar, my cast-off incense clenched in her fist. She dropped it into the smoldering flames quickly, then turned her scraped, triumphant face to Mother and the priestess and waited to be praised.

*"What have you done?"* The old priestess's squawk of outrage shocked my sister back to the brink of tears.

"I . . . I only . . . ," she began, trembling. "Helen dropped the offering, so I—"

"Clytemnestra, what were you thinking?" Mother stepped between my sister and the fuming priestess, her voice unnaturally shrill. "I taught you girls the *proper* way to serve Artemis! Weren't you listening? Didn't you know that if an offering touches the ground, it's no longer fit for the goddess?"

"I'm not the one who dropped it!" Clytemnestra protested, tears streaming down her face. "Helen did that! Why aren't you yelling at her?"

"Because Helen isn't behaving like an infant!" Mother was so rattled by the scene we were making in front of the priestess, the maidens, the other women, and Artemis herself that she continued to scold my sister even when her words made no sense.

"But she *did!*" Clytemnestra stamped her foot. "She threw the offering away on purpose! She—"

"Not another word out of you, Clytemnestra," Mother decreed. "Not *one.*" She called for Ione and commanded her to take my shamed and sobbing sister away. Sometimes even the best parents can be as closed-minded and unreasonable as the gods.

Afterward, as we were returning to the palace citadel, Clytemnestra turned her red-eyed, runny-nosed face to me and said, "It's not fair! *You* do something wrong and Mama yells at *me!* Just because you're pretty, you get away with *everything.* I hate you!" Then she tried to slap me, so I pulled her hair, and poor Ione had to get four other servants to pull us apart and cart us off to separate rooms.

They put me in a storeroom where my father's tallymen kept the bales of sheepskins that were part of the tax payments from our people. I climbed onto a thick pile of fleeces, lay down in comfort, and stared at the ceiling, thinking about what had happened. No matter what else I thought of my sister, she was right: I *had* done something bad at the temple, but I *hadn't* been punished for it. And even when I did earn punishment for fighting with Clytemnestra, how bad was it? I was more comfortable on those fleeces than in my own bed. Was I just lucky, or was Clytemnestra right? Did things go more easily for me because I was *pretty?*

I'd never thought about it before, even though I'd

heard many people say, *What a pretty girl!* when they saw me. It happened whenever guests came to the palace. As soon as our parents presented the four of us to their visitors, the newcomers would praise how big and strong and handsome my brothers were. That made me giggle. Couldn't they see that Castor was a little cross-eyed and that Polydeuces never took his finger out of his nose except to eat? As for my sister, our guests called her things like *charming,* or *sweet,* or *delightful,* but I—

I was *pretty.* It never failed. One man even said that I was *beautiful,* until his fellow envoy was very quick to say that no one could be beautiful in the palace of Tyndareus except his queen.

*Pretty.* What did that mean, really? And was I? I had no way of knowing. I'd caught sight of my reflection in pools of water from time to time, but the image was dark and unclear. I wanted better. My mother owned a mirror that had come all the way from Egypt, but up until that moment I'd never understood why she spent so much time looking into it. I decided that as soon as my punishment was over, I'd sneak into my parents' sleeping chamber and see what *pretty* looked like.

The sun was halfway down the western sky by the time one of our house slaves let me out of the storeroom. She was a grouchy old thing who didn't like to waste time talking. When I asked her where my nurse was, she snapped, "How would I know?" before gathering up an armful of fleeces and waddling off.

I was thrilled! If Ione was busy elsewhere, it meant I had the chance to run to my parents' room and satisfy my curiosity right away. I stole through the corridors of the palace as fast as I could go without drawing attention. Silently I prayed: *O Aphrodite, please let me find Mama's mirror, and see what I want to see, and get away before anyone catches me!* Who better than the goddess of beauty to help me find out exactly what *pretty* meant?

Aphrodite heard my prayers. I didn't run into anyone on my way to my parents' room, the room itself was deserted, and Mother's mirror was lying out in plain sight on a little table, just waiting for me to snatch it up and stare at my reflection. I was still muttering a hasty *thank you* to the goddess when I heard, "Helen! What do you think you're doing?" It was my mother. She'd come into the room and stolen up behind me so silently that the unexpected sound of her voice made me jump half out of my skin. I gave a little yip of shock and dropped the mirror. The loud *clang* it made when it hit the painted tiles shook my bones.

"Oh dear." Mother bent to pick up the mirror while I stood there shamefaced. "It's all scratched and dented. I'm going to look like I've caught the pox. I suppose it's partly my fault for creeping up on you like that. I was a skilled huntress when I was a girl back in Calydon. You have to walk like a shadow when you're tracking deer." She shook her head over the damaged mirror, but she was smiling. "Sweet one, why are you meddling with my things?"

I clasped my hands behind my back and looked away. "I—I wanted to see what I look like."

"*That* much I could figure out," she said dryly. "But why now? Seven is much too young to start worrying about if you're pretty enough to attract a good husband."

"A what?" My head came up sharply. I stared at my mother as if she'd lost her mind. "I don't care if I'm pretty *enough* to get a husband! I don't *want* a husband. When you get married, you have to go away from home. I don't want to leave you or Father, not *ever*."

My mother laughed. She laughed so hard that she had to sit down on a carved folding stool. How *could* she? Didn't she see how upset I was by the idea of having to marry and leave everything I really loved?

When my mother finally caught her breath, she swept me onto her lap and kissed me. "Oh, my precious little girl! Where *do* you get your ideas? First of all, you *will* want a husband one day; that I promise you. But you needn't be afraid of leaving Sparta. You will stay here. It's your sister who'll have to leave when she marries. The two of you shared one birth, but you were the first one to see the light. The midwife tied a red thread around your wrist the instant you were born so that there'd be no mistakes made about your claim to the throne later on. You're older than Clytemnestra by just enough to make you queen of your father's land when the time comes."

"Me?" It was the first I'd heard of *this*.

My mother kissed me again. "Yes, *you*. Why are you so surprised? Has no one told you? Not even Ione?"

I shook my head. "I thought—I thought that Castor and Polydeuces would be the kings of Sparta when they grew up."

"Ah!" My mother nodded. "Well, I can understand why you'd reach that conclusion. You're too young to know that this land has always been ruled by queens. The only time a king rules is when his mother has no daughters. That's why Tyndareus is king but why your brothers won't be."

"Oh." I looked down at my hands, clasped quietly in my lap. I had come stealing into my parents' bedchamber just to see my face, and all at once I was staring at my future. Queen of Sparta! "Will Castor and Polydeuces mind that they're not kings and I'm queen?" I asked, suddenly feeling very sorry for my brothers.

My mother brushed away my fears like summer flies. "Castor and Polydeuces will be fine. They might not be the next kings of Sparta, but they'll have no trouble making great names for themselves in this world. I have faith in my boys. And don't you worry, my dearest one: Whether or not you're their queen, they'll always love you. How could anyone not love you, little Helen? You're such a beautiful child."

So there we were again. I could claim a kingdom, cause a scene at a shrine, refuse to sacrifice to a goddess, and get away with it all. My life would always be easy and pleasant because no matter what I did, everything would be forgiven, forgotten, laughed away because I was pretty. No, I was better than pretty. I was *beautiful.*

I had no reason to doubt that this was true.

I got off my mother's lap and picked up the mirror again. The face that looked back was certainly different from Clytemnestra's. The cheeks were rosier, the chin more rounded, the lips fuller and more clearly shaped, the teeth brighter when I smiled. Our hair was the same color, but mine was shinier, and my eyes were the deep, striking blue of ripe grapes, while hers were ordinary brown. Did all of those small differences add up to beauty? I frowned at my reflection, puzzled. Though it was the first time I'd seen my face so clearly—even a dented mirror shows you a better image than a pool of water—I felt as if I'd seen such a face somewhere else.

Then it hit me—my brother Polydeuces! My face

was a younger, softer version of his. Even our hair was the same in style as well as color, since in Sparta the nobly born men as well as the women wore their hair in long curls as far down their backs as it would grow. Polydeuces and I looked remarkably similar, but no one ever called *him* beautiful.

It was all very confusing. I needed to think about it. Very solemnly, I gave the mirror back to my mother and went to my own room.

Ione was there, spreading a new blanket on my bed. It was dyed the color of ripe barley, and one of my mother's maids had embroidered the corners with bunches of red grapes. There was no fine new blanket for Clytemnestra's bed. The way I saw it, I'd received this new gift as one more reward for being beautiful. I wondered if Polydeuces would be getting a new blanket too.

"What have you been up to?" Ione said, frowning. "Your sister is in the courtyard, working with her spindle. She was starting on her third skein of yarn when I left her. Go get yours and—"

"Ione," I cut in. "Why am I so much prettier than Clytemnestra?"

My nurse gaped at me. "My poor little lamb, has the sun cooked your brains? What a thing to say!"

"I'm serious," I insisted. "I know I'm prettier than she is. I'm beautiful. The queen herself said so. And it's all right for me to say it too, because I'm going to be queen myself someday. I just want to know *why* I'm prettier than she is, that's all."

"*There's* a fine question," Ione snorted. "I thank the gods that I'll be dead long before you rule this land, if that's a sample of your wisdom, O Queen."

"Don't make fun of me!" I cried. My head was still full of the new, dizzying awareness of power, the power of being beautiful. Even my sister said I was treated better than she was because of it. Yet here was Ione—Ione who always gave me my favorite foods, who made me dolls, who adorned my new clothes with embroidery and mended my old ones with care, who watched over me when I was sick—here she was, defying me! Teasing me! Was she blind? Didn't she understand that I deserved to be treated better than anyone else because I was beautiful? It was infuriating.

"Ione, if you don't answer my question I'll— I'll—" I tried to think of something to say that would make this stubborn grown-up take me seriously. Then I remembered what Father's palace manager always said to bring contrary slaves and servants back into line. If it worked for him—

"—I'll have you whipped!"

"I live in mortal terror of your wrath," Ione said, her face unreadable. "Far be it from *me* to keep you from learning the truth. You're more beautiful than your sister or any woman alive because you're not the daughter of a mere mortal like Lord Tyndareus. You must be the child of a god, of Zeus himself, master of the thunderbolt. There, is *that* good enough for you?"

"You are still making fun of me!" I shouted. "I *will* have you punished for that!"

"By all means, *try*, O Queen," she said, with a wry smile. "But first I'm going to show you a great marvel, in honor of your true father." Without warning she grabbed me by the belt of my tunic, sat down on my bed, hauled me across her knees, and declared: "I'm going to make it rain."

# A GIRL'S PLACE

She *spanked* me! It didn't hurt all that much, but the humiliation was horrible. Ione loved me, cared for me, looked after me when Mother was busy, and yet she'd done *that* to me? I loved her with all my heart, but after she finished my punishment and left me alone with my thoughts, those thoughts were murderous. How *dare* she? I cried out my indignation facedown on my bed.

"Helen? Are you all right?" My brother Polydeuces stuck his head around one side of the doorway and peered into my room. "Some of the slaves heard you howling, so they raised an alarm. By the time things quieted down again, Ione was explaining to Mother why she spanked you."

"What did Mama do to *her* when she found out?"

I asked eagerly. I was still smarting with embarrassment, and I wanted Ione to suffer for it too, just a little.

"Nothing," Polydeuces replied. "Mother was surprised when Ione told her she'd never spanked you before, that's all."

I groaned and buried my face in my arms. I felt the bed sag as my brother sat down beside me and patted me on the back in sympathy.

"Don't cry, Helen," he said. "It's happened to all of us. Well, not to Clytemnestra. She's *perfect*." I looked up in time to see his lips curl. "Perfect at not getting caught."

"I'm not crying," I said. "I'm mad. She spanked me for *no reason*. I didn't do anything wrong."

"That happens a lot," Polydeuces said. Was that a snicker? "So, what set her off?"

"Nothing," I maintained. And I told him exactly what had happened between Ione and me so he'd understand the vastness of the injustice I'd suffered.

When I was done, he was silent. Then he let out a long, slow whistle and said, "You threatened her with a *whipping*? Little sister, when Ione comes back, you'd better get down on your knees and thank her for not telling Mother about that."

"Why should I thank her for anything?" I grumped.

"Because if Mother ever hears that you showed Ione that much disrespect, she'll spank you herself."

"Oh." I propped myself up on my elbows and leaned my chin on my hands. Now that the first shock of my punishment had faded, I realized what a little monster I'd been to my devoted nurse. What was the point of being beautiful if my actions were ugly and mean?

I looked earnestly at my brother. "Am I pretty, Polydeuces?"

"Huh? Where did that come from?" he asked, taken by surprise.

"Lots of people say I am, even Mama. Clytemnestra says I get treated better because of it, but it didn't seem to make any difference to Ione. She spanked me anyway, and she's slapped me, and—"

"Ione changed your dirty diapers. How pretty were you then?" Polydeuces grinned. "She loves you, Helen, and she doesn't want you to grow up vain and spoiled, believing you can do or say whatever you like just because you're pretty. Even if you were as beautiful as Aphrodite, you still wouldn't get everything your own way."

"I don't *want* to get everything my own way," I told him. "I just want—I want—"

What *did* I want? I'd never thought about it before. I knew that I hadn't wanted to worship Artemis, but Mother made me go to the temple anyway. I'd told her that I wouldn't want a husband, not ever, but she'd acted like I couldn't decide such things for myself.

Polydeuces was gazing at me, waiting for me to finish my sentence. If I said, *I just want to be free,* would he know what I really meant? Or would he say, *You're already free, silly. You're not a slave, right?*

I wasn't a slave, but as much as I hated carding and spinning and weaving wool, Ione and Mother forced me to spend day after day learning how to do it. What they said was: "This is what all women do, even queens," but what I heard was: *This is all that women can do, and even queens have no choice about it.* Was that being free?

Clytemnestra wasn't a slave, but when she was old enough she'd be married off and sent away to live with her husband. Would she get to choose him, or would she simply be told, *This is the man you're going to marry,* the same way that Ione told us, *This is the dress you're going to wear today?* Was *that* being free?

I sat up. I knew what I wanted. "I just want to say yes or no about my own life," I said. "Always."

"You can *say* yes or no all you want right now, little sister. The trick is getting other people to pay attention." Polydeuces gave one of my curls a playful tug. "You're pretty . . . for a toad"—his smile said he was only joking—"but even Aphrodite herself has to obey Zeus's commands. Now, if she could get her hands on a bundle of his thunderbolts—well, if she *could,* not even Zeus would dare tell her what to do. Of course, that won't happen. Aphrodite's happy with the way things are. She'd rather sip nectar all day than have thunderbolt target practice make her hands rougher than mine."

Polydeuces held out his palms so that I could see the calluses. "That's from all the time I've spent learning to fight," he told me proudly. "Castor's hands aren't half as tough as mine—our teacher Glaucus said so. That reminds me—" He stood up. "I've got to go help Castor rewrap the hilts on our practice swords with rawhide. If we don't, Glaucus will knock them out of our hands tomorrow."

I grabbed his wrist as he started for the door. "If I help you rewrap your swords, will you let me hold one?" A new idea had taken fire in my mind, a fire kindled by my brother's light words about Aphrodite: *If she could get her hands on a bundle of his thunderbolts, not even Zeus would dare tell her what to do.* "Will you teach me how to use it too?" I persisted. "Please?"

Polydeuces stared at me as if I'd grown fins and scales. "Why would you want to do that? Swords are for warriors, not little girls."

"Why can't I be both?" I countered. "I'm just as old as you were when you and Castor first started learning how to fight."

"How hard *did* Ione spank you? I think she rattled your brains." Polydeuces shook his head and tried a second time to walk out of my room.

I ran after him, seized his arm with both hands, and refused to let him go. "Why *can't* I learn the same things you and Castor do?" I demanded. "Why can't you let me *try*?"

"I'll tell you what, little sister," Polydeuces replied, pulling his arm free. "You can learn from me just as soon as you can"—he took off like a rabbit, sprinting out of my room and down the hall, calling back over his shoulder—*"catch me!"*

I tried. I ran as fast as I could, even though I knew I'd be in a lot of fresh trouble if Ione came back to the room and found me gone. I didn't care. Suddenly I knew what I had to do if I was going to have the life I wanted for myself, a life in which *I* was the one who said yes or no, the one who made her own choices.

It was a useless race, one that I lost. Polydeuces had longer legs, and they weren't all tangled up in a dress. He'd also had a lot more practice running; it was part of his warrior's training, along with sword-play, spear-throwing, archery, horse-taming, and racing chariots over the worst terrain.

By the time I gave up trying to catch him and went trailing back to my room, I knew three things:

Even if I was pretty, it wasn't going to be enough to bring me the life I wanted: one where I was free to make choices that mattered, one where people listened to what I had to say.

Aphrodite had the beauty; Zeus had the thunderbolts. Everyone loved Aphrodite, but everyone *listened* to Zeus.

I'd never get my hands on a thunderbolt, so if I wanted to be free, I'd better find a way to get my hands on the next best thing: a sword.

Polydeuces said he'd teach me how to use a sword if I could run fast enough to catch him. I didn't really believe he meant that, but he did make me realize that one of the first things a warrior must know is how to *run*.

Not run *away*—a Spartan would sooner die— just run. Even I knew that a fighter needed strong legs as well as strong arms. When the poets performed in our great hall, I loved to hear them sing about how famous heroes outraced the wind to reach the thick of battle.

No one can run in a dress, so the first thing I did was "borrow" a short tunic from my brother Castor. If my brothers hadn't been too big for a nursemaid, Ione would have turned that shabby old thing into cleaning rags long ago. Castor didn't pay attention to how his clothes looked, or even to where his clothes were. I was thankful for that.

Once I had the tunic, I tied my hair back the way my brothers did when they had their lessons with Glaucus. They called it a "club," because that's what it looked like hanging down the nape of the neck after they'd twisted up the long, thick strands. I'd never had to do anything with my own hair—Ione always washed and combed it for me—so it took a lot of work until I managed to do it.

Then it was only a matter of waiting for a time when I knew Ione would be busy elsewhere in the palace long enough for me to slip away. I waited until one of our countless small household crises popped up—in a household the size of our palace, they always did—and I had my chance.

I pulled on the tunic, rubbed a little dirt on my face, then said a quick prayer to Aphrodite. *Great goddess, Ione says that love makes people see things that aren't really there. If anyone notices me today, please let them think they're seeing my brother Polydeuces.*

And then I ran. I ran without sandals, even though it hurt, because the songs said that was how real warriors ran. As I dashed out through the palace gates, I heard one of our guards call out behind me, "Good day to you, young prince! The gods bless you," and I thanked Aphrodite for having heard my prayer.

From that day on, I ran whenever I had the chance, and the years ran with me. The hardest part was getting away from Ione and from all the times I was supposed to be with my sister and the other women, turning fleece into thread, thread into cloth, cloth into clothing. Before, I'd only disliked those chores because they were so tedious. Now they were obstacles that kept me from doing what I really loved, and I hated them passionately. I ran my best whenever I imagined that every stride was putting more distance between me and the carding combs, the spindle, and the loom.

On my tenth birthday, I was running across a field not far from the palace when a hare broke from cover in front of me and took flight.

*You can learn from me just as soon as you can catch me!*

I don't know why I heard Polydeuces's long-ago taunt at that moment. I only knew that the gods themselves had thrown a challenge my way, and I meant to accept it. Without breaking stride, I veered sharply and ran after the hare. The wind tasted sweet as my shadow flew across the grass. The hare ran, he leaped, he zigzagged wildly, but I matched him every time, move for move, until at last he slowed his pace. That was when I paused, bent my knees, and with a mighty leap flung myself onto the creature.

A moment later the hare was racing off, un-harmed, and I was standing in the middle of the field holding a tuft of fur from his tail and shouting tri-umphantly at the sun, "*Got* you, Polydeuces!" Then I toppled backward into the meadow and watched the sky spin crazily above me as I gasped for breath and grinned.

When I recovered from my mad race, I felt ready

to take every last *You can't!* that the world wanted to throw at me and turn it into *Oh yes I can!*

It was time for me to learn how to do more than run.

I got back on my feet and looked across the field to a grove of olive trees, their silver-green leaves fluttering in the breeze. The palace citadel lay in that direction, and so did the narrow strip of open ground where Glaucus gave my brothers their daily training lessons.

If Polydeuces was so dead set against girls learning the ways of sword and spear, I was certain that his teacher would be even more unreasonable about sharing his lessons. Well, the hare hadn't wanted to give me the little tuft of fur that was now my prized trophy, but I'd still managed to take it. Why couldn't I do the same with those lessons?

I ran to the olive grove but took care to say a prayer to Athena before entering the trees. The goddess of wisdom created the olive tree so that we mortals would enjoy its gifts—especially the oil we used for everything from cooking, to protecting skin and hair, to filling the lamps that brightened our homes. The trees that grew near the citadel were kept sacred to her, their fruits never harvested except by her priests when they wanted oil to light her temple. I was sure that Athena would bless my plan to spy on Glaucus and my brothers, because she was a warrior herself, her images always wearing a helmet, carrying shield and spear.

I overestimated the goddess's kindness and I underestimated Glaucus. I thought I was well hidden, crouched behind one of the sacred olive trees, watching him coach my brothers as they fought one another with wooden swords. How was I to know that the old soldier still had eyesight that a hawk would envy? I didn't suspect a thing when he casually announced that he had to go pee and for them to keep up the good work. I was still spying on Castor and Polydeuces when he circled around the far side of the olive grove and swept down on me before I knew what was going on.

"What are you doing here?" he demanded, holding me by the back of the neck as if I were a puppy and dragging me out onto the training ground. When I squirmed, he shook me until my teeth rattled. "Answer!"

"Put me down!" I shouted at him. "I'm Helen! I'm your princess! I'm going to be your queen!" My brothers had dropped their swords and stood by, snickering.

Glaucus never cracked a smile. "Are you," he said. He set me down, but he didn't let go of my neck. "Queens work with spindles and needles. They card wool and weave cloth. They make medicines and perfumes. Do you see any wool to be carded and spun out here? Do I smell like I use perfume?"

"You smell like you ought to!" I snapped back. He still didn't laugh, but I saw that grim mouth creep up just a bit at the corners.

"Why don't you go back to the citadel and make me some, then," he said. "Or would you rather tell me what's brought you here?"

"I want to learn how to fight!" I declared, staring him right in the eyes to show him I wasn't afraid. "Even if I never have to use a sword, I want to know *how*. When I'm queen, I've got to be strong enough to protect myself. If I can't do that, how can I protect anyone else? And if someone thinks he can control my life and my decisions just because he's got a sword and I don't—I want him to get a *surprise*."

This time, Glaucus laughed. Laughed? He roared! I was positive he was mocking me, and that was so infuriating that, like a fool, I lost my temper. My arms were too short for my fists to reach him, but I flailed at him with my feet. I had to do *something* to show him that I wasn't going to take an insult meekly, not even from a man who could throw me halfway to the citadel walls.

At my first kick, he dropped his hold on my neck, grabbed my foot in mid-arc, and had me dangling upside down in the blink of an eye. I was so startled I couldn't even scream.

"That," said Glaucus, "was your first lesson— keep your temper under control or it's going to control you. Here's your second—pick your battles." Still holding me upside down, he turned toward my brothers. Castor and Polydeuces were now laughing so hard that they'd fallen over and were rolling on the ground. Quietly and gently, Glaucus set me on my feet and gave me one of the boys' discarded swords. His eyes flicked meaningfully from me to them.

I didn't need a second invitation. I thwacked my brothers' backsides so fast and so hard with one of their own practice swords that the bruises left them looking like a pair of leopards. By the time they scrambled to their feet and out of reach, I was breathing hard, but I'd never felt happier. My brothers filled the air with their protests until Glaucus silenced them both with a look.

Then they had no other choice but to stand by, pulling long faces, while their teacher gave his attention to evaluating my improvised performance: "Good energy, even if it's not focused. Bad technique, but that's understandable and it can be corrected. Too much enthusiasm. There's no shame in honorable combat, but there shouldn't be so much unnatural pleasure. The man with the greatest thirst for blood ends up drinking at Hades's table. *Men!*" At the word, my brothers tensed like hunting hounds. I giggled to hear him use that word to address a pair of boys still shy of their fifteenth birthday, but I bit off my laughter the instant Glaucus glared at me. "Men, we welcome your new comrade."

The startled looks on their faces were beyond description.

"Is this a joke?" Polydeuces demanded. "Are you saying it just to punish us because we didn't fight well today? We'll do better tomorrow, I swear it by Zeus!"

"She can't join us," Castor said, shaking his head. "It's—it's—it's just *wrong*."

Glaucus soon put a stop to their protests. "Your sister has explained why she wants to share your lessons, and she makes good points. She's younger than you, but already she knows the wisdom of being able to take care of herself *and* her people, once she's our queen. Good: A weak ruler means a weak land; a weak land means war. Now if *you* can give me any reason why I should not teach her along with you, say it. If it makes sense, I'll heed it, but remember this: It must be a reason that would apply if she'd been born a boy. If all you can say is *She's a girl!* then save your breath. You'll need it to outrun me, and the gods help you when I catch you."

"But—but she's a— She's too *young!*" It was lucky Castor caught himself before he could utter the words that would earn him a beating.

"She doesn't need to worry about protecting herself once she's queen," Polydeuces put in. "We'll do that. We'd do it even if it *weren't* our duty! Helen, don't you trust us to take care of you?"

Before I could reply, Castor plowed on, "And she's weak. Look at her arms! All scrawny. She'll get hurt, and she'll never be able to keep up with us."

Glaucus folded his arms across his chest. "If she can't keep up, she'll get no special treatment. She can give up and go back to the palace anytime she likes. Once she does that, I won't allow her to rejoin us. Understood? *All* of you?" He gave me a hard look. I said nothing, but I clenched my fists and made a private vow to Zeus himself that the only way I'd leave the training ground would be as a small, cold corpse.

I was still enjoying thoughts of *And I'll be dead and then they'll all be sorry!* when Glaucus added, "As for her age, she's older than you were when your father first turned you over to me."

"Father!" Castor cried, like a starving man discovering a loaf of bread. "He'd never risk anything happening to Helen. She *is* going to be queen one day."

"Castor's right," Polydeuces said eagerly, his head bobbing up and down. "He'll *never* hear of her training with us."

"Exactly," said Glaucus, and he smiled.

So we entered into a pact of the deepest secrecy, my brothers and Glaucus and I. It was agreed that I would train in the use of sword and shield and spear whenever I could slip away from the women's world of distaff and spindle and loom inside the palace walls. Glaucus made Castor and Polydeuces promise that they would not speak of my lessons to anyone, not a word, not a hint. They clung to their initial reluctance. Castor kept repeating, "But what if Father finds out *anyway?* What will he do to us *then?*" until Polydeuces pointed out that I'd soon get tired of doing a *man's* work; it would be only a matter of time before I quit on my own. Castor didn't look convinced, but he went where Polydeuces led. Glaucus had them take the gods' own oath, swearing by the dreadful powers of the river Styx, the black water that flows between the lands of the living and the realm of Hades, lord of the dead.

Of course, Glaucus laid down some exceptions to our pact for me. "If you're clumsy enough to make anyone suspicious—anyone to whom you owe honor and obedience, I mean—and you're asked a direct question about where you're going or what you're doing, tell the truth."

I nodded. I knew that lying was wrong, but I drew a broken line around the whole matter of concealing my sword-training from my parents. If I didn't tell them I *was* doing it, it wasn't the same thing as telling them I *wasn't.*

"If you're discovered, it won't be anyone's fault but your own," he went on. "I know how to keep secrets, and your brothers have sworn."

"I'll be careful," I promised. "I'll make sure no one follows me, and I'll always come in disguise. And if Clytemnestra asks me where I'm going, I'll beat her until she stays quiet."

"Do *that*, and we're through," Glaucus told me. "I'm not teaching you how to fight if it means you'll turn into a tyrant. The world's got enough of those. If you want to learn from me, you'll work for the privilege, and you'll know that not all of my lessons will take place on the training ground."

## 3

# LESSONS

My next lesson came between the time Glaucus first agreed to show me how to fight and the time I was at last able to steal away from the palace and join my brothers on the training ground. Seven days! Gods, how could seven days seem like eternity?

On the first day, I leaped out of bed, eager to throw on my "borrowed" tunic and run to the training ground, only to find Ione standing in my doorway with a stack of newly woven fabric.

"You need new dresses," she said, and proceeded to fumble and fuss over how tall I was growing and whether or not to add an extra layer of flounces to my skirt, just in case I grew taller still. I didn't know you could waste a whole day over dressmaking.

The next morning I learned that you can waste

*another* day over the same stupid dresses. Ione decided it was time for me to learn how to sew my own clothes. I objected, saying, "I'm never going to have to do this for myself when I'm grown up!" Ione countered with, "Well, you're not grown up yet."

I did a terrible job. Ione sat me down with a group of the palace women, and they all took turns undoing my mistakes and trying to say something nice about my clumsy efforts. Ione couldn't deny that I had no talent for needlework, but that didn't stop her from putting me to work embroidering dress sleeves on the third day.

Once again I was working in the company of other palace women—servants and specially trained slaves and the daughters of high-ranking nobles who had the honor of attending the queen. As soon as she gave me my work, Ione went off on her own errand, which gave me an idea: If I could find a pretext for leaving the courtyard, I'd be able to escape the palace!

I jabbed myself with the needle deliberately; it was the first inspiration that hit me. "Ow! My finger!" I held up my hand so that everyone could see the blood. I dropped my embroidery and stood up, pretending to be desperate with pain. "I have to find my mother!" I wailed. It was the queen's duty to treat sickness and heal injuries. "Oh, it hurts *so* much!" I started out of the courtyard.

Three of the older servants, all friends of Ione,

flocked around me before I'd taken five steps. "You poor lamb, what a dreadful, dreadful wound," one of them said, shaking her head. "We can't allow you to go to your mother unescorted, not with such a terrible hurt."

"I can find her myself, really," I said, but they wouldn't hear of it.

"And what if you bleed so much that you collapse before you reach her, dear Lady Helen? No, no, we must bring you to the queen. It's our duty."

"But it's not that serious! It's only a small—" I began. Then I stopped, realizing I'd tripped over my own hasty tongue. The women smiled and escorted me back to my place in the courtyard.

The fourth, fifth, and sixth days nearly drove me barking mad. I kept getting up earlier and earlier, hoping to escape before Ione could catch me. That was how I learned that you *can't* get up earlier than a farmer's wife. She was always there, always with a new set of tasks for me. At least she'd given up on the needlework, but that didn't stop her from dumping a herd's worth of fleeces in my lap for carding, or dragging me off to spin thread with my sister, or, worst of all, turning me over to Clytemnestra with the words: "I give up. *You* teach her."

The only advantage to having Clytemnestra for a teacher was that she wasn't an early riser. I suffered through my lesson with her on the sixth day—and if

I had one olive for every time she sneered at my uneven, snapped, snarled thread, I could press a whole jug full of oil! Earlier that year, we'd each been given our own rooms, so on the seventh day I slipped out of my room and past hers while she was still snuffling in her bed.

I hurried down the hall, Castor's tunic wadded up tightly against my chest, wondering where I could find the safest place to change. I was just about to sneak into one of the palace storerooms when a hand fell on my shoulder and Ione's voice sounded in my ear. "Oh good, there you are. I need you for some *very important* work."

"But Clytemnestra has to teach me how to spin better," I said, hoping Ione would accept my excuse. No need to tell her that once she let me go, I had no intention of going anywhere near my spindle or my sister.

"That can wait. Your mother will soon be making our winter medicines. She needs us to gather ingredients." So that was how I lost yet another day, picking herbs and flowers instead of learning how to use a sword.

Glaucus laughed when I finally came limping out of the olive grove to where he had Castor and Polydeuces doing target practice with the throwing spear. "There you are, princess!" he cried. "I thought you'd changed your mind and given up on our pact before it began."

"Do I look like I've changed my mind?" I grumbled. I rubbed my arms, sore and aching, and spat dust from my mouth. My legs were covered with bloody scrapes, and it would take me hours to work the tangles out of my hair.

"Then why so long coming out here?" I liked Glaucus better when he was being stern; he had the most aggravating grin of any man alive. "Forget the path? Lose your way?"

"I'm watched," I said. "Ever since the day you promised to teach me how to fight, it's been next to impossible to get away. Whenever I knew you were taking the boys down here, I'd try to follow, but Ione always seemed to come along with a task for me to do. I wouldn't be here now if I hadn't gotten up *long* before dawn, dressed, and hidden myself in one of the storerooms all morning. Even then, I had to drop from a window and climb down the eastern side of the palace hill to be sure that no one would see me."

"The eastern side . . ." Glaucus rubbed his chin. "That's where the briars grow thickest, isn't it?" And his grin got wider and wider, until suddenly I understood exactly what had been going on.

"You did this!" I shouted. "I don't know what you said to Ione, but you're the reason why she hasn't left me alone for a moment all these days!"

"You look mad enough to throw a rock at my head," Glaucus said calmly. "Did you think I was going to make this easy for you, princess? You say you want to learn a fighter's skills. Well, patience is one of them, cunning's another, and no one can give those to you but yourself. If you'd rather have gifts fall into your lap, go back to the palace and put on a skirt, but if you still want to learn from me, let's see you throw something besides a rock." Instead of giving me the sharpened wooden practice spears he gave my brothers, he handed me his own weapon, a beautiful, bronze-headed spear made to fly to the target with a hawk's clean grace.

It wasn't as massive as the great hunting spears the men used to kill wild boar, but it was heavy enough. I envied my brothers, armed with sharpened sticks. They had no trouble hitting the bales of barley straw at the far end of the training ground. Meanwhile, I spent more time struggling to lift the genuine spear than I did throwing it. *Hit* the target? I was happy when I finally managed to fling that cumbersome weapon more than five paces away from me.

I'd come to the training ground with sore arms. As that day wore on, they felt ready to drop off like dead vine leaves. Still I kept at it, hoisting the spear, throwing the spear, fetching the spear, until I wanted to howl from the pain. Part of my staying power came from fear that if I quit or even complained, Glaucus would decide that I wasn't worth teaching after all.

Then what? My brothers loved me, but they'd never agree to teach me the ways of weapons. They'd just point to my failure as proof that there really were some things boys could do that girls shouldn't even try.

I needed Glaucus. I needed to show him that Castor was wrong, that I *could* keep up with my brothers after all.

"Well," Glaucus said when at last he took the spear from my shaking hands. "That was awful. Next time you'll practice with the same equipment as your brothers do."

I was aching so badly that I could have kissed his hands for those words, but I didn't want to let him know that. I had to make him see that I was strong enough to hold my own on the training ground, so I put on a brave show. "This was only my first day. I want to go on using the real thing. I don't want to learn how to throw some stupid *stick*."

Glaucus's scowl was downright terrifying. "What you will learn, princess," he said grimly, "is *obedience*. Or you'll learn nothing more from me."

I was tired and sore and frustrated. My mouth was dry, and my head was beginning to ache along with my arms. Glaucus was a famous warrior, the one man Father thought worthy to teach princes, but he was also the man who'd agreed to teach me, then made it almost impossible for me to come to my lessons, and now, *now* he was scolding me about obedience! I was so exasperated that I forgot his very first lesson. *Keep your temper under control or it's going to control you.*

"I know all about obedience." I spat out the words as if they were sour pomegranate seeds. "Obey my nurse, obey my parents, obey the gods. If the gods love obedience so much, why didn't they fill the world with sheep?"

I stamped my foot for emphasis. The sharp-edged bit of stone on the training ground wouldn't have hurt my foot if I'd only trod on it, but stamping drove it into my flesh like a dagger. The sudden pain took me by surprise so that I gasped instead of yowling. When I picked up my foot to see what I'd done, there was a lot of blood.

I felt the tears rising, but I also felt Glaucus's eyes on me, and my brothers' as well. I clenched my hands and screwed my eyes tight shut, biting down hard on my lower lip, all in a mighty battle to hold back my tears. *Soldiers never cry*, I thought. *Soldiers never cry.*

I lost that battle. The pain was too great, and my breath tore out of my body in a bone-shaking sob. I expected to see Glaucus turn to my brothers and say, "There, now you see the real difference between men and women. No man would ever act like this over a little blood."

Instead, I was startled out of my tears by the sight of the broad-shouldered warrior kneeling beside me and taking my wounded foot in his hand as gently as if he were my mother.

"Let's see that," he said. "Mmm, this isn't going to be easy to hide from your nurse. That was a stupid thing to do, princess, but I've seen worse. We'll find a way around it. Men! Are you going to stand there like deadwood or have you got any brains to bring to this problem?"

I stopped sobbing as I watched my brothers scramble all over one another like a pair of big-pawed puppies in their haste to help me.

"It's not such a bad wound, Helen," Castor whispered, trying to give me comfort. "It'll heal quickly."

"You actually managed to lift that spear," Polydeuces murmured. "Amazing. Wasn't that something, Castor?"

Castor agreed, echoing Polydeuces's pleasure in my accomplishment. I would have hugged them for their kindness then and there, but I didn't know if that would have embarrassed them in front of their teacher. They did love me, even if they'd have to be convinced that a girl's place was beside them on the training ground.

In the time it took for my tears to dry, Castor and Polydeuces managed to wash my wound, ruin their clothing by tearing strips from the hems for bandages, and wrap my foot as thickly and tightly as if they were swaddling an infant in wintertime. Polydeuces had even been able to scrounge up some spiderwebs to help stop the bleeding. When they were done, they stood back and gazed at Glaucus with happy, expectant faces.

The old warrior examined their bulky handiwork, shook his head, and undid it all. He retied the bandages, discarding most of the tattered cloth, muttering that Sparta was doomed if we were its hope for the future.

If I couldn't thank Castor and Polydeuces for their care any other way, at least I could stand up to Glaucus in their defense. "Don't say that!" I exclaimed, my face hot. "They did a *good* job, better than you're doing now."

Glaucus sat back on his haunches. "Loyalty, princess? That's commendable, but they should earn your praise."

"They're going to be heroes, not healers," I snapped. "So what if they can't tie a bandage? They're going to be the pride of Sparta someday—you just wait!—and when that day comes, the only reason anyone will ever remember *your* name is because you were their teacher!"

"Not all of us care if our names are remembered, in life or after death," Glaucus replied, his face stony. "Better men than I have become food for battlefield crows defending your father's lands. They could have broken away from the Spartan army and rushed into single combat against the enemy, all for their own glory. Instead, they died fighting in the ranks, for the good of all instead of the glory of one. They lost their chance to be remembered, but they won wars. Those are *my* heroes, princess."

"Then I don't want my brothers to be your kind of heroes," I said. "Sheep go where they're led. Are *they* your heroes too?"

I must have looked ridiculous, a small, filthy, scratched, and bleeding child facing up to a seasoned warrior who could have snapped my spine like a dry reed. For a time the two of us sat glaring at one another while Castor and Polydeuces looked on, too nervous to make a sound. Even if my belligerence cost me all future lessons from Glaucus, I wasn't going to back down. He had no right to belittle my brothers. I remembered the second lesson he'd taught me: *Pick your battles.*

Then Glaucus broke the silence with a roar of laughter. "Sheep again!" he crowed. "You drag them into your arguments time after time, yet I'll wager that you've never been closer to them than the meat on your table or the wool on your spindle. You have no idea what they're really like. You've just heard other palace folk say that sheep are stupid, spiritless beasts, so you echo their ignorance. If you'd been raised like me, on an upland farm, you'd soon learn the truth. Sheep *don't* always go where they're led, not half so easily as palace folk do, anyway."

He slapped his knees and stood up. "You're a blunt girl, but praise Athena, you're not stupid. You're just young. You'll learn. The gods know, I'm old and I'm still learning. I only pray they'll let me live to teach you the difference between sheep and heroes, blind obedience and discipline."

"What?" I'd expected to be sent away for being so outspoken. I glanced at my brothers. They'd been with Glaucus for years and knew him better than I did. Was he truly willing to keep teaching me, or was it an ugly joke, punishment for my audacity? I hoped they'd give some sign to let me know whether it was safe to take him at his word.

They were smiling. They looked proud of me.

I looked back at Glaucus. "You—you'll still teach me?"

"That will depend on if you'll learn." He cast a casual glance back toward where the royal palace of Sparta stood high on its fortified hill. "It also seems that right now it's going to depend on luck. While you and I have been bickering, your father's sentries have been watching, wondering why I've stopped instructing the princes just to waste so much time and attention on *this* grubby little creature." He nodded at me. "I helped train those men, and unless I did a rotten

job, they'll follow their suspicions down here to find
out what's going on."

"I—I think I see two of them now," Castor said,
shading his eyes with one hand. "You're right, Glaucus, they're coming this way. Helen, you can't go back
to the palace; they're on the only path. They'll recognize you and tell Father, and that'll be the end of your
training."

"You should be happy, then," I said. "You didn't
want me to train with you."

"That was because I didn't think you were serious
about it," Castor replied. "But after hearing what you
said, seeing you keep trying to use that spear, not giving up, well . . ."

Polydeuces stooped to murmur in my ear. "What
he's trying to say is, anyone who'd stand up to Glaucus
like you did deserves a chance. You stood up for us,
little sister; the least we can do is stand up for you."

I climbed to my feet with a hand up from both
my brothers. I don't think that I ever loved them so
much as I did then. My foot throbbed, but Glaucus
had done a good job of binding it up. It could bear
my weight, which was a good thing because I was
about to ask it to bear more than that. I dug my feet—
both hurt and whole—into the dirt and took off at a
run. Pain shot through my body with every other step,
and I heard the shouts of Father's sentries on my trail,
ordering me to stop, but I ran on.

## 4

# CLYTEMNESTRA'S SECRET

I outran the sentries in spite of my injured foot. I escaped them by dodging through the olive grove, then circling all around the royal citadel until I reached the path back to the great gate. The men on guard there didn't think twice about letting me in. To their eyes I was just another one of the young slaves who worked in the palace kitchens or stables or any of a hundred other places inside our walls. Why should they care about a slave? They waved me inside impatiently, without a second glance. I scrambled past them and vanished into the cool shadows of the palace before their comrades could catch up to me.

I managed to avoid Ione or anyone else who might recognize me in my disguise. I tore off my clothing, hid the ragged tunic in the wooden box that held my dolls, and crawled into my bed, breathing hard. I stayed there the rest of the day, wrapped up in a blazing sheet of agony, until Ione found me at suppertime. She didn't know what to think when she saw my wounded foot and heard me spin a story about treading on a piece of broken pottery in the palace.

"Why didn't you find me when this happened?" she demanded, examining the wound tenderly. In spite of all that my brothers and Glaucus had done, it was a mess. I watched in dismay as Ione plucked a sticky olive leaf out of my foot and held it up between us.

"I—I was—" I began.

Ione raised one hand, silencing me. "Don't bother lying to me. I can't make you tell me the truth, but I don't need to waste my time hearing lies." She turned her head toward the little heap of bandages she'd unwound from my foot and picked up one of the longer strips. "I know who you've been with, at least. I know this cloth. I wove it myself to make a tunic for your brother Castor. My needle made this little pattern of sea creatures along the hem. I knew that my work would be wasted on him—he doesn't care what his clothing looks like as long as it serves its purpose—but I wanted to do it for him anyway." She let the tattered strip drop back onto the small, bloody heap.

"I'm sorry, Ione," I said meekly. She was hurt, and it wasn't because Castor had ruined her embroidery. It was because she'd always trusted me and now I'd tried to deceive her. She loved me, and I'd repaid her with lies. I didn't know how to apologize for that, so instead I said, "I'm sorry Castor tore that. It was very pretty. All the work you—"

Again her hand went up, demanding my silence. "You don't need to apologize to me. You're growing up, all of you, shutting me out of your lives. The boys were taken away from me long ago, because they claim it's bad for future warriors to be raised by women. Soon I'll have no more authority over you and your sister either. I'll be no more than a piece of furniture to you then, something you can ignore unless you need to use me. Keep your secrets. But next time you want to persuade someone that you were hurt inside the palace, get rid of this sort of thing"—she held up the telltale olive leaf—"and *wash* yourself. You look as if you've been wrestling with pigs. As for your hair . . ."

She went on like this for a while, fetching water and salve and fresh bandages for my foot as she chattered on. She sat beside me on my bed and cleaned my face roughly, like a mother cat with a wayward kitten. When she turned her attention to my hair, she yanked the tangles out so hard that I thought she meant to take my scalp off with them. When she was done with me, I looked like a presentable daughter of Sparta again.

"There," she said, holding me at arm's length and

surveying her handiwork. "That will do. Look at you! It won't be long before you're a woman, and what a beautiful woman you'll be."

I felt the tips of my ears turn red. My nurse had never given me such a compliment before.

"Ione, I'm nowhere near being a woman," I told her. "I'm only ten."

"Not forever. One way or the other, you'll fly away." She shook her head and sighed. "That Glaucus is a wise man, even if he's too tight-lipped. He told me to keep an eye on you, but he wouldn't say why. I don't know what you're up to that should involve him, and I don't want to know. All that matters to me is that he asked me to keep you close and I failed. Now look what's happened to you."

I thought I saw tears in her eyes. I tried to throw my arms around her neck, but she was on her feet and beyond my reach before I could do that.

"Go and eat, little bird," she said from the doorway. Then she was gone.

I limped a little as I walked through the palace, following the smell of food. It wasn't coming from the hall where my parents held feasts to honor Spartan nobles or foreign ambassadors. Instead, the aroma led me to the kitchen, where I found my brothers gobbling bread and sheep's milk cheese, with the bony remains of a broiled fish between them.

"Where's Clytemnestra?" I asked as a kitchen

slave hurried to find me a stool. Another fetched my food and some triply-watered wine.

"Been and gone," Castor said cheerfully, through a mouthful of bread crust. "Something's up with her. Every bite she took, she was smiling. I know that sly look: She's got a secret."

Polydeuces agreed with his twin. "I'll bet it's about the guest, the one who came today while we were all on the training ground."

"What guest?" I asked eagerly. It was always exciting when visitors came to our father's court. Visitors meant gifts, thrilling tales of the perils they'd braved to reach Sparta, and news from other kingdoms.

"One of the maids said that her brother was the one summoned to bring bread and salt to the king's hall." All of Sparta's important visitors were welcomed with the ritual that created the sacred bond between host and guest by the sharing of bread and salt. The gods punished any man who violated that holy trust.

"Any idea where he's from?" I asked. My brothers shook their heads ruefully. "I'll bet Clytemnestra knows. That's got to be her secret."

"Good luck making her tell us anything," Castor said sarcastically.

"Why do we have to ask her what we can find out for ourselves?" I said.

My brothers smiled. The next instant my uneaten

dinner was abandoned as the three of us fled the kitchen, off to haunt the great hall for news, to put our ears to a few doors, to talk to the servants, to do whatever it took to discover the identity of Sparta's newest guest. I had a hard time keeping up with Castor and Polydeuces on account of my injured foot, until the two of them made a carry-chair of their linked hands, scooped me up, and carried me along before I could protest.

They might have helped me, but their good intentions hurt our mission. You can't gather secrets when you're making a spectacle of yourself in the palace passageways. They no sooner set me back on my feet beside a pillar in the great hall than we were discovered.

"Why are you three lurking here?" Mother's girl-hood skills as a huntress were as sharp as ever.

We whirled around, my brothers already babbling flimsy excuses. I didn't bother. *Mother's no fool,* I thought. *She knows why we're here.*

Of course she did. She folded her arms, regarded us severely, and said, "He's from Mykenae."

"Who is?" Castor was still trying to keep up the illusion of innocence.

Mother just rolled her eyes. "Do you want to play games, Castor, or do you want to know about our guest?"

"I do if he doesn't," Polydeuces spoke up. "Myke-nae! Mother, is it true what I've heard about their royal house? Did Lord Atreus really make his brother eat his own—?"

"*Silence*," Mother commanded sharply. Her eyes flashed. "I forbid you to mention any of those awful stories while we're entertaining Lord Thyestes's ambassador. I thought you had more sense, Polydeuces."

My brother lowered his head, ashamed. "I'm sorry, Mother," he said.

"What awful stories?" I whispered to Castor, but he refused to tell me anything as long as Mother might overhear.

Which she did. "None you'll hear while that man is our honored guest, Helen. Unless you want to ruin your sister's marriage plans."

"*Marriage!*" I cried. The word bounced wildly off the painted pillars of the great hall. "Clytemnestra? But she's only—"

"Lower your voice," Mother told me. "I won't let that Mykenaean go home and tell his king that Sparta's future queen has no manners."

"So that was Clytemnestra's big secret," Polydeuces mused. He patted my shoulder. "Don't worry, Helen: Father is only making the marriage *agreement* with Mykenae now. Clytemnestra won't leave us for a while yet."

"Long enough for her to lord it over us because *she's* going to be queen of Mykenae." Castor did a deadly accurate imitation of how our sister always sailed through the palace, spine stiff with pride, nose in the air, lips pursed as if she smelled a rotten fish. Even Mother had to laugh. As much as she loved us all, she couldn't deny that Clytemnestra did like to put on airs.

That night, I went to bed with my head spinning from the news. Married! My sister was going to be married. I wondered when she'd have to leave Sparta. I wondered what her husband would be like. I wanted to lean toward her bed and whisper a dozen questions to her, to find out if she was really pleased with the future that Father and the Mykenaean ambassador were giving her. It would have to wait for morning.

Alone in the shadows, I whispered a small prayer to my favorite goddess. "O Aphrodite, make my sister's husband love her as much as Father loves Mother." It was the first time I hadn't called my mother "Mama." My sister was going to be married. Neither one of us was a child anymore. "If he loves her, he'll want her to be happy."

The next morning I rose early, dressed, gobbled my breakfast in the kitchen, and went in search of Clytemnestra. She was carding wool on a courtyard bench when I found her. It was a tedious job, pulling the matted clumps of fleece through the carding combs. I wished her a good day, then sat beside her on the bench and began to pick out some of the knots in the fleece with my fingers. We worked together in silence. It was as if nothing had changed, as if there were no Mykenaean visitor under our roof.

At last I put my clump of wool back into the basket of washed fleece. "Mother told us," I said. "I hope you and Lord Thyestes will be happy together."

Clytemnestra rolled her eyes and gave me a condescending look. "Oh, Helen, Lord Thyestes is *ancient.* I'm marrying his son Prince Tantalus."

"Oh. So you won't be queen of Mykenae?"

"You'd like that, wouldn't you?" She gave the carding combs a hard tug. "Sorry to disappoint you, but my husband will be king of Mykenae after his father dies, so you won't be the only queen in this family. And Mykenae is richer than Sparta too!"

"That's not what I—" I began.

She didn't let me finish. "I can't *wait* to get away from this place. I'm tired of having to listen to Ione and Mother and Father and—and to everyone say how *pretty* you are all the time, as if that's an excuse for why you never do any *real* work."

"But I don't think they—"

It was no use trying to get a word in. My sister had made up her mind: "You never pick up a spindle unless someone makes you do it, and I've never seen you having a lesson at the big loom. As for learning how to make medicines from Mother—" She made a scornful sound. "I feel sorry for Sparta when you're queen. What are you going to do? Tell your husband and the rest of the court that they can wrap your *beauty* around them to keep warm and well all winter?

"*I* made Father a long tunic," she went on. "I made it *myself,* start to finish, from carding the wool to weaving the cloth to embroidering a pattern of waves on the sleeves. When I gave it to him, I told him I chose waves because Aphrodite was born from the sea and I knew how much he loved her. Do you know what he said to me then?" Clytemnestra's eyes narrowed. "He said, 'What a lucky man I am to have one daughter who's as clever as Athena and another who's as beautiful as Aphrodite!' Even when you did *nothing,* even when you weren't there, he praised *you!*"

She threw down her carding combs and swept into the shadows of the palace, leaving me standing like a statue in the courtyard, all my wishes for her future happiness unsaid.

The ambassador from Mykenae stayed with us for ten days. The night before he left, Father gave a great banquet to honor him and to celebrate Clytemnestra's betrothal. Ione helped me get ready for the feast, picking out my dress, fussing over my hair, and chattering away the whole time.

"Ah, look at how well you've healed in just ten days' time!" she exclaimed, examining my feet before slipping them into my best pair of sandals. It was true:

The gash on my foot was almost gone. I only needed one thin strip of cloth to cover it. "You must have made a good sacrifice to Aesculapius the Healer."

She straightened up and began to arrange my hair. As much as I wanted to dress and groom myself, Ione refused. As my nurse, she'd get the credit or blame for how I looked at the banquet.

"What lovely curls!" she said, working diligently with the ivory comb. "That Mykenaean will have to fill his mouth with gold when he describes you to his master, Lord Thyestes."

"Why would he need to do that?" I asked.

My nursemaid chuckled. "Do you imagine that your sister's marrying the only prince of Mykenae? Lord Thyestes has plenty of sons, and his royal brother, Atreus, has at least two that I know of. Those Mykenaeans breed like rabbits."

I giggled, then clapped my hands to my mouth. "Ione, what an awful thing to say!" I exclaimed, still laughing.

"Well, no one can deny it. I only pray that your sister's getting a good man. With a family that large, there's bound to be at least one rotten apple on the tree. If even half the stories I've heard about the kings of Mykenae are true—"

"What stories?" Mother had stopped Polydeuces before he could tell me anything.

"I really shouldn't say a word; nasty things." She

put down the comb and began to weave a strand of freshwater pearls through my hair.

I turned around quickly and grabbed her hands. "*Please* tell me, Ione. I promise I won't repeat anything. You won't get into trouble for telling me."

"Hmph! There's no chance of that unless you come right out and mention my name. *Everyone* knows about those Mykenaeans."

"I don't. And I think I should; my sister *is* going to be their queen." I gave her my most persuasive smile, the one I'd used since babyhood whenever I wanted to get her to bend the rules for me, just a little.

"Oh, all right." She gave in easily. I think she wanted to tell me all the tales. "But turn around and sit still or you'll never be ready for the feast tonight, and then I *will* be in trouble. Your sister is marrying Lord Thyestes's oldest son, but that man wasn't always king of Mykenae. At first his brother, Lord Atreus, ruled."

She made a small scornful sound. "*Brothers.* Not all brothers are like yours, my dear; I helped raise Castor and Polydeuces, so I know. They may quarrel and scuffle, but it's all quickly over and forgotten. There's true affection and loyalty binding those two. If they were stones in a wall, you couldn't fit a knife blade between them.

"But Atreus and Thyestes—! I've heard they hate one another as fiercely as if they came from separate sides of the earth instead of from the same mother's womb. They both want Mykenae, and so they've spent their lives fighting and scheming and betraying one another in order to seize the throne. Back and forth it's gone—first Atreus was king, then Thyestes, then Atreus again—and every time the crown changes hands, it's stained with fresh blood. I heard that Lord Atreus even killed his own wife, a Cretan princess, because she dared to smile at his brother!"

"Just for *smiling* at him?" I couldn't believe it.

Ione coughed nervously. "Well, perhaps she did more than smile. But that's nothing. The worst is this: *I* heard that Lord Atreus actually killed some of his brother's children, then ordered their flesh cooked and served it *to their own father!* Lord Thyestes didn't suspect a thing until after that abominable meal, when Atreus showed him their *heads.*"

For someone who hadn't wanted to tell me one word about the Mykenaeans, Ione was taking unnatural glee in repeating one grisly horror after another.

"What kind of a family is my sister marrying into?" I cried, jerking my head out from under Ione's busy hands.

My nurse seemed unconcerned with Clytemnestra's future among such people. "Tsk. Now look what you've done, torn the pearls loose and mussed your curls. I'll have to start all over."

"But Clytemnestra can't marry a monster!" I protested.

"Oh, hush," Ione said calmly, taking up the comb again. "Prince Tantalus never harmed anyone, and as for the stories about his father and uncle—I'm sure they're only stories. Do you think your royal parents would give their darling girl to Mykenae if the tales were true?

"Of course, you won't have that problem, little bird," she went on. "As our queen-to-be, you'll pick yourself a good husband."

"Husband?" This time I jerked my head so suddenly that my hair got tangled in the comb and I gave a little yelp of pain before I added, "I don't want a husband!" *And after hearing you talk, I* definitely *don't want a Mykenaean,* I thought.

"*Don't* isn't the same as *won't.*" Ione chuckled knowingly as she picked up the pearls.

It was a splendid, lavish feast intended to impress Lord Thyestes's ambassador so that when he went home he'd tell his master all about Sparta's wealth and power. The tables creaked under the weight of platters filled with stewed rabbit and mutton, broiled fish, crackling loaves of barley bread, round white cheeses, fresh salads decorated with mint and parsley, even the special treat of roasted venison. Mounds of almonds and slabs of honeycomb were offered to our guest in dishes that had come all the way from Crete. I loved their beautifully painted patterns of fish, dolphins, and big-eyed octopi.

Midway through the feast, my father made the ceremonial announcement about my sister's betrothal. Because she was the center of attention, Clytemnestra sat in a place of honor, between our parents, and glowed with pleasure when the Spartan nobles raised their voices in congratulations so loud they made the oil lamps flicker.

If my sister truly wanted to leave Sparta right away, Lord Thyestes's ambassador shared her eagerness. I was seated at Mother's left, so I had no trouble hearing when he leaned forward from his place beside Father and said, "Great lady, when can I tell Lord Thyestes to expect your noble daughter's arrival?"

Mother offered him a sweet smile. "Not for two years, at the very least. She's still too much of a child for marriage. I know that a young princess is often raised in her future husband's house, so she can learn her new people's ways, but if she's *too* young, she might become so homesick that she won't be able to think of anything except her family."

"With all respect, great lady," the ambassador said, bowing to my mother just a little bit, "Prince Tantalus will be her family."

I saw Mother's face harden until she looked like

an image of the goddess Artemis just before she sends an arrow through some unlucky mortal's heart. Her voice was icy when she replied, "With all my *royal* respect to your master, we who rule Sparta never employ messengers who think they can instruct a queen."

The Mykenaean turned pale. His apology was coldly formal, and Mother accepted it just as coldly. It took my father's hearty laugh to break the awkward mood and restore the banquet's festivity.

I wondered how disappointed my sister would be when she found out she'd have to spend two more years with us. I hoped she wouldn't feel that this was my fault too.

# 5

# MY MOTHER'S PAST

The day after the banquet, I decided that I'd lost enough training time. I didn't want Glaucus to think that I'd given up my desire to learn a warrior's skills, so I bound my foot with extra cloth and slipped out of the palace to join my brothers. The gods be thanked, there was a big uproar at the gates as the ambassador left us. No one in the crowd noticed me, and Ione had quit being my watchdog.

When I reached the training ground, Glaucus was alone. And he didn't look happy. "Someone had better teach your brothers that only fools and children believe it's a brave thing to drink unwatered wine," he said. He pressed his lips together and shot a poisonous look at the palace walls. "If their heads hurt today, just wait until I get my hands on them tomorrow. Meanwhile, you and I had better find another place to work on your warrior skills, princess."

"Why?" I asked.

"Because once that Mykenaean wine-bag leaves, the guards will go back to their regular duties. They expect to see me training your brothers. Even the sight of a third 'boy' down here doesn't faze them—they probably reckon you for one of the princes' playmates, a servant's kid. But if they saw me spending my time on you alone, they'd smell a dead mouse in the barley and come charging down here to investigate. Understand?"

I nodded. Glaucus smiled, then picked up the bundle of practice javelins as easily as if they were made of straw. He strode off toward the river with me scurrying after him. I tried not to let him know that my heart was about to burst from sheer joy. Glaucus and all that he could teach me were mine alone, at least for one day. He wouldn't have to split his attention between me and my brothers. I felt like singing.

He led me to a narrow part of the river, forested on both banks, out of sight of the palace walls. He dropped the practice javelins and dove into the water without bothering to remove a single piece of clothing, not even his sandals. Once across, he cut rings into the bark of three huge trees on the far bank, then came swimming back before I could wonder whether I was supposed to follow him or stay put. (Just as well. I'd never learned how to swim.)

"Here," he said, handing me one of the practice javelins and nodding at the targets he'd improvised.

"Which one do you want me to hit?" I asked.

That amused him. "I'll be happy if I don't have to spend the rest of the day racing downstream, trying to recapture all the shafts that'll wind up in the river. Just try to get it across the water, princess."

His words made my face go hot. *He's trying to make me mad,* I thought. *He thinks he can control me like that, but it's my life:* I *say yes or no.*

I calmly picked up the first shaft, held it at eye level, and sighted down the length of it.

"I suppose that's all I'll be able to do with this one," I said. "It's warped. It won't fly true."

I picked up each one of the other fake spears and examined them in the same way. They were all just crooked enough to veer away from the target, no matter how skilled the thrower, and I said so.

The old soldier gave me a strange look, then checked the spears for himself. "Well, I'll be Hades's dinner guest!" he exclaimed. "You're right! Good for you, princess."

"I can still throw them across the river," I said, trying not to let him see how much his praise pleased me. "But you carved those targets for nothing."

"I have a better idea," he said. "Wait here."

He was gone for a while. I passed the time by flinging stones over the water. None of them made it to the far bank. Silently I gave thanks that there'd be no spear-throwing practice that day. My arm wasn't strong enough yet; I would have been mortified.

Glaucus came back through the trees, carrying something wrapped up in his cloak. He unfurled it and a short sword fell at my feet. It was the real thing, a bronze blade with a cutting edge that glittered in the sunlight. He must have gone all the way back to the palace to fetch it.

"Pick it up," Glaucus told me, drawing his own sword from his belt. "Let's see how it suits you."

I gazed at the weapon but couldn't bring myself to touch it. To hold a *real* sword—! It was a privilege I longed for and feared. Why was Glaucus giving me this chance so soon? Did he mean it to be an honor or a test? I hesitated, longing and just a bit afraid.

"Go on and take it, princess," Glaucus said. His smile was encouraging. "I just want to see what you can do with that. Don't worry: I promise not to hurt you, and the gods know you won't hurt me."

My hand closed on the hilt and I picked up the sword. "In that case, I'm ready to learn," I said.

My first real sword fight was a worse disaster than my first time using a real spear. The heavy blade was made for a grown man and was beautifully balanced.

That was the only thing that kept me from dropping it more than I did. My first swings were wild. When I swatted a tree trunk, the vibrations made my hand tingle and smart. I didn't even manage to cut the bark. As for my efforts to imitate Glaucus's fighting style, they were clumsier than a pig trying to walk on its hind legs. I know he didn't expect much of me my first time, but I'd expected more of myself.

*I don't care* what *he said about just wanting to see what I can do with this blade,* I thought. *He* must *be judging me. I've got to show him I can do better than this or he might change his mind about letting me train.*

The fear of being dismissed made me redouble my efforts, but with the same lack of effect. Glaucus held me at bay effortlessly, while I panted and stumbled and kept wiping sweat out of my eyes. I finally got so frustrated, trying to break through his guard, that I lost my patience and charged him, holding the bronze sword high over my head and howling like a wolf. He sidestepped and tripped me as I went flying past. When I sprawled on my face in the dirt, he touched the back of my neck lightly with the tip of his own weapon.

"There's no shame in dying in battle, princess," he said. "But this would have been a very stupid death. The lesson's done." Then he picked up my sword and strode away. I was left to trail back into the palace, sore, exhausted, and convinced that I'd made such a fool of myself that Glaucus would never want me on the training ground again. I decided that I wouldn't give him the chance to banish me. Instead, I stayed in the palace the next day, joining my sister and the other women. I sat near Clytemnestra while she worked at the big loom, surrounded by servants, slaves, and ladies of the palace, all of us busy at the woman's work of making cloth. My hands were still sore from my wretched attempt at swordsmanship, my fingers clumsy as I held the distaff and tried to make the spindle obey me. I hated every moment, but I stuck to the tedious chore because I'd decided it was my only future.

The room where we worked was well lit by the sun, heavy with the fresh scent of washed fleece. The women chattered while they worked, hummed old songs, told stories, spoke gently or impatiently to the younger girls who were still learning their skills. It was a peaceful, safe place, but so is a grave.

I looked at my sister. Her face was serene, all her attention focused on the pattern she was creating on the great loom. In that instant, I realized that she no longer envied me anything—not my looks, or the way the grown-ups seemed to favor me, or even the fact that I'd be queen of Sparta someday. Our rivalry was over; she had what she'd always wanted. She, too, was going to be a queen.

I spent five days with the women, inside the

palace walls. Every time I considered stealing back to the training ground I remembered my failure. My face burned with fresh humiliation, and I abandoned the thought once more.

On the sixth day of my self-enforced captivity, something happened that changed everything. We were all working together, as usual. By now it was quite clear that each thread we spun or wove or embroidered was intended for my sister's bride goods. The older women murmured about how strange it was that the queen didn't come to help prepare her daughter's dowry.

"It's natural," one of them remarked, her needle making a pattern of lilies along the hem of a gown. "She doesn't want to face the fact that she's losing her babies."

"That's true," another added. "Didn't you hear about what she said to the ambassador? He wanted our princess to come to Mykenae before winter, but the queen refused."

"What does she think *that* will do?" a third snapped. "Children grow up and leave us. That's how it is, even for queens. Does she think she can stop time by—"

Her voice dropped abruptly into silence. A hush fell over the room. The women around me were laying down their work and rising like a flock of herons taking flight. Even my sister stood up from her bench at the great loom and turned, making a graceful gesture of respect. Queen Leda had come.

I scrambled to my feet and made a quick, clumsy bow, holding up my hands to greet her. In public, even when the only other people present were slaves, we royal children had to salute our parents with the same reverence we would pay to the gods.

Mother acknowledged all of us with a curt nod, then pointed at my discarded distaff and spindle. "Helen, pick those up and come with me." Her voice was almost as sharp as when she'd reprimanded the Mykenaean ambassador. My stomach turned sour. *What have I done?*

We walked down the hallways of the palace in silence. I was almost too frightened to breathe. She led the way up a blue-and-crimson-painted stairway and brought me to the bedroom she shared with my father. It had a window that looked out over a small thicket of bright flowers and sweet-smelling herbs.

Mother sat down on the bed and motioned for me to sit beside her. The air was still and warm. I could hear the bees buzzing as they drank nectar from the courtyard flowers. Without a word, Mother took the spindle and distaff away from me.

"Is this the way you're always going to handle troubles, Helen?" she asked, her voice soft and kind. "By running away?"

I blushed. "I don't know what you mean."

She patted my hand, then without warning grabbed it and turned it over so she could examine the palm. One of her fingers traced the signs that the sword hilt had left on top of the calluses I'd already earned from the wooden spears. Six days hadn't been long enough to erase them.

"Oh, but you do," she said. "Why do your hands look more like your brothers' than Clytemnestra's? Tell me the truth."

"You already know it, don't you," I said. There was no need to make it a question. My mother nodded. "Who told you?" I asked.

"No one had to tell me," Mother replied. "I saw you practicing with the sword on the day Lord Thyestes's ambassador went back to Mykenae. I'd had enough of him, so I left your father to handle the ceremony of farewell without me and went off to hunt rabbits."

"Hunting rabbits?" I stared at my mother as if she'd grown a pair of horns. *"You?"*

She laughed, and twined a lock of my hair around one finger. "Your father loves rabbit stewed with onions. He says the ones I catch just for him taste best."

I tried to picture my tall, elegant mother crouching in the underbrush to set a snare. "Who taught you how to make rabbit traps?" I asked.

"Traps?" she echoed. "I haven't got the patience

for traps." She got up and reached under the big chest at the foot of the bed. The long wooden box she dragged out was painted with curls of ivy, garlands of pine boughs, and a pattern of wild boars, tusked and bristling. When she opened it, I gaped at the black bronze-banded bow and the arrows fletched with pheasant feathers.

"This is what I use to hunt," Mother said, grinning as she strung the bow. She did it as naturally as breathing. "Not just rabbits. I bring home game birds too, and deer, and even foxes, when I can outsmart them. The first time I saw your father, I'd just come home from the hunt. The forests of Calydon are thick with game, but the deer are so clever that it was the first time I'd managed to bring one down. I was so proud of what I'd done that I insisted on carrying the buck into the throne room myself and dropped it at my father's feet before I noticed we had a guest." She smiled at the memory.

"I'll bet Father thought you were Artemis herself," I said.

That made my mother laugh. "Not Artemis. You know how he feels about her. But he did say he mistook me for one of her huntress nymphs. That was just before he told me he had to marry me or die."

I made a face. "Father said *that*?"

"Men say many things when they want to win a woman. Whether or not they mean what they say . . ."

She shrugged. "Your father meant it. Poor soul, it seemed like he *would* die, because none of my father's advisers thought I should marry him. Tyndareus came to Calydon as a landless exile; his brother had stolen his kingdom."

The story of Father's early trouble and final triumph was so well known that the palace stones could tell it. "Did you come to Sparta to marry him after he won back his crown?" I asked. "Or did he have to go back to Calydon for you?"

"Are you asking because you want to know, or because you want to distract me from what we *need* to talk about?" Mother asked, her fingers curled around the polished curve of her bow.

I looked away. She touched my chin and gently turned me back to face her.

"It's all right, Helen," she said. "When I was your age, I, too, believed that if you buried a problem, it would go away."

"There's no problem," I said. "I'm through."

"Why? Because of what Glaucus said to you? I was standing in the shelter of the trees. I saw and heard everything. He was right, you know. You *did* act stupidly, running headlong at him like that, and it was just the sort of thing that would've gotten you killed in a real fight."

"I know," I said, miserable. "That's why I quit!"

"Yes," she said. "But why did you start?"

"I don't know. It was silly."

"We both know that's a lie," my mother said. She set aside her bow and picked up the women's tools I'd brought with me. She studied the thread wound around the spindle and the clump of carded wool tied to the distaff. I knew I'd made a mess of both and waited for her to say so.

Instead, she said, "For once, your distaff doesn't look like you stuck it into a bird's nest. And look at this: It's the smoothest thread I've ever seen you spin."

"It ought to be," I muttered. "I worked on it for five days."

"And how many days did you work with the sword? One. Don't you think the sword deserves at least as much of a chance as the spindle?"

I gave her a startled look. "Are you saying that you *want* me to go back to training with my brothers?"

My mother held my hands in both of hers. "That would be easy, wouldn't it?" she said. "So easy to let someone else make your choices for you. That way, if you fail, it isn't your fault." She clasped my hands more tightly. "You deserve to live a better life than that."

"I—I don't understand." My mother's words confused me. I was only ten years old.

She let go of my hands and leaned back. "You will, if you think about it. Then, whichever choice you make—sword or spindle or both—will be truly yours."

As I stepped out of the bedroom doorway, one

last question made me pause. "Mother?" I rested one hand on the doorpost, with its carved pattern of palm branches. "Mother, will you teach me how to hunt?"

She gave me a strange look. "Gladly. But why?"

"Because if I do choose to go back to the training ground and Father finds out and wants me to stop, I want to bring him a whole *cauldron* of stewed rabbit so he'll change his mind."

When Mother stopped laughing, she took me outside, off into the olive grove, and gave me my first archery lesson. I didn't hit anything, but as Mother told me (with a perfectly straight face), I did manage to scare the olives off a couple of trees.

I went back to the training ground the next morning. Glaucus didn't say a word about my absence. He was busy working with my brothers, so the only welcome I got from him was a silent nod and the hint of a satisfied smile.

He had the boys practicing with wooden swords, fighting both of them at once and winning. He made it look so easy, even though they outnumbered him and were younger and faster on their feet. When he smacked Castor's sword aside with one blow and disarmed Polydeuces on the backstroke, I first thought: *There's no shame in losing a match to someone like that.*

While my brothers scrambled to pick up their swords, Glaucus turned to me. "Well, princess," he said. "Will you be staying, or is this just a visit?"

I let his sarcasm wash past me. "I'm staying," I said simply. "If you'll take me back."

This time his smile was wide. "*She* spoke with you, didn't she," he stated. "The queen. I thought I caught sight of her in the woods that day."

"What? *Mother* told you to come back?" Castor exchanged a bewildered look with his twin.

"She didn't *tell* me to do anything," I said.

"No," Glaucus said, looking at me thoughtfully. "I don't suppose anyone could do that." I didn't know whether to be pleased or insulted.

The first day of my return to training didn't go well. I was rusty, and my brothers each took full advantage of that when paired off against me. Wooden swords leave wide, purple bruises, but by the end of the day I'd given back one for every five I got, which was good enough for me.

I knew I wouldn't be able to outshine my brothers anytime soon. Even if I trained with them daily and sacrificed a whole herd of sheep to Ares, it couldn't happen: They were five years older than me, and they'd begun their training when I was still an infant. Worse for me, at fifteen my brothers were already tough and strong. How I envied them for the way their bodies had changed, and how I wished mine would do the same!

# NEWS FROM MYKENAE

I got my wish for a changed body the year I turned twelve, though not the changes I'd been hoping for. Overnight, my legs and arms became so long that I couldn't govern them. That made me clumsy, both in the house and on the training ground. Clytemnestra hadn't been cursed by any such sudden growth. She was still small and graceful. I hoped no one else had noticed how awkward, how *different* I'd become.

I had to give up that hope once and for all on a late-winter day halfway through my twelfth year. While cold rain pelted down outdoors, I stayed in the palace, helping Mother, Clytemnestra, and Ione store some of my sister's bride goods. Father came in to see how we were doing. If he intended to inspect the piles of carefully folded cloth, he forgot all about it when he took a good look at me.

"By Ceres, Ione, what have you been feeding her?" Father exclaimed, resting his hands on my shoulders. "She's taller than a boar spear!"

"You needn't tell *me*." My nurse snorted. "I'm the one who's got to make her new clothes all the time, so she still looks like she's wearing a dress instead of a boy's tunic."

"Well, Helen, whatever you've been eating that's made you sprout up like this, you could use a little more," he told me. He held out one of my arms. "Tsk. It's a reed." His tone was fond, but his words stung me anyhow.

Clytemnestra chimed in, oh-so-sweetly. "Father, don't make fun of Helen. I'm sure she feels bad enough about her face without you teasing about what's happened to the rest of her."

"What's this nonsense?" Father demanded, giving her a severe look. "There's nothing wrong with Helen's face!"

"Of course not," Mother said calmly. "My looks changed in just the same way when I was her age—my face, my body, everything so bony and bumbling! But after a couple more years passed, it was quite a different story." She smiled.

How could she tell such obvious lies? She'd *never*

been as scrawny and clumsy as me. It wasn't possible! A stork didn't turn into a swan. I couldn't stand to hear any more. "Will you all stop talking about me as if I were a stone?" I exclaimed. "I'm right here!" And with that, I *wasn't* right there. I ran off, my cheeks flaming with embarrassment, leaving my family to pick apart my appearance to their hearts' content.

The awful thing was, Clytemnestra was right. My face had changed along with my body. When guests came to Sparta, all their compliments now seemed to be about my height. I learned that *regal* is just a polite way to say spindle-thin and sapling-tall. I didn't need Mother's mirror to tell me that I was no longer "the pretty one," but every year on my birthday I stole a peek at it anyway. It told me what I already knew: My face was thinner, the cheekbones and chin sharper, the nose more prominent, and the mouth wider-looking.

I didn't *need* to be "the pretty one," but I needed to be *something*. If I wasn't pretty anymore, what was I? Who was I now?

I was glad to have the training ground for my refuge. When I was there, I didn't have time to brood over my changed looks. I used Glaucus's lessons to get my gawky arms and legs back under control.

By the time I was thirteen, I not only looked like a younger version of Polydeuces, I was fighting like one too. Sometimes I was even able to give my brothers better than I got during our sparring matches, though by that time they were eighteen, full-grown young men, using real swords except when I challenged them to a bout. They complained that I won because they'd forgotten how to handle a wooden blade. Glaucus just told them to shut up and accept defeat like honorable men. As for me, I told them that as soon as Glaucus let me use a real sword all the time, they'd need to find some new excuse when I beat them.

That day finally came when I turned fourteen. There had been a great fuss in the palace that morning. Clytemnestra and I stood beside Father while he made a thanksgiving sacrifice to his favorite goddess, Aphrodite, in our honor. After that, we were given sweetened, watered wine and plate after plate of cake drenched with honey and sprinkled with chopped figs and almonds. After just a few bites it got too sweet for me, but Clytemnestra made a pig of herself, honey dribbling down her chin.

I couldn't wait to get away. Glaucus had been dropping hints for a whole month about how there'd be something special waiting for me when my fourteenth birthday came. As soon as I could manage it, I ducked away, changed my clothes, and raced to the training ground.

My brothers were already there, grinning, nudging each other, and whispering until Glaucus reminded them that even though they had beards and brawn, he could still put a sandal up their backsides. They dropped their clowning, and only then he gave me the sword.

It was more like a large hunter's knife than the warrior's blades my brothers used, but it was new. I could tell that Glaucus had had it made specially for me. I was so overjoyed, I felt ready to fly.

Two months after our fourteenth birthday, on the very day that Clytemnestra sewed the final stitch of crimson thread into the delicate, saffron-yellow wool of her last and finest of her bridal dresses, a courier from Mykenae came running up the steep, rocky path to the palace. It was a most wonderful coincidence; you could almost hear the gods laughing.

We royal sons and daughters all knew that something significant was happening. Father sent word for us to put on our most splendid clothes and come to the great hall. This was the room where all important visitors were greeted and where Father handed down his most vital decisions about the future of Sparta.

There was a small blaze burning in the large, circular hearth that lay in the middle of the room, in front of Father's throne. The thin thread of smoke wafted up and out past the second-floor balconies that ran all around the wide square opening above. The sun was still high enough to pour light into the hall, so no one had to light the stone oil lamps.

My brothers were at Father's right, sunlight and flame flickering over their tanned faces. My place was at Mother's left, and Clytemnestra was between our parents. We were all supposed to keep our eyes straight ahead, the picture of dignity, but even though I stood as if my feet had taken root among the brightly painted patterns on the floor, I couldn't help letting my eyes wander.

The messenger stood on the far side of the fire, on travel-weary legs. He'd been given wine and other refreshments the moment that he arrived (we Spartans knew how to be good hosts) and was even offered some time to rest after the long journey from the north, but apparently he'd refused.

*What he's got to say must be urgent,* I thought. *I wonder if he's brought us good news or bad?*

Father's throne was carved from stone, massive and immovable, but for certain occasions a smaller, wooden throne was brought in for Mother. When I saw her sitting beside him like that, tall and proud and beautiful as a goddess, I found it hard to believe that this was the same woman who'd gone hunting through the hills with me just the other day. The deer we'd shot was in the hands of the kitchen slaves. My arrow was the first to hit it, but hers was the one that brought it down.

I saw how the messenger stared at Queen Leda, drinking in her beauty. *He's probably thinking that it's all true, the story about how Zeus himself fell in love with Mother,* I thought. He was so distracted that Father had to ask him twice to speak. *Finally* he did. "Hail, Lord Tyndareus! Greetings and love from my noble master, Lord Thyestes of Mykenae. My king asks the gods to bless you and your house and bids me say that the day you have all prayed for has come. Prince Tantalus is ready to receive his bride. Lord Thyestes has made rich sacrifices in all the temples of Mykenae and even sent offerings to Apollo's shrine at Delphi, asking for blessings on your children's future. The omens are good; the gods approve."

"May the gods bless Lord Thyestes and all his royal house," Father replied, speaking as formally as the occasion demanded. "You will feast with us tonight to celebrate the happy news you've brought us. You will then return to Lord Thyestes tomorrow and tell him to prepare to receive my daughter, the princess Clytemnestra. She'll leave in five days' time, accompanied by her bridal goods and attendants, including her brothers, the princes Castor and Polydeuces, the royal sons of Sparta. Tell your master that my queen and I pray our daughter will be a wife worthy of Lord Thyestes's son."

I looked at my sister. She'd spent the past four years of her life preparing to become Prince Tantalus's bride, the future queen of Mykenae. Now the waiting was over. In only five days, she'd leave her land, her home, her family. What was she feeling? I tried to read her face. Her lips were pressed together tightly and I saw a little red rising to her cheeks, but that was all.

*She always did say she was eager to leave us,* I thought. *I know we're supposed to stand here like statues, but if I were the one getting my heart's desire, at least I'd smile, just a little.*

After the feast that night, I took the earliest possible opportunity to go back to my room. I didn't bother calling for Ione to fetch a little oil lamp—the moon was almost full, and the stars washed the sky with light. I could see well enough, and I wanted to be alone. I needed some time to myself, to think about what my life was going to be like after Clytemnestra left.

My sister and I might not have gotten along as well as Castor and Polydeuces, yet there was still a bond between us. I treasured the times that she'd treated me like a friend, not a rival. What would she say if I let her know that I envied her as much as she seemed to envy me? She had such a talent for making beautiful things! The blouse she'd embroidered as a gift for me was the finest thing I owned. When she helped me with my own dreadful needlework, she did it without making fun of my poor skills. I think that was the best way she had to let me know she cared about me. I wished I had a way to show how deeply I cared about her.

A cool breeze came in through the window,

bringing the green scent of cedars and pine from the hills. I stood there gazing out toward the mountains, wondering if my sister would believe me if I told her how much I'd miss her.

A strange sound from behind me made me turn quickly. The moonlight couldn't reach every corner of my room; the small, half-choked sound was coming from a deep pool of darkness in the corner nearest the doorway.

"Who's there?" I called. The sound came again, and now I recognized it: a sob.

Before I could say another word, the sob broke into a harsh bout of weeping as a shadow came rushing out of the corner and into my arms. Soft hands clung to me, a tear-streaked face pressed itself against my cheek, and in my ear my sister's anguished voice cried, "Oh, Helen, it's really *happening*. I just realized that it . . . I'm scared. I don't care if I'm never queen of anything, I don't want to marry a *stranger*! Sister, save me; you're our future queen, there must be *something* you can do. Talk to Father, to Mother, beg them to change their minds; they'll listen to *you*. Don't let them do this to me! Oh, Helen, please help me. I want to die!"

I let her cry in my arms until we heard the sound of footsteps and Ione came running into my room, carrying a lamp.

"There you are!" she exclaimed when the light

fell on Clytemnestra. "When you weren't in your room, I—"

My sister threw herself into our nurse's arms and wept louder while I told Ione what was wrong. She was sympathetic, but coldly practical. "A fine time to change your mind!" she told Clytemnestra. Then she turned to me. "Not that it would've mattered if she'd said no to this four years ago. It's Lord Tyndareus's decision. You can talk to your father all you like, child, but don't expect him to call off the marriage. Didn't you hear the messenger? The gods have spoken."

Ione had a point. The gods desired my sister's marriage. More important, the king of Mykenae desired it, and Mykenae was powerful and proud. If Father called off the wedding, the insult could bring war. One girl's unhappiness was nothing next to the safety of all Sparta. He'd never budge, but I couldn't just accept that without doing something for my sister. At least I had to *try*.

Lord Thyestes's messenger headed back north the next morning. As soon as he was out of the palace, I went to my parents and said I needed to speak with them about an urgent, private matter. The three of us went up to their sleeping chamber, where I told them that when Clytemnestra and my brothers set out for Mykenae, I wanted to go too.

"Out of the question," Father said almost before I'd finished speaking.

"Tyndareus, wait," Mother said, taking my hand. "Let her tell you her reasons before you say no."

"What reasons could she have that would be more important than her safety?" he countered. "The roads are full of dangers."

"But you're sending Clytemnestra over those same roads," I pointed out.

"She *has* to go," he said. "You don't."

"But I *want* to," I said. "My sister needs me. She's going to a strange land, a strange house, a total stranger for a husband. It's terrifying! If I travel with her, she'll have something familiar to hold on to, someone to talk to on the journey."

"She'll have the boys," Father replied.

"They'll be on horseback all the way to Myke- nae," Mother told him. "And they won't have time to talk to her or even listen to her: They'll be too busy staying alert for any perils on the road."

"She'll be riding in a cart, all alone," I put in. "Fa- ther, *please.* She's so unhappy. Let me go!"

"Let you go?" he echoed. "Have you forgotten you're the heir to Sparta? Do you expect me to put all of my children into Thyestes's power? Why don't I just hand him my sword and let him cut my throat?"

"But Thyestes is our kinsman now," Mother maintained. "He'd never—"

"A lot that means to a Mykenaean!" Father countered. "You know the stories."

"So do you," Mother said bitterly. "You still gave him our daughter."

"What choice did I have?" Father's jaw tightened. "He wanted an alliance, guaranteed by marriage. Clytemnestra is the price of peace."

"Is that what you want me to do when I'm queen of Sparta?" I asked. "*Buy* peace?"

Father gave me a sad look. "I don't do this gladly, Helen. We Spartans are never afraid to fight, but even if we'd win a war with Mykenae, it would take so many years and cost us so many lives that Sparta would be defenseless afterward. Your enemies will always be watching for any signs of weakness. Remember *that* when you're queen."

"Then why not show Lord Thyestes just how strong we *really* are?" I asked. "Father, if you let me go to Mykenae with Clytemnestra, it will be like saying, *See the power of Sparta, Lord Thyestes! We're so mighty that we have no fear of letting all of our children travel beyond our borders at once, even our future queen! We have no fear of you at all.*"

"That," said Father, "is a bad idea." And he sent me away.

In the days that followed, my sister did nothing but weep quietly in her bed while the servants packed her things. I spent my days at her side, trying to cheer her, telling her how much I envied her the chance to travel, to see new places, new people. Who knew what adventures the road to Mykenae might hold? She only sobbed that she didn't *want* any adventures, she just wanted to stay home or die.

She refused to eat, making Ione so frantic that she fetched Mother. Mother took one look at Clytemnestra's haggard face and went to speak with Father. Soon the palace halls echoed with sharp words and loud arguments as Father's counselors and highest-ranking noblemen were drawn into the matter.

On the afternoon of the fourth day, Mother sat beside me on Clytemnestra's bed and told me to go to my room. Puzzled, I obeyed, and when I got there I found Ione busily packing my clothes. Father came in before I could question her.

"Your idea about going to Mykenae with Clytemnestra isn't so bad after all," he said wearily. "It's certainly the best I've heard, these past few days. Others have just said everything from 'Call off the marriage' to 'Just send her, weeping or not; she's Lord Thyestes's problem now.' It's bad enough that I must give her in marriage to Mykenae. I'll tear out my own heart before I cause her any further pain. Your brothers will look after you, and you'll ride with my best soldiers for guards. Do what you can to comfort your sister, and may the gods watch over all my children."

# PART II
# MYKENAE

## 7

# THYESTES'S SNARE

The next dawn found me seated beside my sister as our ox-drawn cart began the tedious overland trek to Mykenae. Even though the hard wooden slats we sat on were thickly cushioned with folded cloaks and blankets, I still felt as though my spine was going to be jounced out of my body when the lumbering wheels rolled over the next rock in our path.

And the smell! The gods alone knew what the oxen had been eating, to give off such a stench. I tried breathing through my mouth, but it didn't help.

Clytemnestra dealt with the discomforts of the road by complaining, her voice crowding my ears so thoroughly that it often blotted out the creaking of the cart, the tramping of our guards' sandaled feet, and the clash, clatter, and jangle of the wagons behind us, all loaded with my sister's bridal goods. I let her grumble all she liked—it was better than her helpless tears. Sometimes I persuaded my brothers to ride their horses alongside our cart and let her gnaw on their ears, for a change.

It worked, but it was tiring for all of us. By the time we reached the outskirts of Mykenae, the four of us were heartily sick and tired of each other's company. As our train of wagons began the climb up to the great gates of the city, two colossal stone lions above the entrance to the citadel glared down at us in vain. We were all too worn out to be impressed.

We were welcomed with bread and salt by Lord Thyestes himself. The ruler of Mykenae looked like one of Zeus's own thunderclouds, his hair and beard a stormy gray, his eyes flashing like lightning. I didn't believe his words of friendship for a minute. He had a wolf's smile. It made my skin creep every time he looked at me, and he looked at me much too long and too often for comfort.

That night I couldn't sleep. Lord Thyestes had given me a queenly room all to myself. Though there were two loyal Spartan soldiers standing guard outside my door, I was too tense to close my eyes. I'd wanted to share a room with my sister, but the king wouldn't allow that. He claimed it would be an insult to all Sparta if I weren't given lodging worthy of my rank. Maybe he was telling the truth, but I still felt like the deer that the hunting hounds isolate from the herd before they bring her down.

I tossed and turned, then got up and looked for the long, narrow box that held my jewelry and ornaments. As the heir of Sparta I'd been sent to Mykenae with enough necklaces, pins, and earrings to show off our land's prosperity. The box holding them was Glaucus's gift to me, and only the two of us knew its secret: When I tilted back the lid, with its inlaid patterns of pomegranates, and touched a secret catch inside, the false bottom of the box came loose, revealing my sword.

It comforted me to hold the little blade and practice some of the fighting moves that Glaucus had taught me. Just knowing that I wasn't helpless was enough to push my fear of Lord Thyestes and his wolfish grin back into the shadows. Smiling, I hid the sword away again and went to sleep.

My sister was married on the third day of our visit. It was a grand event, with lavish sacrifices made to all the gods and two nights of feasting. Clytemnestra's husband, Tantalus, wasn't young or handsome, but he wasn't *too* old or ugly either, and his homely face was so kind that it was impossible to believe he was Lord Thyestes's son.

"When he saw how frightened I was, he made it a point to tell me that even though we're married, we won't live as husband and wife until I'm ready," Clytemnestra confided in me as we sat together at the table during the first banqueting night. Her fears had begun to fade and she looked like her old self again. "Look at the wedding gift he gave me!" She proudly showed off the gold diadem in her hair with its embossed design of ivy leaves.

"I helped him choose it!" The boy seated beside me blurted out the words as though he'd been saving them up all his life. I knew who he was, because he'd been presented to us along with all the rest of the Mykenaean nobility: Prince Aegisthus, Lord Thyestes's youngest living son. He was skinny, dark, about the same age as my sister and me, and had the first soft sprouting of whiskers on his upper lip.

"It's beautiful," I said. "You did a good job."

The simple compliment made him blush crimson. "I just told Tantalus that girls like plant patterns more than animals," he muttered. "That's right, isn't it? Or do you like animal patterns better?"

I smiled at him. "I like both."

"Because if you'll tell me what you *really* like, I'll make sure to get it for you."

My smile wavered. "You don't need to—"

"But I want to!" Suddenly, Aegisthus was gazing at me as if I were something he feared and wanted at the same time. "At first I didn't, but now that I've seen you"—he gulped for air—"I want you to like me."

"I *do* like you." I said it without thinking. "You don't need to give me an expensive gift for that."

"But you've got to have a bridal gift from me," he said. "One that's good enough for someone like you."

I don't know how the rest of the banquet went. I was too stunned by Aegisthus's declaration. Only the bride's husband could give her a gift as rich and gorgeous as a gold diadem. Suddenly it was clear: Without anyone bothering to ask or tell me *or* my father, it had been decided that I was going to marry Aegisthus. No need to wonder who'd made *that* decision. How convenient for Mykenae.

That night I sent one of my guards to fetch my brothers. I sat in the dark, clutching the hilt of my sword, until they came. When I told them what I'd learned, they wanted to scoop me up and race back to Sparta as fast as their horses could run. Polydeuces wanted to kick Thyestes over a cliff first.

"Stop it," Castor said. "You know we can't do any of that. If we run away, the Mykenaeans will use the insult as an excuse to start a war."

"Even if they don't do that, they'll take it out on Clytemnestra," I added. "This is all my fault for insisting on coming here. I'm going to have to deal with the consequences." I took a deep breath to slow my racing heart. "It'll be all right. As long as Thyestes doesn't do anything to *force* me into marrying his son, I'll just have to put up with the rest of it until it's time for us to go home."

"*I* say it's time to go home *now*," Polydeuces insisted. "Before Thyestes can come up with some scheme to keep you here until you agree to the marriage."

"He can keep me here until the sky shatters," I replied. "I won't marry Aegisthus or any other Mykenaean princeling, and he can't make me!"

My brothers just shook their heads.

Castor and Polydeuces tried to stay with me as much as possible the next day. They were waiting for me the instant I stepped out of my room.

"What are you doing here?" I asked.

"Protecting you," Castor said.

"I don't think you need to do that," I said. "I doubt he's going to abduct me. Where would he take me? I'm already inside his walls." I was trying to make a joke of a tense situation, but my brothers didn't see the humor. They also didn't see that Thyestes's strength wasn't in direct attack but in subtlety.

Though my brothers did their best to stay by my side all day, Thyestes found one excuse after another to separate us. In the morning he told my brothers that the young warriors of Mykenae wanted to test their skills against the princes of Sparta. How could Castor and Polydeuces refuse? And how could I be allowed to go with them when girls were forbidden to watch men's athletic contests? In the afternoon he told them that they had to speak for Sparta before the Mykenaean nobles. That was no place for a girl either, even the Spartan queen-to-be.

Keeping my brothers and me apart was only part of the old fox's plan. While Castor and Polydeuces were elsewhere, the king pushed Aegisthus and me together. I could have hidden myself away in my room until the banquet, but I was no coward. I was Helen of Sparta, and I wouldn't run away when I could fight.

The gods must have approved of my bravery, though poor Aegisthus suffered for his father's arrogance. It was sad. He tried his awkward best to entertain and impress me, while I pretended he wasn't there. My coldness confused and hurt him, I could tell, but I didn't want to give him any false encouragement and I didn't know what else to do.

That night, during the second wedding banquet, my brothers tried to introduce the subject of our return to Sparta. Predictably, Lord Thyestes refused to hear a word about it. "How can you go so soon? You'll break your sister's heart." He gave Clytemnestra a look of false fondness that quickly became a frown when she made no move to look appropriately heartbroken. He tried a different tactic. "Of course, if you haven't found our hospitality here to be good enough for you, I'll understand if you leave."

What could my brothers say to that without insulting the king of Mykenae? Castor and Polydeuces had to assure the king that they'd only offered to leave because they didn't want to burden Mykenae with the expense of lodging and feeding us and all our followers.

*That* was a mistake.

"I see." Lord Thyestes steepled his fingers. "How kind of you to consider the welfare of your sister's new home. By all means, then, send half your men back to Sparta tomorrow. I did wonder why you felt you had to come here surrounded by a small army. The roads between Sparta and Mykenae have bandits, not monsters."

Castor and Polydeuces exchanged a stricken look. They were not much of a match for the old king's wit. Now, if they refused to send home half our soldiers, they'd be liars. If they complied, we'd never have enough men on our side if Thyestes decided that the time had come to force me into marrying his youngest son.

So we discovered that words as well as swords could win battles.

My brothers yielded, telling the king that we were very grateful for his generosity and we'd stay as long as he liked. They made no mention of sending away any of our men, but Thyestes let that pass. As he sat there, stuffing his face with food, the chief steward of the palace approached and whispered something in his ear. Thyestes sat up straight, annoyed at being disturbed while he was eating.

"Yes, yes, I know he's been waiting all day; I've been busy," he said irritably, wiping the grease from his lips with the back of his hand. "Send him in."

The steward bowed and withdrew. He returned shortly, followed by a short, scowling man whose hair and clothes were still heavy with the dust of the road.

"Hail, Lord Thyestes of Mykenae," the man declaimed. "I bring greetings from my master, Lord Oeneus of Calydon."

Thyestes's eyebrows rose. Calydon, my mother's native land, lay far to the northwest, across the isthmus of Corinth. The messenger had a tale of wonders to tell us, a tale of the gods themselves. Old men at Lord Thyestes's table listened like spellbound children while the road-worn man told about how his master had made the worst mistake any mortal can. When he sacrificed to the gods in thanks for a good harvest, he forgot to include them all. Artemis, goddess of the moon and the hunt, received no sacrifice. It was an oversight, but the gods don't care about mortal excuses: They only know that the payment for any insult is revenge.

"Now a wild boar is ravaging Calydon," the messenger said. "A monstrous boar like a mountain, with hooves of bronze and tusks as big and sharp as scythes. The goddess Artemis sent him to punish my lord Oeneus. The beast destroys everything that crosses his path. His hooves and tusks tear up fields of grain; he breaks down the walls of houses and rampages through the streets of towns. He slaughters our herds and chases all the other game from our forests. The people starve. The hunters who've tried to kill him are gutted with a single slash of his tusks, their hounds trampled into bloody muck under the monster's hooves. And that is why, Lord Thyestes, my master has at last realized that this beast can't be killed by ordinary men. For this hunt, he wants heroes."

There was a great murmuring when the messenger fell silent. Many of the Mykenaeans rose to their feet, eager to start out for wild Calydon that very moment. Every young man there was ready to proclaim himself a hero. My brothers were no exception, but not because they wanted glory. "Lord Oeneus is our uncle!" Castor cried, leaping up from his place at the table. "His queen, Althea, is our mother's sister."

"Our kinsmen need us!" Polydeuces, too, leaped up. He gave our host a wicked grin as he added, "My lord Thyestes, we have no choice. We must go." I could have kissed him.

Before the king could open his mouth to offer a word of protest or argument, I rose from my place. "My brothers, the gods bless your bravery." I pictured myself as Mother at her most queenly as I announced, "I make a sacred vow, by Artemis the huntress, that on

the day you kill the boar, I'll make a thanksgiving sacrifice at her temple in Calydon with my own hands.
May the gods destroy me or any other who keeps me
from fulfilling this promise."

The Mykenaeans cheered my sisterly devotion as
I sat down. I stole a sideways look at our host. He
wasn't cheering. Instead, he looked ready to bite
through bronze. Between my brothers and me, the old
fox had been outfoxed. It was all I could do not to
crow in triumph.

# PART III
# CALYDON

‹o›‑ ‑ 8 ‑ ‑‹o›

# THE HUNTRESS

The journey to Calydon was long and grueling, but I felt like singing all the way. Being free of Lord Thyestes was worth a thousand jolts in the oxcart.

During the trip north, I came to realize that my brothers really were all grown up, men in fact as well as name. As soon as we were out of sight of Mykenae, they began to take precautions for our protection, in case Thyestes decided to try to regain what he'd lost. It made me proud to see how Polydeuces organized our soldiers to stand double watches by night and how he commanded them to scout the land by day. A mouse couldn't have sneaked up on us.

As for Castor, he opened all the supplies that Thyestes had given us and called for volunteers to taste a mouthful of everything, down to the smallest clay jar of water. Even then, he insisted that half of our men eat first while the other half waited to see if the food and drink had any ill effects. (They didn't. Lord Thyestes wasn't *that* desperate to recapture me.)

All of this made it slow going for us until we reached Corinth, where we were able to get supplies we could trust. It was also in Corinth that my brothers suggested I go home.

"Go back?" I said. "You might as well have handed me over to Thyestes in the first place."

"You won't have to go through Mykenaean territory," Castor argued. "You can go home by ship; we'll send word to Mother and Father to have you met at the coast—"

"And break my vow to Artemis?" I asked sweetly. I had him there. A messenger was sent to Sparta to let our parents know that I would be traveling safely with my brothers, returning to Mother's homeland.

From Corinth, we were lucky enough to find a ship that was ready to sail for Calydon. My brothers and I had never traveled by sea, but Poseidon blessed us with a calm, swift, comfortable voyage, a real relief after that miserable, tooth-clattering oxcart. *I could get used to this,* I thought as I stood in the prow and watched sunlight glint across the water.

We arrived safely in Calydon and were welcomed by our aunt, Lady Althea, and her husband, Lord Oeneus. The king beamed when he saw how tall and strong my brothers were, worthy additions to his hunting party. He took them away at once to introduce them to the other warriors and to see what they could do on the training field.

My aunt took care of me, which meant she led me to my room, summoned a slave to attend me, told me that someone would come for me when it was time to eat, and left. I felt I'd been dropped like a bundle of old clothes.

"Tsk, poor Lady Althea," the slave muttered while she shook dust from my mattress. She was a fat, gray-haired woman, sweet-faced and motherly. "She has so much to do these days, I pity her."

A slave pitying a queen? This was new. "What's keeping her that busy?" I asked.

"Why, the great hunt, my lady; what else? So many guests, and more arriving every day! It's doubled and redoubled the work we've got to do inside these walls. And the queen must oversee it all constantly, to make sure that everything is worthy of her husband's hospitality."

I was eager to begin exploring the palace of Calydon, but I didn't get the chance to do it on my first day there. When the slave finished tidying my room and left, I stretched out on my bed just for a moment—so I told myself—and woke up to the last glow of the setting sun. I was still yawning and stretching when the motherly slave returned with a lamp and helped me prepare for dinner.

The palace hall was filled with tables, the tables packed with the great men of over twenty lands. My brothers and I were given places of honor, not because we'd done anything to earn them but because we were the queen's kin. I knew that where you sat at the king's table was the king's choice, so your seat told everyone exactly how much or how little he respected you.

Polydeuces must have impressed Lord Oeneus already. After just one day's display of his skill with sword and spear, he was seated between the king and the queen. Castor sat at Lord Oeneus's other side, and I was next to him. It was a good spot for observing the hall.

The place beside me was empty, which was odd. With so many heroes under Lord Oeneus's roof, a seat so near the king *had* to be filled. If not, it was as if Lord Oeneus were telling his guests, *None of you is worthy to sit this close to me.* It would be an unforgivable insult; all the warriors would leave, and the boar hunt would end before it began.

Castor saw me eyeing the empty seat and quickly put my puzzlement to rest. "That's for our cousin Prince Meleager," he whispered. "Polydeuces and I already met him, out on the training ground today. He's twenty-one, a couple of years older than us, but he looks much younger, and sickly in the bargain. Lady Althea was with him, asking him if he wouldn't rather go inside and rest, fussing over him as if he were a child. Thank the gods Mother would never embarrass *us* like that! Finally Lord Oeneus sent her on her way.

"Once she was gone, we saw the *real* Meleager. Helen, he's incredible. The instant he picked up a spear, you forgot how pale and thin and fragile he looks. Fast? He outran every one of us. Strong? I'm still aching from the wrestling match I lost to him." Castor chuckled.

"You didn't mind losing?" I asked.

He reached for a bowl of olives and dropped a handful on my plate. "Glaucus taught me better than to resent the man who beats you in a fair fight. Or the girl." He winked at me.

"Oh, *now* you admit I beat you fairly?" I teased.

"Who says I'm talking about you?" With that, my brother indicated a table that stood at the far end of the great hall. The men seated there were plainly dressed, young, and nowhere near as well muscled or imposing as Lord Oeneus's other guests.

"Who are they?" I asked.

"Servants," Castor replied. "Weapons bearers who came here with their masters. And one more. I'm surprised at you, Helen: Can't you recognize your own trick when someone else plays it?"

"What are you talking about, Castor?" I demanded.

"Open your eyes, little sister."

I did, and I saw something wonderful.

She wore an unadorned tunic, like most of the young men at that distant table, with her dark bronze hair pulled back and tied horse-tail style. The flickering light of the oil lamps made it easy to mistake her for a man, especially when I wasn't expecting to see a woman among the weapons bearers.

"Who is she?" I asked Castor. And then, in a whisper: "She doesn't *look* like a man; she's just dressed like one. If she's trying to disguise herself, it's not—"

"I was only teasing you about her having stolen your trick, Helen," Castor said fondly. "She's never tried to hide the fact that she's a woman from anyone; she's proud of it, if you ask me. Her name's Atalanta, and she's the daughter of Lord Iasius of Arcadia."

"A king's daughter? And our uncle sat her all the way down there?" I asked, nodding to the far end of the great hall. "With *servants*?" I was flabbergasted. The king had placed her so far away from him that she might as well have been in another room. The insult didn't seem to bother her or affect her appetite. She was eating heartily and had all of her dinner companions laughing at jokes I couldn't hear. "Does Lord Oeneus *want* war with Arcadia?"

"Oh, she's not here as a daughter of Arcadia," Castor replied, smiling. "She's here as one of us; she's come to hunt the boar."

"That's disgraceful," a new voice spoke in my other ear, making me turn sharply from Castor at the sound. While I'd been staring at Atalanta, our cousin Meleager had taken his place beside me at the table. He was just as frail-looking as Castor had described him, but there was nothing weak about the anger burning in his eyes.

"What's disgraceful, cousin, that a woman's a huntress?" I asked coolly. As a guest, I had to keep my own anger under control, but I didn't like my cousin's attitude toward Atalanta at all. "I'm surprised that something like that bothers you. I thought that in this land it's acceptable for royal women to know how to hunt. My own mother, your aunt, taught me the same tracking and archery skills she'd learned when she was still a Calydonian princess."

"That's not what I mean," Meleager replied. "The disgrace is how Father treats her. Maybe it's because he's only king of Calydon by marriage. If he'd been raised here, he might be more willing to accept her for what she is. Atalanta's at least as strong and brave as half the men here, and she can outrace us all. The day she came riding up to the gates, some oafish palace guard tried to send her away. When she dismounted and told him she refused to go until she'd seen the king, he tried to—what was that stupid thing he said?—to 'teach her she's a woman.'" My cousin had a wicked smile. "It was an unforgettable lesson . . .

for the teacher. She didn't even have to use a weapon to disarm him, knock him off his feet, and hold him helpless until the king arrived."

"I wish I'd seen that," I said.

"And I wish Father could remember that he did. He says that it's one thing for a girl to bring down a rabbit or two with her bow but that there's something unnatural about one who also knows how to use sword and spear, who can wrestle, ride, and race like a man. He acts as if each of her achievements is a fluke."

"True," Castor put in. "When she beat me at wrestling, Lord Oeneus took me aside and apologized for the poor condition of the ground. According to him, the only reason I lost was that my foot must've slipped on a stone. I know better than that. I have to admit it. She's not bad."

"You mean for a woman?" I asked, putting a little bite into the question.

"Don't put words in my mouth, little sister," Castor responded. "After just a short while on the training ground with her, I saw what she can do. I *felt* it. I don't know about the rest of the hunters, but Polydeuces agrees with me: She's a worthy companion. A pity that our uncle won't see that."

Meleager shook his head over his father's obstinacy. "How many times can he blame her wins on luck? He can't stand to see a mere girl outdo men time after time. Hasn't he heard of her exploits? The singers already know at least half a dozen stories about her triumphs as an athlete and a hunter."

"Maybe he thinks they're just stories," I said. "That's why he won't believe them."

Meleager snorted with disgust. "Then why is he so eager to believe the high-flown tales the singers recite about all of *them*?" He made a sweeping gesture that included every man feasting in his father's hall. Two red spots flared on his pasty cheeks as he spoke with even more indignation. "They don't even need the singers' tales. They do their own boasting well enough. *Too* well. They come here with stories about how they've slain giants and monsters, but where's the proof?"

I smiled, liking my cousin more and more. "What do you want them to do? Haul a dragon's head around with them everywhere they go?"

I was teasing, but he took me seriously. "A dragon's tooth would be enough. The hunter who kills the boar will be given its hide as a trophy—Father said so. The tusks go with the hide. I'll bet that whoever wins that prize will always carry one tusk with him from then on and show it proudly. That's because *this* beast is real. Anyone can destroy a thousand imaginary monsters."

He took a long drink of wine and fell silent. His eyes never left Atalanta for the rest of the meal.

As the feast went on, I saw what Meleager meant

about the other hunters' love of boasting. It didn't take much to get them started. Mention the weather and someone would claim to be the son of Zeus, master of the thunderbolt; say that you couldn't eat another bite and someone would start telling the tale of how he'd slain a giant who could eat a whole ox in one mouthful. As soon as one of them would finish, another would start.

I leaned toward Castor and whispered, "Want to play a game? If we hear ten stories about dead monsters before we hear ten about who's a god's son, I win. Otherwise, you do."

"Not fair! We've already heard at least six men speak." He lined up six olive pits on the table in front of him. "*All* of them claimed their fathers were gods. If I can't count them—"

"No, the game starts now, but you can count four of those, because I'm generous," I teased, snagging away two of the six pits. "I'm still going to win."

I had seven olive pits to Castor's nine when Pirithous of Thessaly stood up. He must have been a famous man, because he was seated just three places away from Lord Oeneus. He began by letting all of us know that he was the son of Zeus. Castor ate another olive, spat the pit into his hand, set it down with the others, and mouthed *I win* at me. I was just about to ask him for a rematch when Pirithous finished his brag with the words: "But my lone adventures are only half of it. For the rest, Lord Oeneus, we must hear my dearest friend, my heart's brother, Lord Theseus, king of Athens!"

At the sound of his name, Theseus rose from the seat next to Pirithous, a seat even closer to the king. I gaped at the sight of the handsomest man I'd ever seen, tanned and strong, with a ready smile. We were close enough for me to see his sea-green eyes and the streaks of gold running through his long, chestnut-colored hair. I didn't know why the sight of him made my blood pound in my ears and my breath grow short. Even though he was much older than I, I couldn't help feeling drawn to him. I even found myself thinking, *My sister's husband is much older than she is too.* When he caught me gazing at him and flashed me a grin, I blushed from neck to hair.

Then he opened his mouth to speak.

To hear him talk about his adventures, you'd think he and Pirithous had fought their way to the throne of Hades and back. Not only was he Poseidon's son, but he claimed a human father as well, the previous king of Athens. The monsters he'd slaughtered as a young man were the human sort—bandits who murdered innocent travelers—and then came his greatest victory: the minotaur! He'd sailed to Crete to face that terrible creature, half bull and half man. It feasted on human flesh, and Athens was compelled to send Crete seven youths and seven maidens every nine years to feed the beast. He slew it single-handedly, of course, freed the Athenian captives, and carried off heaps of Cretan gold, but not before he'd won the ardent love of the king's own daughter, Princess Ariadne.

"*I* put an end to the minotaur," Theseus declared. "Just as I'll put an end to the Calydonian boar!" No one challenged his story—or even thought to ask what had become of that devoted Cretan princess—partly because the scars crisscrossing his chest and arms proved he wasn't afraid of a real fight, but mostly because the other men soon went on to tell equally far-fetched tales of their own exploits.

So much for finding *that* attractive. I sighed. Theseus was handsome, but he was loud and arrogant. I remembered how Clytemnestra used to claim that my looks earned me unfair privileges, back when I was still a pretty child instead of the gangly girl I'd become. If someone would say the same of Theseus's appearance, I bet he'd simply reply, *Why, yes, of course I get special treatment, I'm entitled to it.* Ariadne could keep him, if she even existed in the first place.

While the hunters took turns praising themselves, I nudged Castor and whispered, "Where's the training ground?"

He thought he knew my reason for asking. "Oh

no you don't," he said. "This isn't Sparta. You heard what Lord Oeneus thinks of women who act like men. You'll offend him."

"What offends him is women who do *better* than men," I said. "Don't worry, I don't want to do sword practice with any of them." I indicated the still-swaggering hunters. "If one of them beats me, he'll claim I had twelve arms, six heads, and spat poison. I just want to watch how you're all preparing for the hunt."

"Well, well, so you want to watch *men* exercising?" Castor snickered. "My little sister's growing up!"

I gave him a hard look. "The boar isn't the *only* pig around here."

That made him laugh outright. "Ah, Helen, I'm only joking. But never mind where the training ground is. You can't go. Lord Oeneus has forbidden any woman from lingering there, distracting us. He wants us to concentrate on getting ready to hunt the boar."

I didn't say another word on the subject. My brother was wrong. I didn't want to go to the training ground to see the men; I wanted to watch Atalanta. I wanted to see for myself what a woman could achieve and how she did it.

I knew there was no question of sneaking there in my old disguise. My brothers would recognize me at once and send me away. They were honor-bound to respect the rules that our uncle had laid down.

That was all right. The training ground wasn't the only place where I might be able to observe that astonishing woman. I'd find a way to get what I wanted: I was a huntress too.

It took me three days before I was able to find Atalanta away from the training ground, even though my aunt's hectic life as hostess to all the hunters left me completely free. Each morning I disguised myself as a boy again and explored. No one bothered me. The coming boar hunt had filled the court of Calydon with dozens of new faces. I passed for just another one of the hunters' servants.

My plan was simple. Meleager said that Atalanta had come riding up to the gates of Calydon. I didn't know how to ride or much about horses, but I'd heard my brothers talk about the beasts often enough to know they needed to be exercised. I'd wait until Atalanta came to the stables to exercise her horse and follow her from there. I might not get to watch her practicing with weapons, but just being able to *see* her would be enough for me.

I went to the stables, made friends with one of the workers, and got a good look at Atalanta's horse. He was a fine animal, short and sturdy, with a broad back the color of autumn oak leaves and a sooty muzzle, mane, and tail. *She'd never let anyone else take care of him,* I thought.

I'd guessed right: Atalanta did exercise her own horse daily. The problem was *when* she did it: She didn't devote one set time for that activity. The first day I came to the stables, I learned she'd already been and gone. The second day, I loitered so long that one of the stablehands grew suspicious of a "servant" with no work to do. He chased me away before she got there. The third day, I thought my luck had changed: Atalanta arrived and mounted her horse while I was waiting.

That was when I learned that my simple plan to follow Atalanta from the stables had a simple flaw: No matter how fast I could run, a horse could run faster. She and her steed were away from the palace and lost in a cloud of dust, heading for the woodlands, before I even managed to pass through the citadel gates.

Running after her wasn't the answer. I looked down at the trail the horse had left and began to track it. The fresh hoofprints showed how horse and rider left the road and took a hunter's path into the foothills. Once or twice I lost the trail and prayed to keen-eyed Hermes to help me find it again. The trickster god answered my prayers with a fresh pile of horse dung right in the middle of my path.

I marched on without any sight of them until I began to worry whether I'd gone so deeply into the forest that I risked finding the boar before I found

Atalanta. Plus I hadn't thought to bring my sword, so I was defenseless.

*Stop that!* I told myself severely. *Have you seen or heard the beast nearby? Or do you think that a gigantic boar's like a forest nymph, able to slip through the trees and brush silently? You know he'd make enough noise to give you lots of warning. By the time he crossed your path, you'd be safe. Can he climb trees?*

That was when I heard hooves pounding through the undergrowth. I ducked behind a big beech tree just in time to see Atalanta come riding back down the path. I stayed hidden until she was well out of sight, then continued up the trail. If she had a favorite spot for exercising her horse, I intended to find it. On the other hand, if she only rode him into the hills and back to the palace, I needed to know that too.

I continued uphill, eyes on the horse's path, until I came to a clearing. It was ringed with ancient oak trees, and a little freshwater spring bubbled out of mossy rocks that cropped out of the earth at the northern end. The grass was torn up, and there were too many hoofprints for it to be a place she'd come to only once.

I crouched beside the spring and said a prayer of thanks to the unknown god who dwelled there, letting him know that he had my sincere gratitude for permitting me to find what I'd been seeking. Tomorrow I wouldn't try to follow Atalanta. I'd wait for her to come to me.

## 9

# ATALANTA'S STORY

The following day, I was up and out of the gates with the sunrise. In my hurry to reach the clearing, I forgot to bring any food or drink along with me, so by the time Atalanta appeared, my stomach was grumbling. I didn't care. I was convinced that any sacrifice of comfort was worth it, just to watch her. I found a venerable oak tree whose branches made for an easy climb and scaled it high enough for the foliage to conceal me. Then I waited.

I had no way of knowing how long I'd have to wait or even if this might be the one day that Atalanta decided to take her horse elsewhere for his exercise. My stomach kept up a long recitation of complaints until at last I decided it might be wise to ask the gods' help.

But which god? The answer was obvious, even though I didn't like it. Atalanta was a huntress; therefore, Artemis the huntress was the only one who could answer my prayer.

I muttered my petition quickly, not really expecting the goddess to hear me. Like Father, I disliked Artemis for her heartlessness, her readiness to punish the smallest insult, even if it happened only by oversight. I'd sworn an oath in her name, and though I fully intended to fulfill it once the hunt was over—I knew better than to cheat the gods—wouldn't she know I'd only used her as an excuse to escape Mykenae? Couldn't she tell how little I cared for her? Why should she do anything for me?

As I sat straddling the branch, alone with my thoughts and a very unhappy stomach, I heard the sound of hoofbeats approaching from farther down the hill. The next moment, Atalanta's horse burst into the clearing. I whispered my thanks to Artemis, though the part of me that didn't like that goddess still wondered whether I could trust her gift.

It was a joy to watch Atalanta ride. She moved smoothly and naturally with her horse, making it look as though together they were one miraculous creature. I forgot all about my empty stomach as I watched her put the little stallion through his paces. Sometimes, while riding him around the clearing at a gallop, she'd drop lightly to the ground and race beside him. She had no trouble matching his stride, and there were moments when I believed she could have outdistanced him, if she'd wanted to do it. When she grabbed the dangling reins and leaped back onto him as easily as if she had wings, I had to bite my tongue to keep from cheering her name and giving myself away.

I might as well have cheered, because she caught me.

"What are you staring at, boy?" Atalanta drove her horse straight at the tree where I was sitting and shouted up into the branches. Until that moment, I'd thought my shelter was impenetrable.

"Nothing," I muttered, clinging to a leafy limb of the ancient oak.

"Oh?" She raised one eyebrow. "Then what are you doing up there? Building a nest?"

"I'm picking acorns," I replied with as much dignity as I could manage. It was a stupid thing to say, but it made her laugh.

"Get down, little squirrel," she commanded me. "I won't hurt you."

I hung by my hands from the branch for a moment, then dropped to the ground in front of her, landing on an oak root and sprawling into last autumn's fallen leaves. My tumble startled her horse, but she controlled the huge creature with just a touch of her knees to his barrel.

When I stumbled back to my feet, brushing crushed leaves from my clothes, the horsewoman studied me closely. "Ah," she said at last. "I was wrong. You're no boy. You're the twins' sister Helen, the Spartan princess. I've seen you at dinner, always sitting next to Prince Meleager. Hasn't anyone ever told you that queens-to-be don't belong in trees?"

"And you're Atalanta the huntress, the one all the men are talking about. Hasn't anyone ever told you that women don't belong on horseback?" I shot back deliberately.

That made her laugh even more. "You tell *me* where we belong," she said, and before I could catch a breath, she leaned down, hooked one arm around me, and swept me up in front of her on the horse. With a shout and a light flick of her heels, she set the stallion into a gallop through the forest.

We left the little clearing far behind. The horse laid back his ears and ran flat out, threading a break-neck path around the trees. Atalanta shoved me forward just in time to dodge low-hanging branches and kept me from slipping off sideways whenever her steed made a sharp turn. I felt the wind whip across my face and thought, *So this is what it's like to fly!* I knotted my hands into the horse's mane and felt all my fears blow away behind us like so many dead leaves. I let out a whoop of joy and didn't want our wild ride to end until we'd ridden across the world.

Atalanta finally reined the horse back to a canter, then a trot, and finally a slow walk. We were on a rise just above the royal palace of Calydon. She dismounted gracefully and offered me a hand down, but I decided I'd show her I could do that for myself.

I swung one leg up and back, lost my balance for the second time that day, and hit the ground, splayed out like a starfish on a rock. I took the sheepskin pad with me. Atalanta's horse looked down at me, snorted, and walked away, flicking his tail disdainfully.

"Did he just laugh at me?" I asked, slowly sitting up. Every bone in my body felt like it'd been beaten with sticks.

"I hope so," she replied, grinning. "You earned it." She picked up the sheepskin, sat down on a large boulder, and rested one arm across her updrawn knees. "Now, care to tell me why you're wandering through the woods, dressed like that?" She indicated the sleeveless tunic I'd filched from Castor. It was much too big for me, even belted tightly. "Is it some Spartan custom, raising daughters to be sons?"

"My father's got sons," I said, standing up and shaking the dirt from my "borrowed" clothes.

"Mine didn't." Atalanta's mouth turned up at one corner, but it wasn't a smile. "When I was born, he was so disappointed that he ordered one of his servants to take me out to the mountains and leave me there to die." She gave me a sudden, penetrating stare. "I guess you've heard the stories?"

"The men say that you were fed and protected by

a she-bear until a party of hunters found you." I looked her in the eye. "I don't believe it."

"Good for you, girl," she said. "The part about the she-bear makes a good story, but it's not the truth. The rest is." She shrugged, then spoke matter-of-factly about what came of her father's coldhearted decision. "I was abandoned to die but found by the sort of people my father wouldn't understand. To them, a child was a child. To him, children were . . . tools. He only wanted a certain number and a specific kind; the rest were disposable. It was probably good that he didn't need a daughter; otherwise, I'd have spent my life being forced to fit the mold of what *he* decided I should be."

Her face was grim, and I saw her hands tighten into fists as she told me her story. I didn't want to make her dwell on so much ugliness, but I had to ask. "How do you know all this? About your father, I mean."

She relaxed a little and even smiled. "Oh, I like you! You can think. Yes, how *would* I know anything about either of my parents if I was abandoned as a baby? Well, the person my father sent off to do his dirty work was a slave, a man with no choice except to obey. The king might have owned his body, but his heart was his own. He wrapped me in a good, warm blanket before he followed my father's orders to abandon me in the wilderness, and he didn't lay me on the ground until he caught sight of a hunting party coming through the trees. Even then, he hid until he saw they'd found me." She looked into the forest, as if hoping to catch sight of that good man's spirit. "Then he came forward and told them who I was and why I'd been thrown away like an old rag. The only thing of any value that he owned was a single carnelian bead with a bear carved on it, but he offered the huntsmen that if they'd agree to help me."

"So that's where the she-bear in the story comes from," I said.

"Probably." Atalanta reached into her tunic and drew up a loop of leather cord. The brilliant burnt orange of carnelian glittered in the sunlight. "The man who became my foster father accepted this from the slave who saved my life. He didn't need it, but he took it because it was the only way he could make that good man believe he'd keep his promise to raise me. When he was dying, he gave it to me and told me the whole story." She cupped the carnelian bead in her palm and gazed at it as if it held her soul. "He never thought to ask the slave's name, but the gods know it, and I pray to them all to reward him."

She shook off the somber memories and tucked the necklace back out of sight. "Maybe I ought to thank my father for throwing me away. He'll never know it, but he gave me my freedom. I intend to keep it, and thanks to my foster father, I've got the means to do it."

"Is he the one who taught you to hunt?" I asked. Atalanta's reputation as a master of spear and arrow was already legendary.

"Yes, and how to ride a horse too." She whistled softly, and her stallion came trotting up, as obedient as a well-trained hound. She stroked his muzzle fondly. "There aren't enough men like him."

Something puzzled me. "The first time I saw you, my brother Castor told me you're the daughter of Lord Iasius of Arcadia. If your father abandoned you—"

"Why am I burdened with his name?" Atalanta finished the question for me. "Simple. Because men, even slaves, reveal many secrets on their deathbeds, and so when that good man died, my father found out what really had become of me. By then he'd changed his mind about needing a daughter, so he ordered my return, as if I were a borrowed cloak." She blew softly into the stallion's nostrils, a strange action that seemed to please the animal. "You can guess how well *that* worked. But he did acknowledge our blood tie so that now all the world knows it. I can't evade or deny it, much as I'd like to."

She took the bit out of the stallion's mouth, then looked back to me and said, "You still haven't answered my question: Why are you dressed like that?"

"It was the easiest way to get out of the palace and follow you," I replied. "No one stops a boy."

"That's clever," Atalanta admitted. "Though I wouldn't say you *followed* me. And why would you want to do that, anyway? Am I so fascinating because I'm a curiosity, the woman who hunts and rides like a man?"

"Is that what you think you are?" I said stiffly. "Back home, the warrior who taught my brothers how to fight with sword and spear taught me too. My mother taught me how to hunt. I hoped that you'd have something new to teach me; that's why I've been watching you. But if you say you're just a curiosity—" I turned away and started down the hillside.

Her hand fell on my shoulder before I'd gone ten paces. "The way to learn is face to face, not hiding in the treetops, little squirrel," she said. "Especially if I'm going to teach you how to ride."

"You'll do it?" I was her devoted worshipper once more. "You'll really teach me how to ri—?"

Just then, my belly gave a growl worthy of an earthquake, loud enough to silence me in mid-word. I lowered my eyes, embarrassed, but the huntress patted me on the back, and when I looked up again, I saw that she was smiling.

"I will, Helen. And the first thing I'll teach you is

this: Don't come to your riding lessons on an empty stomach!"

We sat down together on a nearby rock while the stallion grazed. Atalanta had some sheep's milk cheese wrapped in oak leaves stowed in the pouch at her belt, also a bit of bread and an apple. She was happy to give me the bread and cheese, but when I eyed the apple too she said, "No, greedy squirrel. This is for Aristos." She whistled, and the horse came trotting up to claim his treat.

While he gobbled the fruit, she stroked his neck and told me, "Aristos *is* the best. Why should I give him any other name? When you're on his back, see to it that you respect him or he'll have you off again before you can blink."

"I will, I promise, but . . . how could he tell if I didn't?" I asked.

"Trust me, horses *know* things." Atalanta offered me a drink of water from the leather flask she carried.

"I can believe that," I said, gazing at the stallion's dark, intelligent eyes.

"Now, the important thing for you to know before we begin is not to be afraid of him," Atalanta went on. "Aristos is very patient with children."

"I'm no child!"

"To him, you're an infant, which is good and bad at the same time. The bad part is that you know absolutely nothing about horses. The good part is that infants learn fast. Well, infant, are you ready?" She replaced Aristos's bit.

I stood up and wiped crumbs of bread and cheese from my hands and tunic. "Try me."

I had grand visions of mastering Aristos that very day, before the sun reached noon, and racing him all the way back to the palace. I was so taken by that image, I didn't bother including a place in it for Atalanta. It was just me and Aristos and a chorus of admiring gasps from everyone who saw us come galloping through the citadel gates.

Instead, I spent what was left of that morning just learning to get on the horse. Better to say *trying* to get on the horse. As Atalanta said, it didn't count as *on* if I just went toppling *off* the stallion's back as soon as I mounted him.

We began with Atalanta positioned by the horse's head, with me facing his left side. She offered her linked hands and told me, "Take hold of the reins, then put your left foot here and I'll give you a boost up."

"But I want to do this the same way you do," I objected. "No one helps *you* mount."

"Humor me." She bent forward a little so that her linked hands were lower. "You can try it without my help next time. For now, just do as I say and, whatever you do, *don't* let go of the reins."

I wanted to say, *You told me that already,* but decided to

hold my tongue. I was sure that once Atalanta saw how well I sat that horse, she'd realize I was ready for more-advanced lessons. I grabbed the reins in my left hand, rested my right on the sheepskin pad covering Aristos's back, placed my left foot in the huntress's hands, and bounded upward just as she gave me the promised boost.

I went over the top and off the far side, dropping the reins in mid-flight. Luckily for me, I rolled when I hit the ground and only got a light bruising. Aristos gave me a disdainful look over one shoulder, then ambled away.

Atalanta stood over me, arms folded. "Would you like to try that again?" she asked, doing her best not to smile.

I got up, trudged over to Aristos, took his bridle, and led him back to his mistress. "As many times as it takes."

It took many, *many* times. My second attempt at mounting ended when I dropped the reins just as I landed on the fleecy pad and Aristos bolted, sending me tumbling. My third failed when I knocked the sheepskin off on my way up and found nothing between me and the stallion's back. That was when I learned just how slippery horsehair is. By good fortune, Atalanta managed to catch me when I slid off.

On the fourth try, I held tight to the reins, landed on the sheepskin, and straddled the horse proudly. Atalanta looked pleased, or perhaps just relieved.

And then I looked down. Sweet Aphrodite, was the ground *that* far away? Aristos's back hadn't seemed so high up when I'd ridden under Atalanta's protection, but now I was all by myself atop a horse who was suddenly tall as an oak tree! I yelped and leaned forward, clutching for his mane and neck, trying to hold on to his body the way I'd held on to that branch.

The branch was narrower. The branch didn't *breathe,* shifting shape constantly, making itself wider and narrower by turns and far more difficult for my legs to grasp. The branch didn't decide to start moving without warning. I made the mistake of leaning even farther forward, lost my balance, and fell off once more.

Aristos took about ten steps, then came back to give me a long look that as good as asked, *What are you doing down there?*

By the time Atalanta announced that the lesson was over, I'd managed to mount Aristos and stay mounted, but just barely. Dismounting—deliberately and with some style, not merely falling off the horse—was another story. I begged her to give me more time.

"I'd like to, little squirrel, but I need to go back to the citadel, to join the others. If I don't show up on the training ground, they'll all say it's because I'm just another undependable woman."

"Not *all* of them," I said. "My brothers respect you, and Prince Meleager thinks you're skilled *and* beautiful."

The moment the words left my lips, I regretted blurting them out. Atalanta gave me a quizzical look. "Did he *say* that? That I'm beautiful?"

I shrugged, hoping she'd let the matter drop. No matter how my cousin had praised Atalanta, it wasn't my right to repeat it.

"Mmm. I see. Well, Helen, if you ever find your tongue again, feel free to tell your cousin that I thank him for thinking highly of my abilities but to save his opinion of my looks. I didn't choose my face. It's a random gift from the gods. But I am pleased to know that he appreciates my *true* accomplishments. That compliment's worth even more to me, coming from a man whose own athletic skills are so impressive."

"Do you—do you *like* my cousin?" I asked.

A strange, thoughtful expression crossed the huntress's face before she replied. "I do like him, but not the way I think *you* mean it. And I respect him. You can tell him that too."

I'd seen the longing in Meleager's eyes when he looked at Atalanta at dinner. I had the feeling that he wanted more than her *respect.*

Holding the reins herself, Atalanta gave me a lift onto Aristos, then jumped up in back of me. We rode most of the way back to the citadel together. I asked her to stop and let me down in the shade of some pine trees beside the road at a point from which the stronghold gates still looked as small as the first joint of my thumb. I could see the citadel, but as long as I stayed behind the trees, no one there, however hawkeyed, could see me.

"I'll walk from here," I told her as I stood stroking Aristos's neck. "I don't want anyone paying too much attention to me when I go back inside, and if I come riding in with you, it'd be too conspicuous. One of the guards might take a *good* look at me and realize I'm not a boy. Then he might start asking questions."

"I think you give those men too much credit," Atalanta replied. "If you don't look like a threat or an oddity, they won't give you a second glance. But be as cautious as you like."

"I'd rather do that than risk discovery," I said. "Especially when that might mean I'd be forbidden to leave the citadel again *and* be watched." I remembered how Glaucus's way of testing my dedication and Ione's vigilance kept me from the training ground for so many days. I refused to have to deal with a nuisance like *that* again. "Nothing's going to interfere with my riding lessons."

"Well said." The huntress was pleased, and my heart rejoiced to have her approval. "Tomorrow I'll leave the palace at sunrise. You'll be safe enough from discovery if you meet me here, then we'll ride on together. Oh, and make sure you wear something that protects your legs a little more than that tunic."

"Like what?" I asked. "You're wearing a man's tunic too."

"I wear more than this when I ride Aristos over longer distances," she told me. "Mykenaean horsemen have a reputation for endurance because they wear short breeches when they need to make long journeys; so do I. Even now I'm wearing a loinwrap that covers my upper thighs. If you don't wear something that gives you at least that much protection tomorrow morning, you'll regret it by tomorrow night, believe me." She pressed her heels to the stallion's sides and was gone.

She was wrong. I didn't regret wearing inadequate leg covering the next day. I regretted it that very night. I was sore from all the bruises I'd gathered in one fall after another, and my legs were badly chafed and aching after straddling Aristos's wide body.

I also had more problems to deal with than my aches and pains. After that morning in the hills, I was filthy and reeked of horse. Though I'd tied up my hair, my repeated tumbles had left it snarled. How I missed Ione! My long strands of black curls fell well below my waist, and the tedious work of washing and unsnarling them had always been her job.

Though Ione was still in Sparta, I *did* have someone to help me with this sort of thing here in Calydon—in theory, anyway. My aunt had ordered the motherly slave woman I'd met on my first night in Calydon to attend me, but after she'd neaten my room in the morning for the day, she'd vanish until it was time to help me get ready for dinner. I had no idea of how to summon her if I needed her between those times, and I didn't dare go searching for her while I was still dressed as a boy.

I had to do what I could for myself before I could even begin to seek her out. There was some water in a large jug by my bedside, so I used that to wash off the worst of the grime on my face, arms, and feet. Next I put on a dress and wrestled a comb through my tangles. I had to remove any telltale bits of twig or leaf before I got the slave woman to help me wash my hair thoroughly. I didn't want her to start asking questions, or even thinking of them.

As I passed through the palace halls looking for her, I came across the large room where my aunt and her women sat working. It was like a glimpse of home. The great loom stood in the best light, with the queen herself making the shuttle fly back and forth between the up-and-down threads. Three nobly born ladies of Calydon sat nearby on low stools, one spinning thread, two doing needlework while they gossiped. The gold ornaments in their hair and decorating their brightly patterned gowns proclaimed their rank. The remaining five women at work were plainly dressed—slaves or servants, by the look of them—two using spindles, three toiling through a huge basket of raw fleece with their carding combs.

As I watched them from the doorway, unnoticed, I caught sight of the shallow basket standing next to the loom. It was filled with newly made cloth. Atalanta wanted me to protect my legs better for tomorrow's lesson, and this looked like my chance to get something for the purpose.

*I'll tell the queen that I've lost my mantle and I need some cloth for a new one,* I thought. I wasn't sure of exactly *how* I'd alter the simple length of woven wool to shield my legs, but I decided Atalanta could help me with that. My task was to get the cloth in the first place.

Without pausing to think things through any further, I stepped into the room and greeted my aunt with reverence. She was pleased to see me and insisted that I sit beside her at the loom.

"Helen, my dear, you've found me! I've been so busy, I hope you haven't been *too* bored? Have you found enough to do?" Abruptly, her affectionate expression froze. She wrinkled her nose grotesquely, then leaned a little closer, sniffed, and asked, "What *have* you been doing? Er, I mean, what have you been doing to entertain yourself so—*strenuously?*"

One of the noblewomen sniffed as well, then

smiled. "I'd say she's found the stables." She squeezed my hand gently. "I loved horses when I was your age too. My nurse had to drag me away from them almost every day. When she caught me helping the grooms brush my father's stallion, she was scandalized." She mimicked her long-gone nurse's gruff, scolding voice: " '*What* do you think you're doing, my lady? What evil spirit told you that *this* is fit work for any woman? What would your mother say if she could see you now?' "

When we all finished laughing, I lowered my head and said, "You're right; I was with the horses. I'm sorry if I . . . brought some of the stables along with me." I looked up and grinned. That brought fresh laughter.

My aunt patted my cheek. "You're Leda's daughter, right enough. She was just the same, when we were girls together. If it weren't for the stables, you'd never find her inside the palace at all."

"Did she know how to ride?" I asked eagerly.

Lady Althea shook her head. "She got into enough mischief without that. She just thought they were beautiful, fascinating animals. Besides, she was such a formidable runner that I think being on horseback would've only slowed her down. Did you know that she was quite the huntress?"

"Just like Atalanta." I was proud to compare my mother to my new friend and teacher.

My aunt didn't share my enthusiasm or my opinion. Her face darkened. "Don't liken my sister to that unnatural creature. Leda might have known how to run and hunt, but she also knew how to do a woman's *rightful* work. As soon as she married your father, she was glad to give up all those silly girlhood pastimes."

I thought of my mother's pleasure when she'd taught me archery, her joy when my arrow brought down my first quarry. *And when did she learn that "rightful" woman's work if you say she was never in the palace?* I wondered. But I decided not to voice my thoughts to the queen. What would it accomplish except to irritate her even more?

"All that Atalanta needs is a good husband and a house full of babies," the second noblewoman spoke up. "*That* will cure her quickly enough."

"Cure her of what?" I asked. I couldn't help it. "She's not *sick*, she's just not like you."

"I should hope not!" The lady looked smug about it. "And I thank Hera for it. If I were anything like that—that—that want-to-be man, I'd throw myself into the sea!"

I decided that if I didn't leave then and there, I'd say something to my aunt's self-righteous companion that would cause unnecessary trouble for everyone. A guest who broke the peace of her host's home wasn't worthy of the sacred bread and salt. I mumbled my tale about the lost mantle, Lady Althea cheerfully gave me a suitable piece of cloth from the basket beside her, and I ran from the room.

As I fled down the corridor, I heard the smug noblewoman tell my aunt, "Such a sweet child. What a pity she's such a sharp-faced, skinny thing."

"*Exactly* like her mother," my aunt's voice trailed after me. "And you *know* what a beauty she grew up to be."

# 10

# THE BOAR COMES

The cloth I'd been given by my aunt turned out to be useless. I tried several ways of wearing it under my tunic, wrapped and tucked this way and that, but it kept slipping off or bunching up when I walked. I had enough trouble getting up on Aristos without a wad of wool snaring my legs and getting in the way. I wound up leaving it behind in my room before I ran out to meet Atalanta by the pines.

We rode into the hills before the early-morning mist was completely gone from between the trees. The silvery haze held secrets. Once I thought I saw the slim, swift shape of a dryad slipping back into the bark of her tree, but it might have been nothing more than an ordinary shadow. The sun burned the mist away by the time we reached the clearing.

My second morning of riding lessons went only a little better than the first. As soon as I mastered mounting Aristos with a boost from Atalanta, she decreed I was ready to try getting up on the horse without her helping hands.

"Like this," she said, demonstrating the proper way to do it. It was much the same business as the assisted mount—reins in the left hand, a little jump, a little push upward with the right hand, the right leg swung over the horse's back, and there she was.

There *she* was; not me.

The best thing you could say about my attempts was that at least I'd stopped dropping the reins. At first my jump up wasn't high enough, and I slammed my chest into Aristos's side. When I jumped harder, I still couldn't manage to swing my leg over the horse and ended up hanging over his back on my stomach before sliding back down.

Atalanta let me have half a dozen tries before she stepped in and showed me how to use both hands to help me make the midair turn without losing my grip on the reins. That was the only reason I was finally able to mount Aristos, though not without a lot of squirming myself into a proper seat once I was on the stallion's back.

Then the *real* lessons began.

By the time Atalanta had to return to the citadel,

she seemed pleased with my progress. "Not bad, little squirrel; not bad at all," she said as she watched me guide Aristos around the clearing at a walk. "You're still sitting too far forward—that's why you fell off both times today—but you have the right instinct for balancing control between your hands and your legs. Tomorrow we'll see if you can stay on him when he picks up his pace. Here's a taste."

She gave the horse a light swat on the rump and he went into a lively trot. My teeth clattered together as I bounced along, but I pulled back firmly on the reins, and brought him to a stop before every bone in my back shook loose. I turned Aristos's head toward Atalanta, touched his side with my heels, and walked him back to her.

"I think I'll be ready," I said, smiling feebly through the fresh pains of that day's lesson.

I wasn't smiling when she dropped me off at the little roadside pine grove. The insides of my legs were hurting too much. I was used to dealing with aches and bruises from all the time I'd spent learning weaponry with Glaucus and my brothers, but having my skin rubbed raw by a horse's flanks was something new. My flesh stung as if I'd landed on my behind in a beehive. The simple act of putting one foot in front of the other to walk back to the citadel became a bizarre, agonizing dance.

I was lucky that Atalanta didn't simply go galloping off as soon as she let me off Aristos. She saw my pain and she knew the reason.

"Didn't I tell you to protect your thighs?" she asked.

"I tried," I replied. "I tried, and I *really* wish I'd succeeded, believe me." I went on to explain my failed attempts at turning that length of cloth from my aunt into a usable undergarment.

"Hmm. Where's that cloth now?" Atalanta asked.

"I left it on my bed this morning."

"Good; easy enough to find. If there's enough material to make myself a new pair of Mykenaean riding breeches, I'll swap it for my old ones. They won't fit you perfectly, but they'll do, and I could use a new pair."

"You know how to sew?" I was unwilling to believe it.

Atalanta was amused by my incredulity. "Don't gape at me like that, girl. It's not as if I knew how to *fly*." And with that, she rode off.

It took me a long, painful time to walk back to the citadel. As I limped through the gates, one of the guards jeered, "Next time work harder, boy, and your master won't beat you so badly!" I gritted my teeth and ignored him as I made my way back to my room.

Pain or no pain, I had to move much more

quickly once I was inside the palace, in order to avoid being seen and questioned. A scruffy, ragged "boy" could have a dozen excuses for passing through those parts of the Calydonian citadel where people did real labor, but next to none for being caught on the upper floor where the highborn had rooms.

I was climbing the stairs to the upper level when I ran into one of the hunters coming down. He took one look at me and his eyes widened. "By Zeus, boy, what happened to *you*?"

"I fell off a horse." There was no harm in telling the truth, as far as I could tell. I tried to move past him before anyone else might happen to come along.

He stayed where he was, blocking the narrow stairway. "A horse?" he echoed. "Are you all right? Did you get hurt?"

I shrugged. "It's nothing." Again I tried to move past him, adding, "Please excuse me, sir; I have to see if my master needs me."

I only wanted an excuse to get away from him, back to my own room. In my haste, I'd picked a poor one, because the next thing the man asked, quite reasonably, was, "Who is your master? I doubt you'll find him in his room at this time of day. Why don't you come along with me to the training ground? I'll help you look for him."

He sounded genuinely concerned, as if he really

cared about helping a grubby, unimportant "boy" like me. He seemed to be only slightly older than my brothers, with nothing remarkable about his looks— he was shorter than most of the other hunters, had dull black hair, brown eyes, pockmarked skin, and a body as solid and ordinary as a bullock's—yet it was clear he had a good heart. Even though his concern was bringing him dreadfully close to undoing my disguise, I found myself drawn to him.

"Thank you, sir, but I still have to go back to my master's room," I replied, evading his question. "I'm responsible for carrying his weapons. If he's not still there, he'll be waiting for me at the training ground, and he's not a patient man. *Please* let me pass!"

"Ah, so you're one of the weapons bearers?" (Under other circumstances I might have appreciated his friendliness, but not when it was delaying me, no matter *how* attractive I found him.) "It's a thankless job, isn't it? I remember my days serving my uncle on his adventures. Talk about a man with no patience! But a celebrated hero, then as now. The places he took me, the exploits we shared, the marvels I saw him perform, sometimes with his bare hands! It was an honor to serve—" He stopped, suddenly self-conscious. "I'm sorry, lad—you're in a hurry and I'm keeping you from your duties." He stepped to one side on the stairs.

But I made no move to go on my way. All at once I recognized the face I'd only glimpsed at my uncle's table. "Sir, are you—are you Iolaus, great Herakles's nephew?"

He gave an uncomfortable laugh and scratched his head. "I can't deny it. How did you know me?"

"I saw you at dinner." That was the truth, even if he'd believe I'd done so from a place at the servants' table, not the king's. "I've heard the poets sing of your exploits. It's an honor to meet you."

His mouth curved into a charming smile. "The real honor would be to meet Herakles. Surely you've heard what some of the other hunters say about me? That Lord Oeneus allowed me to join the hunt only because of my uncle's deeds, not mine."

"If you ask me, some of the men who scoff at you wouldn't fare so well if anyone looked closely at *their* claims to fame," I replied hotly. "Everyone knows that you were the one who helped Herakles slay the nine-headed Hydra!"

"Yes, well . . ." He took a deep breath. "Lad, did you ever *see* a nine-headed beast of any sort, mouse or monster?"

"No, but—"

"No one has, including me *and* my uncle. But the poets who sing for their living know they won't earn a full belly from spinning tales about how Herakles and his nephew slew an ordinary swamp snake; a monstrously *big* swamp snake, as thick around the body as a pillar, but with just one head, after all."

"Oh." I was deeply disappointed.

"Now, now, cheer up." Iolaus put on a jolly face. "No need to lose heart just because *my* adventures are such trivial things. All the more reason for you to grow up strong and brave and perform *truly* heroic deeds. Show the rest of us how it's done, eh? Now run along. Your master's waiting and I'll feel awful if he punishes you because I kept you chatting here." He turned and bounded down the stairs. I was sorry to see him go.

I made it to my chamber without further incident and saw that Atalanta had been there. The length of cloth was gone, replaced by an unfamiliar piece of clothing. My bedside water jug had been refilled to the brim, and there was a small, sealed clay pot next to it. I broke the seal, removed the lid, and dipped one finger into the thick yellow salve inside. It felt cool, smelled like honey, and brought me sweet relief as soon as I smoothed it over my suffering skin. I blessed Atalanta's name.

My third day of riding lessons slipped by in a dance of walk, trot, and canter. My style when mounting and dismounting the horse still left a lot to be desired, but Atalanta was satisfied with how much better I sat once I was on the stallion. When Aristos moved, I straightened my spine without making it rigid and leaned back a bit, instead of bending forward to steady myself. The Mykenaean breeches helped, giving my legs a more secure grip on his sides.

Trotting still jounced me almost as much as an oxcart ride, but I didn't fall off. The canter was a smoother gait—I loved it!—but what I really wanted to do was recapture the amazing sensation I'd experienced when Atalanta first swept me up onto horseback and gave Aristos his wings.

"Can I run him?" I asked. "*Really* run him?"

"Don't let me stop you," Atalanta replied. "If you think you can—"

I was off before she could finish her sentence. A kick of my heels to Aristos's flanks and we were off. The first burst of speed stole my breath. I was ecstatic, feeling the wind, skimming across the ground—

—sliding too far forward to control the horse properly, sheepskin or no sheepskin beneath my seat, breeches or no breeches on my legs. I wasn't ready to deal with how slippery a horse's back could become once he worked up a sweat. As if horsehair needed something to make it even more slippery than it already was! The stallion wasn't just running, he was running away with me, heading for the trees. If I hit a low branch head-on—

I panicked and pulled back on the reins, trying to turn him, but I used too heavy a hand and Aristos wouldn't stand for it. He jerked his head up sharply, tearing the reins from my hand, then down, humping his back and flinging out his heels.

I'd wanted to fly *on* horseback, not *from* it. The gods were merciful and let me plunge well clear of the stallion's flashing hooves and all of the larger rocks in the area.

I was still lying on my stomach, getting a close view of mud and grass roots, when I heard Atalanta's shrill whistle and Aristos's footsteps, deceptively dainty for such a powerful creature. The two of them walked over to where I lay so that I got a good look at the huntress's bare feet and the horse's mucky hooves before I pushed myself up to sit.

"Do you know what you did wrong?" Atalanta asked me.

"Everything?"

It wasn't as bad as that, according to her, but bad enough. Aristos had to be sweet-talked for a while before he'd allow me to approach him again. I found myself apologizing to a horse for having acted heedlessly. At first I felt silly doing it, but the longer I spoke to him, quietly asking him for another chance, the more his attitude toward me seemed to soften. When I finished begging his pardon, I swear by Zeus himself that Aristos turned sideways as if to offer me his back once more!

We finished the morning with a few more attempts at galloping, though nowhere near as headlong as the first try. Atalanta told me to sit back, and I was so eager not to repeat my initial mistakes that I made a bunch of new ones, toppling backward over the stallion's rump two times out of three. I was lucky I didn't break my neck.

"Well, one good thing about today's work," Atalanta said when it was time for us to return to the citadel. "You've spent so little time actually *on* the horse that you might not be quite as sore as yesterday."

As if he understood and agreed with his mistress, Aristos let loose a long, scornful whinny in my face.

"Just you wait until tomorrow," I told him.

The next morning, long before the sun was up, I was jolted awake by the sound of running feet, voices shouting curses and commands, and the clash and jangle of weapons. My room on the second floor of Lord Oeneus's palace opened onto a pillared gallery that ringed a courtyard. I threw my blanket around me, stepped out of my room, and gazed down. The huge space below was mobbed—the gathered heroes, their weapons bearers, palace servants, and Lord Oeneus himself—all of them milling around, weaving between the pillars, everyone trying to find someone else, all of them blundering in a dozen directions at once.

Then I heard the sound of my brothers' voices

sweeping along the gallery, racing toward me. I turned to greet them and was bowled off my feet.

"Agh! Who'd I just knock down?" The sky above the courtyard was still dark and the moon was already set; Castor never did have good night vision. "Are you all right?"

"I'm fine, stupid," I replied, holding on to the gallery railing and hauling myself back to my feet.

"Helen?" Polydeuces peered at me. "Go back to sleep; there's still plenty of time before you have to get up."

"*You're* up," I pointed out. "What's going on?"

"The boar," he replied shortly. "Once Lord Oeneus decided there were enough of us for a successful hunt, he sent out teams of men to search for it. They've been scouting the countryside for days. One of them spotted it and sent a runner back with word. It's been living on the great mountain to the west of the palace, the one with the big slash of trees burned off by lightning."

"The gods are on our side," Castor added. "I heard that mountain's got plenty of places we can corner the beast for the kill. I hope I'm the one who brings it down. Wouldn't Father be proud to see me come home wrapped in a monstrous wild boar's hide!"

"It'd go well with your manners," I said, but both of my brothers hustled past me and were already gone.

I hurried to dress, putting on the same tunic I'd

worn every time I went to meet Atalanta. I threaded the scabbard of my small sword through the belt, then secured my dark curls into a club even more carefully than usual. It took me longer than I liked. By the time I'd tied the last knot in the thin strip of cloth, the courtyard was empty. The hunt was on the move.

The guard must have thought I was some hero's servant who'd overslept. He shouted good-natured threats after me as I ran through the gate. "Run faster, boy! You'll get a whipping from your master when he sees you lagging behind!"

The night sky was paling to smoky blue, and the rising sun was just beginning to show a few thin strands of pink and gold over the eastern hills. It was simple enough for me to track the hunters. They'd all set out on foot because there was no way of knowing when the boar would turn to a mountain path too steep or thickly grown to let horses pass. They left a clear trail to follow, and the dogs—let's just say that dogs have a way of making it easy for you to know where they've been. I heard the hounds baying in the distance, their voices echoing among the trees above when I reached the base of the mountain. Following the tracks of so many feet and the cry of the hunting pack, I plunged into the forests of Calydon.

The sun was well over the horizon before I caught up to them. By that time, they'd scattered through the woods. I said a quiet prayer to Hermes, patron of thieves and tricksters, asking him to see to it that I didn't run into my brothers. Dressed as I was, only Castor and Polydeuces would recognize me at a glance. No one else could imagine the princess of Sparta to be here, with a sword at her hip.

My brothers would be livid if they caught me. Though they might have accepted my presence on the training ground back home, they'd never stand for my being a part of the boar hunt, with all its thrills and perils. They'd force me to go back to the citadel, even if it meant one of them would have to drop out of this grand adventure in order to enforce their decision. The unlucky twin would never forgive me for stealing his first chance at fame.

*O Hermes, be with me! Let me find the hunt, but not my brothers!*

The trickster heard, and being a trickster he answered my prayer in his own special way. The first hunters I found weren't my brothers. They were that handsome braggart Theseus of Athens and his friend Pirithous.

"Well, what's this?" Theseus boomed when he saw me loping through the underbrush. He was leaning on a huge boar spear, the shaft as thick as a young tree, the bronze point bigger than my hand. "Lost your way, boy? Don't be afraid, we'll protect you." He and Pirithous roared with laughter.

"I can protect myself," I told them calmly, drawing my blade.

It only made them laugh harder. "Who told you we were hunting bunnies?" Pirithous sneered. He was carrying a bundle of lighter spears and had a weighted net slung over one shoulder. "Ever *seen* a wild boar, puppy? Even a young one can open a man's belly with one stroke of his tusks."

"I've seen wild boars," I lied. "This is at least as long as any boar's tusk." I held up my sword proudly. "When I meet the Calydonian boar today, we'll see whose belly gets torn open."

It was a silly, empty boast, like those they spouted about themselves, but it seemed to win me some friends. The two men traded a look of amusement, then Theseus said, "I like your nerve, boy. What's your name?"

"Glaucus."

He didn't ask me where I was from; he must've assumed I was a Calydonian. "Well, Glaucus, Theseus and I travel light, so we didn't come to Calydon with a whole crew of servants like some of these other so-called heroes. Why don't you give us a hand with our gear?" Pirithous held out the bundle of spears. "When I kill the boar, I'll give you one of his teeth to wear 'round your neck as a reward."

I shook my head. "I only work for one person."

"A servant with a sword?" Theseus's eyebrows rose. "Who'd allow that?"

I looked him steadily in the eye. "Atalanta."

"*Her?*" Pirithous spat. "This is the first I've heard that she kept servants. Theseus, didn't we see her arrive at the palace gates alone?"

"I'm not hers," I said quickly. "I serve Prince Meleager. He ordered me to attend her on the hunt, but she outran me. He's the one who gave me this." I made a great show of brandishing my sword.

"That explains it." Theseus's mouth twisted into a mocking smile. "Meleager's in love with that monstrosity, the gods alone know why. The way he looks at her makes me want to puke."

"He'd better watch himself," Pirithous put in. "A woman like that devours men. I heard that when he was born, the Fates told his mother that he'd live only as long as the log burning on the hearth. She poured water on it, wrapped it up, and put it away somewhere safe, but I don't think it worked. Call me a liar, but I swear there are times he looks like he's burning to ashes from the inside out."

"He's still a good warrior," Theseus said. "*And* a fine hunter, who'll beat us to the boar if we don't stop jabbering with this brat and get going." He shouldered his massive spear and started off.

Pirithous followed, though he did spare me one backward glance. "Go back to the palace, Glaucus;

this isn't for you," he told me. "You're almost as weak and soft-looking as a girl. Your hands should hold a lyre, not a sword." Then he, too, was gone.

I went after them, but only because the whole hunting party was heading in the same direction, higher up the mountain. As I made my way through the trees, I heard a new note in the music of the hunt. The howls and wails of injured dogs, the shrieks of men in pain, and, over all, the bone-chilling bellow of the Calydonian boar.

Then the trees ended. I stepped out onto a spear-head-shaped swath of open ground, the old forest all burned away by a lightning strike, just as Polydeuces had said. There were only a few brave sprouts of new green beginning to poke up from the charred earth, among the blackened stumps of trees. About halfway up that bleak terrain was a small, narrow ravine, like the bite of an ax. That was where the sounds were coming from.

Other stragglers were running toward it, men sweating and shouting, brandishing their weapons and cheering for the kill. I ran with them. I recognized my brothers from the back, already moving toward the front rank of the hunters, but I no longer cared if they saw me. The hunt was almost over; let them send me back to the palace now and it wouldn't matter. In fact, I *wanted* them to see me. I'd enjoy their look of surprise when I tapped them on the shoulder and—

My hand was already outstretched to touch them when my sandal slipped and I fell on my face. I pushed myself up on my forearms and stared at the ground.

No wonder I'd fallen. The earth was slick with blood.

# 11

# THE GREAT HUNT

I was still sprawled on the blood-soaked ground when a strong hand hauled me upright and a familiar voice commanded: "Get up or get trampled, lad."

I regained my feet and found myself again face to face with Iolaus. "Thank you, sir," I said. "I got separated from my master in the woods. What's happening? Do we have the boar?"

He grimaced. "That depends on if you ask the boar or the hunters. He's got his back to the wall and there's no way he can fight his way through so many of us. He's got no choice but to surrender." Another heartrending howl tore through the air. A hound as big as me went flying up and over the hunters' heads, its body streaked with red. The cornered boar had

tossed the poor creature as easily as if it were a wisp of
straw. "Too bad he disagrees."

"Where's Atalanta?" I cried, clutching Iolaus's
arm. The blood underfoot, the unlucky dog's fate, the
uproar from the ravine all suddenly combined to
strike my heart with terror. But I wasn't afraid for my
own life. I feared for my friend. Without thinking, I
grabbed Iolaus's shoulders and sprang up, desperate to
see over the heads of the hunters in front of me. I
would have clambered all the way up his back to gain
a better view if he hadn't shaken me off like water.

"Calm yourself, lad. You'll see her if it's the gods'
will. She's the one who found the beast. The way that
woman can run, no wonder! With the hounds, she
drove him into that narrow spot, and her spear drew
first blood." Iolaus looked grave. "That was when he
turned and attacked."

"No!" In my head I could see the boar turning,
charging, and who would be his nearest target? I threw
myself forward, into the mob, and shoved my way
through.

I struggled past men holding a whole forest of
heavy boar spears—unwieldy weapons that were made
to be braced against the earth, to meet the infuriated
beast's charge and let his own strength impale him. As
I squirmed my way through, I encountered someone
whose luck had run out. The body lay face to the sun,

arms and legs flung out at strange angles, one hand still curled around a spear's splintered shaft. His face looked like a smashed piece of fruit. The boar had trampled him, then ripped his side open. I saw the white slivers of exposed ribs just before I vomited.

Someone grabbed my shoulder and shook me. "Help or get out of the way, pup." It was Theseus and he was unarmed. "The monster broke my spear," he said tersely. "Get me another!"

"Get it yourself," I growled, wiping my mouth on the back of my hand before lunging away from him.

Atalanta was standing at the entrance to the ravine, behind Meleager and about four other men. She had her boar spear in hand and was trying to elbow her way ahead of them. I was so happy to see her alive that my voice broke when I called out her name.

"What are you doing here, you idiot?" she shouted. She broke away from Meleager and the others to confront me. "Do you *want* to die?" She slapped my face so hard it made echoes.

Then she looked at her hand, smeared with blood, mud, and ashes from my face. Her anger turned to alarm. "What's this? Are you wounded? Show me!"

I began babbling out a rapid explanation of what had happened, but she stopped me as soon as she saw

I wasn't hurt. "Never mind. I have to finish what I started. I'd have had that beast on my spear by now, except for Prince Meleager. He saw me wound it and thought I was in danger. The gods protect me from men who mean well! Those others with him got between me and my prize because they want to steal the honor of the kill. They're too stupid to know what they're up against. I don't think half these men ever faced a boar on their own."

"But there are so many hunters here—" I began.

She raised her hand to silence me: "No matter how many hunters set out together, we each face the boar alone."

As if the gods heard her words, there was a fresh chorus of screams as the boar broke through the mob of armed men. He was a moving mountain of flesh, blood, and bristle, draped in shredded hunting nets. Foam streamed from his mouth, and a wake of blood sprayed out behind him from the dozen shallow wounds on his flanks. Hounds held on to his ears, throat, and haunches, their jaws locked. Only death would make them lose their grip. Their ferocious loyalty to their masters' orders was a gallant, tragic thing to see.

"He's heading up the mountain!" Atalanta shouldered her spear and took off, her feet flying fast as dragonfly wings. But instead of rushing up the steep, naked slope after the boar, she raced back into the trees and down through the forest.

"What are you doing?" I gasped as I tried to keep up with her.

She paused. "Trust me. He's gone up the mountain, but he's got to come down again. I know where to meet him when he does." And she was off.

I don't remember the path we took. I was too anxious about keeping up with Atalanta to notice much. Twigs scratched my face, and brambles clawed my legs. I panted for breath as I ran and inhaled a spiderweb. While I stopped for a moment to spit out the sticky strands, I heard the sound of the hunt up the mountain, dogs and men making an uproar loud enough to shake boulders from their beds.

"Not much farther!" Atalanta called over one shoulder. I wanted to shout back that I didn't care how much farther we went, I could do it, I wasn't tired at all, except . . . I was too tired. By the time she stopped and wedged her spear into the earth, I was ready to collapse.

I didn't dare. Atalanta's eyes were fixed on the trail, a steep, twisting, narrow path marked by the prints of cloven hooves and the smell of boar droppings. The clamor was getting louder.

*This is real*, I thought, staring at Atalanta. My mind filled with images of the dogs, of the dead man I'd seen. I stood frozen, feeling danger rolling down on me like a flood and unable to do anything but wait for it to wash me away.

*"Here!"* Atalanta's shout shattered my trance. "Get behind me. Hold the spear straight and steady. The slope will give him speed and power. Hold him until the spear point reaches his heart!"

I obeyed, imitating her grip on the spear, the way she braced her feet in the earth. There was a thin, slippery covering of fallen pine needles underfoot, making it hard to stand firmly. My nose filled with the pungent scent of the pines around us, the musky, spicy smell of mushrooms and ferns from the forest floor, the reek of my own sweat. The dazzle of sunlight through the boughs and the kiss of a breeze on my cheek were unbearably sweet. Even through the din of the oncoming hunt, I could hear the beauty of a bird's song.

*I could die here.* I was surprised that the thought didn't frighten me. I was sad, but for my parents, my brothers, even for Clytemnestra. *I could die here,* I thought. *But not without a fight.*

I closed my eyes, tightened my grip on the spear, dug in my feet even more deeply, wedged my left shoulder against Atalanta's back, and waited for the boar.

His roar crashed over me the instant that he hit our spear. The impact threw us down the path like a rockslide. Baying dogs came rushing past us, unable to stop their mad chase of the boar and overshooting their prey. I fell to one knee, scraping it raw, but I never let go of the spear.

As swiftly as it happened, it ended. There was a deafening crack as Atalanta's spearhead broke off in the boar's shoulder. We were swept to one side as the beast took off down the trail.

Atalanta was still cursing his escape when we both heard the twang of a bowstring, the whiz of an arrow, the hit, and the boar's last squeal of rage and pain. The beast toppled like a tower into the dust, the hounds swarming over him in bloody triumph.

The men were cheering. Their exultant cries soon changed to one word, one name, a name they roared over and over again: "Me-lea-*ger*! Me-lea-*ger*! Me-lea-*ger*!"

As the hunters forced the dogs to retreat from the dead boar, my cousin stepped forward and laid one hand on the monstrous body: The kill was his.

Tears joined the sweat streaming down my face as he claimed the quarry. *It isn't fair!* My thoughts blazed with frustration. *This should be Atalanta's glory! They should be shouting* her *name!*

But as the servants struggled to hoist the dead boar onto their shoulders and the still-cheering hunters began the trek down the mountain, back to the citadel of Calydon, I heard Atalanta's voice ringing out, chanting, "Me-lea-*ger*! Me-lea-*ger*!" as heartily as them all.

I let the jubilant procession pass well ahead of me before I started back to the palace. Even though it was all over, I still didn't want to run into my brothers; I was too bone-weary to be bothered with their reactions if they discovered my presence.

I returned to find the citadel transformed into a storm of wild rejoicing and headlong preparations for the victory banquet. No one noticed me as I trailed back to my room, stripped, scrubbed away the day's dirt and blood, crawled under my blanket, and collapsed into a dreamless sleep.

My brothers woke me when the sun was beginning to set. "What's the matter with you, Helen?" Castor cried, shaking me by the shoulder. "How can you sleep at a time like this?"

"Are you all right?" Polydeuces put in. "You're not ill, are you?" He touched my forehead to check for fever.

I brushed his hand away gently. "I'm *fine,* 'Ione.' You don't need to fuss over me just because I'm smart enough to catch some sleep before the feast. I'll still be awake when the two of you are snoring with your heads on the table."

"Ha! If not for us, you'd've slept right *through* the feast," Castor countered.

"I'll build a temple in your honor to show my thanks," I said, straight-faced. "Now if you really want to lend a hand, go find a servant to help me get ready. This is a special occasion and I want to look my best."

"Ooooooh, our little sister wants to look *nice*, does she?" Polydeuces crooned. "I wonder why?" I saw him wink at Castor and knew I was doomed to be teased to death.

"Don't you mean, 'I wonder *who*?'" Castor replied. He tried to look sly and all-knowing, but his tendency to go cross-eyed ruined the effect. "Do you think it's Meleager himself?"

"He's the hero of the day, but I think she'd rather have a *brawnier* man," Polydeuces said. "I'll bet I can guess who. I saw how you looked at him the first night we were here." He flung his arms around his twin, pitched his voice high, and cried, "Oh, Theseus, you're *sooooooo* strong! Make me queen of Athens too!"

"*Out!*" I shouted, snatching up my nearly empty water jug. My brothers retreated at a run, laughing.

I was doing my best to arrange my hair and dress for the banquet when the slave woman showed up, carrying a small oil lamp. She also brought me gifts from the queen: a new dress in all the colors of a springtime sunrise and a necklace of rock crystal and gold beads.

"The lady Althea asks you to accept and wear these, to celebrate the prince's triumph," she explained. Then she picked up a comb and set to work on my hair.

When I was finally ready, I went downstairs to the

great hall. My brothers were already waiting for me at the king's table. We were seated together, close enough to the king to satisfy the pride of Sparta, but nowhere near the place of greatest honor, between Lord Oeneus and his queen.

I knew for whom that seat was reserved, but I didn't know why it was still empty.

The hide of the Calydonian boar was spread out on the floor in front of the royal table, the heavy head propped up on a chair so that everyone could see Meleager's arrow still sticking out of the beast's left eye socket.

Every table in the hall was laden with a token piece of meat from the great kill. Even the slaves and servants would have the privilege of tasting broth made from the monster's bones, but the meatiest ones went to the surviving hounds. While we all shared a taste of Meleager's victory, Lord Oeneus added so much more food to the banquet that even the mice under his table would be waddling back to their nests that night.

And yet we ate with ghosts. The boar had killed four of the hunters. Two more were gravely wounded. The king swore that they were all heroes whose names would live through the songs of the hunt. No one bothered to count or name the servants who'd died that day, even though they'd lost their lives for venturing closer to the boar than many of the "heroes."

Only the master of the royal hunting pack mourned for the slaughtered dogs.

My brothers couldn't be bothered by phantoms. Tomorrow the dead would be burned, their ashes entombed with honor, the survivors would compete in athletic contests to please their spirits. Tonight Castor and Polydeuces sat near the king and basked in the congratulations of their fellow hunters. Apparently they'd done great deeds during the hunt—there were witnesses!—and had earned the right to be called heroes. If they'd noticed my presence on the mountainside that day, they washed the memory from their minds with cup after cup of wine.

And still the place between the king and queen of Calydon stayed empty.

"Where is he?" I whispered to Polydeuces. "Where's Meleager? Is something wrong?"

"Nothing, nothing." The wine slurred his speech just a bit. "This is all the king's idea, keeping us waiting for Meleager just to make us cheer him even louder when he finally shows up." He hiccuped.

As if in response to Polydeuces's words, Lord Oeneus rose up from his chair, bawled for silence, then spread his arms wide and called out, "Come forward, Meleager, my son!" If there hadn't been enough oil lamps to light the great hall that night, his face was radiant enough to do the job. "Come and claim your prize!"

Cheers shook the pillars of the hall as Meleager entered, but my cousin seemed indifferent to the praises thundering in his ears. His face was clouded as he approached his father and the boar. Something dark rode his shoulders, something that touched my heart with foreboding. I wasn't the only one who felt it: I was seated near enough to his mother, the queen, to see how anxiously she leaned forward.

Meleager ran one hand down the boar's bristly crest. He touched the bloodstained tusks, closed his eyes, and sighed, then opened them and said, "I can't accept what isn't mine. This beast would still be alive, ravaging our land, if not for the hero who truly deserves this trophy. My arrow never would have been enough to kill the monster if her spear hadn't weakened it. Atalanta! Take your rightful prize!"

He seized the hide, head and all, and slung it over his shoulder. He strode down the hall to where Atalanta still sat among the weapons bearers. He dropped it at her feet and gazed at her with all the worship in his heart.

I don't know who sprang up first, crying out against him, calling her a hundred vicious names. Several men leaped over the tables like deer in order to grab the skin.

"If you don't want it, Meleager, it's mine!" someone shouted. "*My* spear made the boar bleed; *I* deserve the prize. You insult us all."

Atalanta was too wise to try to stop them. I couldn't hear whether she flung their insults back in their faces, but I could see her laughing at them just as if they were a bunch of rowdy little boys who needed a good spanking. My cousin didn't share her wisdom. His white face was streaked with feverish color as he drew his sword and attacked the men who tried to take the boar's hide from Atalanta.

"This is bad," Polydeuces muttered, suddenly sober. Before I knew what he was going to do, he and Castor grabbed me. As we ran from the hall I heard weapons clashing, Lord Oeneus bawling for his guards, and the queen screaming. My brothers whisked me up the stairs, down the gallery, and into my room, where they barricaded the door with one of my travel chests and spent the night with their swords in hand.

I don't know whether or not my brothers were able to keep watch all night or whether, like me, they fell into a light doze. I only know that I was startled awake by a loud pounding. As I blinked in the morning sunlight, I saw Polydeuces on guard at the door, demanding to know who was there.

"It's me, Iolaus! Let me in; it's safe. I've got news."

Polydeuces admitted him. Iolaus looked terrible: his face haggard, his eyes red with dark circles under them. He moved unsteadily across the floor and sat down heavily at the foot of my bed, head bowed.

"Well, it's over," he said. "Artemis has her revenge.

Even after death, the boar she sent still had the power to kill. Ah, what a waste! Once the king gave Meleager the hide, it was his property; he could do whatever he liked with it. So what if he gave it to that girl? It was his choice, not an insult to anyone's honor. Where's their precious honor now that they're dead?"

"Who's dead?" Polydeuces asked.

I bit my lip and prayed that Iolaus wouldn't say *Atalanta.*

"Five men that I know of, though I couldn't tell you who four of them were. You know how many of us were here, and I don't pretend to have a praise singer's memory for names. I can't even figure out who they were by seeing who's missing this morning. After what happened last night, a lot of the hunters left Calydon at dawn. Some of the ones who stayed are saying that the dead men were Meleager's uncles." Iolaus made a disgusted face. "That's the way to heap filth on a man, calling him a kin-slayer when he can't defend himself anymore."

"What are you saying?" Castor asked. "Our cousin's dead?"

Iolaus nodded. "Those four men . . . well, Meleager killed them. He slashed the neck of the first man to lay hands on that stinking trophy. That was when the whole room erupted. Half the lamps were knocked over; it's a marvel that the palace didn't catch fire and burn to the ground. By the time Lord Oeneus's braver servants brought fresh light, the floor was red with blood and five bodies lay over the boar. Your cousin was the fifth. He had a few minor wounds, nothing that should have killed him. His skin was scarred with fire too—someone must have flung one of the lamps at him—but again, nothing serious enough to take his life."

"Then how *did* he die?" Polydeuces demanded.

Iolaus shrugged. "Depends whose story you hear. They say that when Lady Althea saw that her son had killed his uncles, she ran back to her room and—"

"The log." I hardly spoke above a whisper, remembering what Pirithous had told me, but Iolaus had good hearing.

"That's right, the one from the tale about the Fates coming to his mother when he was a baby." He stood up again and sighed. "They say she was so blinded by grief for her brothers' deaths that she threw that log back into the flames. It burned to ashes and Meleager died."

"But it's not *true*," Castor protested. "Althea is our mother's sister. We *know* that none of their brothers is still alive!"

"The truth steps aside for a good story," Iolaus said dryly.

"Let people entertain themselves some other

way," Castor snarled. "To say that the queen killed her own son! If I catch any man spreading that slime about Lady Althea, I'll—"

"Save your anger," Iolaus said, resting one hand on my brother's shoulder. And as kindly as he could, he told us my mother's sister was dead too.

The best lies hold a small, withered seed of truth. The queen *had* rushed back to her room after the slaughter in the feasting hall, but not to throw some nonexistent piece of wood into the fire. As soon as she saw her son's dead body, her heart broke, her mind shattered. She hanged herself with her own sash from one of the beams in her room before any of her maid-servants could reach her.

My brothers and I remained in Calydon for ten days after that cursed feast. We attended too many funeral pyres—for my cousin, my aunt, the victims of the boar, and the victims of stupidity. Castor and Poly-deuces won enough prizes at the funeral games after-ward to confirm their budding reputation as heroes. I sat on the sidelines like an ordinary girl, feeling the sting of the hidden, slowly healing scrapes and scratches I'd gotten during the hunt. I didn't see Ata-lanta anywhere.

The palace of Calydon was a house of mourning. Meleager's father moved through the corridors like an avenging wraith. The slaves and servants walked softly, afraid of the king's sudden, senseless outbursts of rage. Once I saw him beat a boy black-and-blue with his own fists for whispering the queen's name to one of his fellow slaves. When I tried to stop him, he gave me a crazed, red-eyed look that reminded me of the maddened boar. I fled, terrified and ashamed.

Many times during those ten endless days, I wished that my brothers and I could have left Calydon as soon as the other boar hunters did. Once the funeral games were over, my uncle's former guests couldn't wait to put plenty of distance between themselves and Lord Oeneus. Castor and Polydeuces and I were among the last to go. Our family ties forced us to linger. Meleager was my cousin, and the lady Althea was my aunt. I dreaded having to tell Mother that both of them were dead.

As I watched my uncle perform the daily sacrifice for his dead wife and son, I wondered whether anyone but my brothers and I would ever tell the truth about what happened that night. As Iolaus said, *The truth steps aside for a good story.*

At least Iolaus had the kindness to remain in Calydon a little longer. Men like Theseus and Pirithous might have sneered at him behind his back, calling him a poor substitute for his uncle Herakles, but they were the cowards who ran away as soon as possible. Iolaus stayed. I saw how he took pains to approach Lord Oeneus at meals, even when the king was sunk deep in despair, and spoke words of comfort to him. It wasn't his fault that my uncle's grief had left him too numb to respond. I loved Iolaus for trying. I wanted to tell him so, but the thought of saying something like that to a man was more daunting than facing the boar all over again. By the time I found the courage to do so, he'd traveled on.

At last it was our turn to leave. My brothers agreed that we'd done our family duty to our uncle and to the spirits of our dead kin. Polydeuces came bearing the good news to me as I sat alone in the room where my aunt's loom stood untouched and abandoned. None of the palace women had found the backbone to return to that place just yet; Lady Althea's last weaving still waited unfinished in the tall wooden frame.

"We'll leave tomorrow," Polydeuces said, sitting beside me on the bench before the loom. "Can you be ready?"

"Of course." I spoke listlessly, even though he'd brought me the news I'd been hoping to hear for days.

He got up to go, then looked back at me. "You don't sound like yourself. What's troubling you, little sister? Are you still mourning Lady Althea and Meleager?"

"Yes," I whispered, because it was easier than telling him the truth. But then I set aside the easy answer and told him, "No. No, that's not it. I'm sad because . . . because . . . Oh, Polydeuces, do you know what happened to her, to Atalanta? I haven't seen her since that night when—"

"No one has," he replied, his face stern. "Vanishing like that, avoiding the funeral games for the man who *died* because of her, running away—"

"She didn't *want* him to die!" I shouted, springing to my feet. "You were there! You *know* she didn't ask for the boar's hide! And you know she'd never run away."

"Then where is she, little sister?" he asked softly.

I shook my head. "I don't know." I sank back onto the bench, tears rolling down my cheeks. "I don't know."

He sat beside me and hugged me. "I'm sorry, Helen," he said. "You're right. She's gone, but she didn't run away like a coward. I can't blame her for leaving, not with Lord Oeneus out of his mind over what happened. If he'd seen her at the funeral games, the gods know what he'd have done to her. May the gods protect her, wherever she is. It was an honor to be her companion in the hunt."

*It was a greater honor to be her friend,* I thought as I clung to my brother.

The morning of our departure was glorious, with fat white clouds gliding across a brilliant sky. Our soldiers were gathering by twos and threes, chatting with one another or just standing around patiently until they were given the word to go. Some of them were awkwardly saying good-bye to teary maidservants, while their comrades looked on and laughed.

I was standing beside the oxcart, waiting for my brothers to finish the official ceremony of farewell inside the palace, when someone called my name. It was the same slave boy who'd earned my uncle's mindless wrath for whispering my aunt's name. He clung to the shadow of the palace's outermost defensive wall, gazing at me through a thatch of dirty brown hair with owl eyes, huge and golden. He looked about my age and even skinnier than I was, if that was possible. Even at that distance I could see the fading marks of my uncle's fists on his scrawny arms and chest, the purple and red bruises dappling his pinched cheeks. He clutched a cloth-wrapped bundle under one arm and beckoned me.

As soon as I came near, he bowed his head and held the bundle out for me to take. "She left this for you," he said.

I didn't need to ask who *she* was. I opened the bundle and found the bronze head of Atalanta's broken spear. It was still flecked with the boar's blood.

"I wanted to clean it, lady," the boy said. "She said no. She said that even if the blood ate up the blade, you'd earned it all, blood and bronze together."

"When was this?" I asked, my eyes never moving from the trophy in my hands. "When did she give this to you?"

"The day she left," the boy replied. "The day before I—the day before I angered the king." He lowered his eyes.

So she hadn't disappeared right away. She'd stayed to honor the dead, even if from a distance. A hunter knows how to hide.

I held the spearhead to my heart. "What's your name?" I asked the boy.

"Milo."

"Milo," I repeated. "How did she come to choose you to bring me this?"

His smile was hesitant. "The cook sent me out to gather mushrooms in the hills. I found her there, camped high up on a slope that had a view of the citadel. She asked me if I was going to tell Lord Oeneus where she was. She wasn't *afraid* I'd tell; she just wanted to know. I said no. I was the one who fetched fresh water to the hunters' rooms. She always thanked me, and sometimes she'd even give me extra food. While she was still up there"—he gestured out the open gate, toward the mountains—"I did the same for her, when I could."

"But she's gone now?" I asked. "You're sure?"

"When I could go back to her camp again— when it didn't hurt to walk—it was deserted." He bowed his head. "I'm sorry."

I took his hand. "Come with me, Milo."

He cringed. "Have I done something wrong,

lady? Have I displeased you? Please don't tell the king that I saw her! He'll have me killed!"

"We're not going to see the king, Milo," I told him, pulling him firmly after me as if he were a small child. "You'll never have to see the king again."

In the palace, I questioned one servant after another until I found the person I sought, my uncle's chief steward. That big-bellied, easygoing man was in one of the storerooms, checking the supply of olive oil, but as soon as he recognized me, he left his work and raised both hands in deferential greeting.

"Lady Helen, what a joy to see you still here!" His voice dripped honey. "I thought that you and your noble brothers were leaving us?"

"We are," I told him. "But there's something I want before we can go."

"What might that be, Lady Helen?" He pressed his palms together. "If one as humble as myself can be of any help to you at all, you only need to ask."

"The gods will bless you for your kindness," I said, smiling as I reached up and removed my gold earrings. They glittered even in the dim, dusty light. "There's something I wish to take away with me when I leave Calydon. I don't want to trouble my royal uncle with the details."

The steward's bright eyes darted from me to Milo and back again. He gave me a questioning look. I nodded and placed the earrings in his plump, soft palm. His fingers closed around them and he beamed.

"Great Lady Helen, you're as wise as you're beautiful." False flattery came easily to him. "There will be no need to burden Lord Oeneus with such a trivial matter at all."

Later that morning, when we were finally free to leave the citadel, my brothers asked the obvious questions about Milo's presence beside me in the oxcart.

"I bought him and freed him," I said casually, as if it were something I did every day. "You know I promised to make a sacrifice of thanksgiving to Artemis if you did well in the boar hunt. I've chosen to sacrifice this boy's former life as a slave. Artemis should approve. A huntress values freedom." I patted Milo's shoulder and added, "He's going to stay with us, though, at least until he finds a way to feed himself."

Polydeuces reached out and grabbed Milo's chin, turning his head from side to side. He frowned as he surveyed the boy's battered face, then glanced down at the bruises on his body. "A fitting sacrifice, then," was all he said.

We rode away from Calydon, down the citadel road, past the little pine grove, into the hills where I'd learned how to ride a horse—a little—and where Milo said Atalanta had made her now-abandoned camp.

*Is she really gone?* I wondered. *We couldn't say good-bye, but wouldn't she wait* somewhere *out there in the forests of Calydon to watch me leave?*

As I stared with longing into the trees, trying to read their secrets, I thought I heard the sound of a horse whinnying. *Aristos . . . Atalanta . . .* I raised my hand in a gesture of farewell.

"Lady, what do you see?" Milo asked.

"Nothing," I said, lowering my hand. "Nothing at all."

# PART IV
# DELPHI

# 12

# AN UNEXPECTED HARBOR

Our trip home from Calydon was to be the reverse of the route we'd taken to go there, sailing east as far as the isthmus of Corinth and then going by land south and west to Sparta.

The voyage was uneventful, with fair skies above and calm waters under our keel. The only bad thing was that we weren't blessed with favorable winds to speed us along. The crewmen complained loudly as they bent their brown backs over the oars, but I was happy. I loved to feel the gentle roll and swell of the sea, to see gulls and pelicans swooping and soaring overhead, to lean out over the rail and wave to the folk on other ships, and to watch the ever-changing coast-line slipping past. As long as I was on the water, I was surrounded by beauty and peace, but once I reached home, I had dreadful news to give to my parents. I'd gladly delay it. I wished the voyage could go on forever.

My brothers, too, were at home on the water. They passed the time talking to the crewmen, asking countless questions about the workings of a ship. How do you steer? What are all the ropes for? Which prayers and sacrifices did Poseidon like best? How do you keep the ship from running aground or going too far from the safety of the coastline and becoming lost? They even insisted on taking a daily turn at the oars. This left some of our Spartan guardsmen ill at ease, not knowing whether my brothers expected them to join them on the rowing benches or just stand by and watch. The ship's master turned down the few who volunteered. On our third day out, I overheard him re-mark to one of his crew: "Bad enough trying to sail a ship with no wind and *two* inexperienced newcomers tangling up the oars!" I was so intent on smothering my giggles that I didn't bother pointing out that my brothers had become very good very fast at the work of sailing.

If the ship's master didn't know what to make of two princes who wanted to be sailors, he would have been even more perplexed if he'd known how much I wanted to do the same. As it was, I managed to share a little of their lessons on seamanship by listening and lingering nearby. That was easy. It was a small ship.

After each day's voyage, once the ship had been

beached for the night, we all lay out on the shore, under the frosty swirl of stars. My brothers and Milo were soon snoring, but I thought that the night sky was far more interesting and enchanting than any painted palace ceiling. I'd have time enough for sleep when we got home.

One of the ship's crew noticed my wakefulness and my fascination with the stars. He was a friendly, talkative old man with leathery brown skin and the only hair on his head a short white beard that traced his jawline. He delighted in filling my ears with tales of the beings—human and animal, beast and hero—whom the gods had placed among the stars as reward or punishment. I knew most of those stories already, but I enjoyed hearing him retell them.

"Who knows, my lady?" he said. "Maybe one day when you're a grown woman, your beauty will make Zeus himself fall in love with you and put your image up there as well, for us ordinary men to see and envy."

"I can think of better reasons to end up among the stars," I said, smiling at such harmless flattery.

Milo didn't share any of my brothers' or my pleasure aboard the little ship. Sailing didn't agree with him, except when he took shelter in sleep. My new friend, the seasoned sailor, took pity on Milo and offered one infallible cure for seasickness after another. None worked.

"I can't understand it," he said as the two of us

watched Milo giving the latest potion back to the sea. It was our fourth day on the water, and the poor boy was limp and green as seaweed. "I even put in *three* extra anchovies, just to make sure it would take effect."

"Well, it did," I pointed out. "Just not the effect we were hoping for."

The old man shook his head over this latest defeat. "That last tonic saved my stomach back when I was just a lad aboard a trading ship bound for the tin mountains of Hyperborea! Here we've got easy sailing across a gulf that cradles our ship and steals the teeth of serious gales, but may Poseidon never send you beyond the Middle Sea, my lady. The waves out to the west are ferocious things that'll devour your ship out from under you. And before that happens, you'll be so miserably sick that you'll pray for the mercy of shipwreck and drowning!"

I did my best to look suitably terrified at the very thought of those western storms—the old man took such joy in seeing his tales have their intended effect!—but secretly I was thrilled at the possibility of riding wild waves.

"What's going on, Helen?" Polydeuces came up behind us, followed closely by Castor. They'd been working hard down among the oarsmen again, and it was no pleasure to stand too near them on that windless day.

"The usual, from the look of things," Castor said,

glancing at Milo's sagging body at the rail. He gave the boy an encouraging pat on the back. "Try to drink something, even if you can't keep your food down, lad," he said. "Shall I bring you a little watered wine?"

Milo lifted his sallow, haggard face and tried to thank my brother for his kindness but had to turn away quickly and spew over the side again.

Polydeuces sighed. "How can he still do that? I haven't seen him eat a bite of food since we boarded. You'd think his gut would be empty by now."

"Maybe it's a sacred mystery and only the gods know the answer," Castor said, smiling. "Like the horn of the she-goat who suckled the infant Zeus, the horn he broke off and blessed as soon as he was king of the gods so that it poured out a never-ending stream of food and drink."

"I always thought it was a strange way to thank the poor beast, breaking off one of her horns," Polydeuces said. "But it's not my place to question the gods." He, too, patted Milo's shivering back and added, "So, boy, how does it feel to be pouring out a never-ending stream of—?"

"*Stop that!*" I scowled at my brothers as I shooed them away from Milo. "How can you make such jokes in front of him?"

"To be honest, the only thing in front of him right now is the sea and the supper he ate three days ago." Castor's grin got wider.

Polydeuces was contrite. "We mean well, Helen. We're only trying to make him laugh. A good laugh might take his mind off being so ill."

"It's a shame we're bound straight for Corinth," the old sailor said, rubbing the back of his neck. "Since nothing else seems to be working for this lad, could be that a short rest on dry land would steady his stomach."

"You think we'd ever be able to get him back on board afterward?" Castor asked.

The sailor shrugged. "What would he have to say about it? He's your slave, isn't he?"

"He's our sister's slave, or was," Castor replied. "She freed him as soon as she bought him."

"And still he came onto this ship with you, sick as seafaring makes him?"

"This is his first voyage," I said, stooping beside Milo to place one arm protectively around him. "He didn't *know* he'd get sick."

"Oh, he'd have come along even if he'd known that a sea monster was waiting to gobble him up," Castor said, with another of those annoying, conspiratorial winks to his twin. "Anything rather than be separated from *you*, little sister."

Polydeuces eagerly took up his brother's game. "That's true," he hastened to tell the old sailor. "If you could have seen the way he's been gazing at her, all the way from Calydon!"

"Can we blame him, Polydeuces?" Castor asked with mock sincerity. "Our little sister is the most beautiful woman in the world." They collapsed laughing into each other's arms.

Milo made a great effort and pushed himself away from the rail, away from me. He took two staggering steps, fists clenched. "She *is.*" Then he spun around and lurched for the ship's side once more.

My brothers exchanged a look of pure astonishment. The old sailor chuckled. "He may have been a slave, Lady Helen, but he's braver than many a free man, to talk back to princes that way! But it wouldn't be the first time a man found courage he never knew he had until he met the right woman."

My face flamed. I wanted to thank Milo for putting an end to my brothers' teasing—whether or not it was all in fun, I still found it annoying—but I was strangely tongue-tied.

Fortunately for me, the old sailor chose that moment to say, "That's not something you see every day, a mouse trying to take a bite from a lion's tail. Mark my words, this lad has the makings of a great hero. Why, if I had it my way, I'd put in at the next port and carry him all the way to Apollo's temple at Delphi, just to see what marvels the Pythia would have to predict about his future."

"*Delphi?*" my brothers echoed as one.

We all knew the name of Delphi, we just hadn't realized it was so near. The town was a famous place of prophecy where Apollo's chief priestess, the Pythia, foretold the future. The poets who'd sung of Delphi in our father's hall told how she answered questions and made her predictions in a small room under the sun god's temple, a cave where a crack in the rocky floor released strangely scented vapors from the earth's core. Seated in a giant tripod set above that crevice, holding a twig from Apollo's holy laurel tree, she inhaled the rising mist, then spouted a jumble of weird gibberish. Only the priests of Apollo could interpret it for you.

Now my brothers felt the inescapable need to hear what the Pythia might have to say to them. So that was why, after a short conversation with the old sailor and a shorter one with the ship's master, we all came to be put ashore at the port just south of Apollo's sacred city.

The old sailor who'd become my friend insisted on carrying me from the ship to the land, so I wouldn't wet my feet. As we said our good-byes, he gave me a leave-taking present, a little carving he'd made out of a smooth, creamy white nub of material too hard to be wood, too soft to be stone. When I asked what it was, he told me, "That's the tip of a genuine monster's tooth, a beast that was a gray, five-legged mountain! I saw it with my own eyes in the lands south of the Middle Sea."

"*Five* legs?"

His head bobbed emphatically. "Four where you'd expect 'em to be and the fifth not so much a leg as a long, boneless arm growing right out of the middle of its face."

I smiled at him. "Now you're teasing me as badly as my brothers."

He held both hands out, palms upward, as if to show me he was hiding nothing, not even the truth. "Lady, if I'm lying, may Poseidon the earth shaker, ruler of the seas, make this my last voyage! The world is full of marvels, if you're willing to travel far enough to see them."

I looked at the carving he'd given me. It was the image of a goddess, her feet resting on the back of a dolphin.

"Do you like it?" he asked eagerly. "That's Aphrodite."

"I know," I whispered. My goddess had found me. I wondered if this meant that someday she'd bring me luck enough to see even one of the world's marvels.

Once we were ashore, it didn't take long for our escort of Spartan guardsmen to attract the attention of one of Apollo's priests. The sun god's shrine kept several of them on daily watch down by the waterside solely to deal with the arrival of unexpected, important guests. The man who hurried forward to place himself in our service was overjoyed to learn that Delphi was about to be honored by a visit from the royal house of Sparta. He wasn't much older than my brothers, fresh-faced, and struggling gamely to grow a beard that was only coming out in tufts and patches. He took a slender branch of sweet-scented laurel leaves from his belt and used it to direct the three temple servants attending him. One wave of that branch and our travel chests were hoisted onto their backs, one word of command and they were heading up the road to Apollo's shrine.

"Lady Helen?" Milo spoke my name timidly as we fell into line behind the priest's entourage. Even though his health and appearance had improved miraculously the instant he'd stepped onto dry land, now his large eyes were filled with distress. "There's nothing left for me to carry." He pointed at the servants' slowly retreating backs.

"Don't worry about it," I told him. "You wouldn't have been able to lift those things anyway."

He stared at me as if I'd slapped his face. I was only telling the truth. He was too small and skinny to budge a packed wooden chest, besides which he was drained by his recent unfortunate voyage. I never meant to hurt his feelings.

"I'm *not* useless!" he protested. "There *has* to be something I can do to serve you!" He looked all around him desperately at every step we took and finally dashed into the trees along the roadside. He emerged proudly carrying a newly broken branch of pine needles. He waved it diligently back and forth near my head as we trudged along. It stirred up a nice little breeze, kept off the flies, and made him happy.

To reach Delphi, all roads led up, up, up. The sun god's shrine was set high amid looming crags and deep fissures in the earth, and as steep and sun-baked as the road was, it was thick with pilgrims. Some had come to Delphi the same way we had, by water, but others were so covered with dust that it was obvious they'd come solely by land.

Our priestly guide kept up a pleasant, nonstop stream of chatter all the way from the seaside to the gates of Apollo's temple, though most of it was directed at my brothers.

"Noble princes, surely Apollo himself brought you to us," he said. "This place calls out to heroes. It was here, in the depths of a lightless cavern, that the young sun god performed his first and best heroic feat, killing Python, a hideous, man-eating monster. That's why his chosen priestess here, his all-knowing oracle, is always known as the Pythia, to commemorate Apollo's greatest foe."

"How soon will we be able to see her?" Castor asked.

The priest rubbed his hands together. "Oh, soon, soon! I'm certain she'll have wonderful things to tell you about the splendid futures awaiting you when you rule Sparta someday."

Castor stopped dead in his tracks. *"May the gods forbid it!"*

Polydeuces spoke more quietly, but with just as much heat. "What sort of oracle doesn't know that our *sister* is the heir of Sparta? If you think ill-wishing her will make us favor you, you're a jackass."

Oh, that unhappy priest! If he could have squirmed out of his skin and slithered off into the bushes, he'd have done it in a heartbeat. As it was, he fidgeted and stammered and nervously plucked laurel leaves from the branch that was his badge of office, crushing them one by one until their fragrance was overwhelming.

I couldn't stand to watch his ever-growing embarrassment. "Weren't you two listening?" I said, nudging my brothers. *"He's* not the oracle. You can't blame him for not knowing everything." When they continued to glower at the priest, I turned to him also. "But you *can* tell us what we'll have to do in order to understand what the Pythia says to us, can't you?" I asked lightly. "I've heard that her words are sometimes confusing." I already knew the answer, but I wanted to divert attention from his blunder.

"Yes, yes, surely!" The priest was almost quivering with relief. "In his wisdom, the sun god makes the Pythia speak in his divine voice to those who bring him worthy offerings. Just so Apollo gives us, his humble servants, the power to interpret whatever he inspires her to say—"

"We know that," Castor remarked.

"—for a small additional offering," the priest concluded. Then he was off chattering again, telling us all about the glories of Delphi, assuring us that we'd have no need to find an inn, that it would be an honor to provide us with the best lodgings on the temple grounds.

The higher we climbed, the thicker the crowds grew, until by the time we entered Delphi itself we were surrounded. So many people! The streets teemed with them. Delphi was an ever-growing weed of a town that sprang up to serve the visitors to Apollo's shrine. People came from all over Greece to lay their questions at the Pythia's feet. I was dazzled by the sight of such crowds, rich and poor from every corner of the mainland and even from the islands scattered over the Middle Sea.

But soon the excitement of being part of that hubbub faded. The brightly colored clothes, the flash of gold ornaments, the sudden appearance of a chariot rolling by, all of the initial glamour shrank down into a clogged mass of hot, aggravated, pushy, impatient savages. All of them seemed to have been born with at least six knobby elbows, and each person acted like he owned the street. Milo's ever-waving pine branch was knocked aside and trampled. Even with our guardsmen at our sides, we were lucky that the same thing didn't happen to us.

"Are all of these people dying to know how they're going to die?" I muttered.

The priest mistook my grumble for a real question. "That's not the only reason that brings people to Delphi. Heroes seek to learn which road will take them to their next triumph. Kings ask the oracle's guidance when they wish to know whether or not to make war. Those who are fortunate enough to be granted an audience with the Pythia come away with the blessing of knowing their destiny."

"But what good does it do to know your *destiny*?" I argued. "You can't escape it. The three Fates spin, measure, and cut the life thread of every human being. Their decisions are final. Even Zeus can't change them."

"But Lady Helen, surely you're skilled enough with the spindle to know that every length of thread is made of many smaller fibers twisted tightly together?" the priest said smoothly. "The Fates themselves grant us one or two places in our lives where the thread untwists and we can follow either one strand or the other. Better to know when and where those choices will come to us instead of being taken by surprise."

"Why only one or two?" I asked, thinking of all the moments my life had already accumulated in which I'd chosen to follow a different path than the one most people would expect of me. "Why not say that every day lets me choose my own future?"

The priest chuckled. "What a gift you have for joking, Lady Helen! You *know* your future. You'll be Sparta's queen, living a life blessed by the gods. Your only surprises will be the name of your husband and whether your babies will be sons or daughters. You don't need to visit the Pythia. But your noble brothers will be heroes, making their own futures; heroes should know what awaits them."

"He's right, Helen," Castor said. "Polydeuces and I should know our fate."

Castor's fate? He didn't need an oracle to discover that; I could tell him exactly what it would be. The young priest's glib words were better than under-ground fumes for giving me a vision of what lay in store for both of my brothers: They were going to have their ears filled with flattery, then be persuaded to leave a rich gift at Apollo's shrine just to hear some poor girl babble riddles while she choked half to death on smoke. Then they'd make *another* offering just to have Apollo's priests translate the Pythia's wild words. If their gifts to the sun god were too extravagant, I could also predict what Father would have to say about it when we got home.

As soon as our party came through the shrine gates, we were greeted by one of the senior priests. He directed the servants to take our baggage to the finest room the temple could offer.

"Unfortunately, noble guests, it is only *one* room," he said. "My apologies, it's all we can provide. Perhaps as you passed through the town, you saw how busy things are at the moment. Your attendants will have to find other lodgings. There are many fine inns at Delphi."

Polydeuces frowned. "Our sister is the heir of Sparta and it's our duty to protect her. Separating her from her guards . . . I don't like it."

The priest gave him a reassuring smile. "Noble prince, if you doubt that your strength alone will be enough to safeguard her, are you also unwilling to trust your sister to Apollo's own protection? Do you believe that a few armed men can shield her better than the sun god himself? The temple grounds are sacred and secure. Of course, if you insist . . ."

"No, no." Polydeuces turned a little pale at the thought of insulting Apollo, even accidentally. "I was only worried about what might happen if she left the shrine."

"Why would she want to do that?" the priest asked. He had begun to talk about me as if I weren't there, or worse, as if I were just another traveler's chest to be stowed in one room or another. "If you tell her to stay on the temple grounds, you have no problem."

Castor's mouth twisted into a wry smile. "That's our sister, all right—just as tame and obedient as every other girl." I jabbed him with my elbow.

"Perhaps you could help us find lodgings for our men at the inn that's *closest* to the shrine?" Polydeuces asked the priest.

"A fine idea, noble prince." He was all smiles. "It's the best in Delphi. I know it well: It belongs to my cousin. Your men are lucky to have such a generous master."

As he spoke, I became aware that Milo was edging closer to me. He looked fearful and unhappy. "Lady Helen, must I go away too?" he whispered. "You need me, don't you?"

"Of course I do," I whispered back to reassure him. "Go follow the men who carried our traveling chests and see what the room we've been given is like."

He brightened immediately. "I'll do better than that for you, Lady Helen! I'll make sure that it's clean, and that you have the best bed, and that—"

Either we'd been incautious and not whispered softly enough or the senior priest had the ears of a greyhound. Suddenly he was standing between us, and though he was still smiling, his words had a hard edge to them. "My deepest regrets, Lady Helen, but your slave cannot be lodged here with you."

"Milo is *free*," I said sternly, standing very tall. "He serves us very well, and my brothers and I need him with us. It's not going to insult Apollo's ability to protect me if he stays. He's no guard."

"So I see." The priest gave Milo a patronizing look. "Gracious Lady Helen, how kind of you to tell me what will or won't insult the god I've served since childhood. Alas, how deeply I regret to tell you that you are . . . mistaken. Do you believe that great Apollo would allow his noble guests to enjoy his hospitality unattended? You might as well say that you'll need to provide your own food and drink because the sun god is too poor or too ungenerous to do so in his own house! Or perhaps you think that those who are good enough to serve Apollo *aren't* good enough to serve you?"

"That isn't why I—" I began, but Polydeuces cut my protest short.

"Our sister would *never* offend Apollo, would you, Helen?" I saw real fear in his eyes when he looked at me. It was clear that the sun god's wrath had the power to terrify my bold, strong brother even when nothing else could.

I couldn't let him be so afraid. I bowed my head to Apollo's priest and said, "We'll do as you tell us. Our guards and servants will all sleep elsewhere."

"Oh, I'd never dare to *tell* you what to do, Lady Helen," the priest replied. I didn't have to look at his face. His voice alone told me that he was wearing a smug, victorious smile.

## 13

# ENCOUNTER IN DELPHI

The senior priest did tell the truth about our lodgings. We were given a fine, comfortable room and spent a restful night. Early the next morning, one of the temple servants arrived with bread, wine, cheese, and news: "Noble guests, you will be permitted to see the holy Pythia today, as soon as you feel you are prepared to hear her voice."

Castor and Polydeuces almost danced for joy. They talked together intensely, debating whether they'd do better to give Apollo two identical offerings or a single, truly impressive one. I stood by the doorway, arms folded, and said nothing.

At last they noticed my silence. "What about you, Helen?" Polydeuces asked. "What will you give to Apollo?"

"Nothing."

"Helen, you can't—" Polydeuces began to object.

I stopped him cold. "I'm giving the god nothing because I'm not coming with you to the temple. Why should I? You heard that priest. *My* future's set."

"We all know you don't believe that," Castor said, smirking. "Or is this your way of telling us that you've decided to put down the sword?"

"Oh, but I do believe it," I replied. And I did. My future *was* set: The choices it held belonged to no one but me. I didn't need or want the Pythia's prophecies to guide me through them.

"This is about those two priests, isn't it?" Polydeuces said. "You can't fool me, little sister. I saw the look on your face, especially when you were listening to the young one. You were as skilled and gracious as Mother at changing the subject to save him from his own foolish remarks. He repaid your help by dismissing you as just another little girl."

"You know, they were only *two* men," Castor put in. "I doubt that all of Apollo's priests here are like them."

"And what if they are?" I countered. "Is Delphi about prophecy or greed?"

"So you think Apollo's oracle is a fake?" Polydeuces asked quietly. He genuinely revered the gods.

"I didn't say that and I don't believe it," I replied

truthfully. "I'd gladly see Apollo's oracle if it didn't mean I'd have to see his priests."

My brothers exchanged a look of resignation. "No use trying to talk her out of it, is there?" Castor asked.

"We know better than that," Polydeuces replied. "Much better." He turned to me. "Are you sure you won't be too bored here, waiting for us to come back? We don't know how long our time with the Pythia will last; I hope you'll find something to do."

"Of course I will," I told him. "I'll be exploring Delphi."

"No you won't," my brothers responded in perfect unison. Then they took turns telling me exactly why I couldn't do what I wanted.

"You wouldn't be safe," Castor said.

"You'd get lost if you went wandering around the city on your own," Polydeuces added.

"It's too big."

"Too noisy."

"Too confusing."

"Too busy."

"You could run into the wrong sort of people."

"Dangerous types."

"But sneaky enough so you couldn't tell they're dangerous until it's too late."

"We're responsible for your safety."

"We have to know where you are at all times."

"It's not that we don't trust *you*, Helen."

"It's *them*."

"It's for your own good."

I flopped down on my bed. "Fine. Go. I'll stay here," I told the ceiling.

Castor and Polydeuces each grabbed one of my wrists and pulled me back to my feet. "I don't think so," Castor said, chuckling. "You'd stay here, all right. You'd stay here just until you saw us go into Apollo's temple, and then you'd be a little cloud of dust sailing out through the gates."

"You don't have to come with us," Polydeuces said. "But if you want to tour this city, you'll have to do it on *our* terms."

With that, he left me in Castor's company.

"Where's he going?" I asked.

"Probably to see if the priests of Apollo have an oil jar big enough to stuff you inside for safekeeping." He winked at me.

No matter how much I loved my brothers, I wasn't in the mood for more teasing. "Aren't you afraid you'll insult the Pythia if you don't go to see her right now? You *were* summoned. She could foretell terrible fates for the two of you if you keep her waiting."

Castor didn't seem worried. "If she's truly blessed with the gift of prophecy, she already knows we're going to be delayed. And if she can't foretell that, she's as much of an oracle as I am, so why should I care *what* she predicts?" He laughed out loud, then added, "But don't tell Polydeuces I said that. He's the devout one."

Polydeuces returned only a little while later, accompanied by two of our Spartan soldiers. "I sent a messenger to the inn where they're staying," he told us. "They'll look after you while Castor and I are with the Pythia. Have a good time in Delphi." He acted as though he'd just solved every problem in the world.

I didn't see it that way.

As we crossed the temple grounds together, I asked Polydeuces, "Is there a *good* reason you're treating me like a silly sheep?" I indicated the two soldiers behind me. "Or are you embarrassing me like this just because you *can?*"

Castor spoke up before his twin could answer. "Stop making a fuss over nothing, Helen. These men will protect you, not steer you."

"That's right, Lady Helen," the taller of the two said. "We're your shadows, not your sheepdogs. Go anywhere you want."

I gave him a sweet, innocent smile. Then I barked at him.

The soldiers and I watched my brothers enter Apollo's temple. Then the taller one asked me where I'd like to go.

"I want to see Milo," I replied. "He's going to come with me while I look around Delphi."

"Milo?" the other soldier echoed as we left the sanctuary grounds.

"You know, the little Calydonian," his comrade said. "How stupid are you? It's not like he blends in with the rest of us. A good lad, but fretful. He was up half the night worrying about how he'd ever know whether Lady Helen would need him to run errands for her while we're at Delphi."

"Is that right?" I asked.

The soldier nodded. "Yes, Lady Helen. It was a great kindness you did, freeing him from slavery, but now gratitude's made him enslave himself to you. You've got a fine servant in that boy."

"Not forever," I said. "Right now there's no choice about it—he's got no family, no way to feed himself—but once we get home I'll apprentice him to one of the palace craftsmen. Then he can live his own life."

"A jug of wine says he'll only be happy if he can live it close to *her*," the first soldier muttered to the other, but when I demanded he repeat his words to my face, he claimed he'd said nothing at all.

My sheepdogs took me to the place where Milo was staying along with some of their companions. Even if the senior priest wanted his cousin's inn alone to get our business, it wasn't big enough to accommodate all of our Spartan guards together, so they'd split up into smaller groups staying at a handful of different lodgings.

As soon as Milo heard I had come for him, he ran out of the inn, overjoyed. "Lady Helen, are you well? What do you need me to do for you? How can I serve you?"

The soldiers escorting me snickered over his eagerness, until I silenced them both with a look colder than the snows of Mount Olympus. "Well, Milo, are you ready to get that cloak I promised you?" I asked.

"Cloak?" Of course he didn't know what I was talking about, but he didn't have to. After only a moment's hesitation, he raised both hands to me, bowed his head, and said, "Whatever pleases you, Lady Helen."

I walked through the streets of Delphi with one soldier ahead of me, one behind me, and Milo at my side. The day was new, but the city was already bustling. The crowded streets with all their noise and commotion were still annoying, but now that I'd had a good night's sleep they were also exciting and challenging. I felt as if Delphi herself were calling out to me: *Come and know me if you can! It takes a special kind of person to learn my secrets. Are you strong or nimble enough to fight through my crowds? Are you smart enough to find your way through my streets? Are you wise enough to deal with any peril or adventure I might choose to throw across your path? I am Delphi, and I dare you to conquer me!*

*And* I *am Helen of Sparta,* I thought. *I'm your match, just wait and see. But first . . .*

First I'd have to slip away from my sheepdogs.

The two Spartan soldiers escorting Milo and me were puzzled by my intention to get him a cloak, and they didn't hesitate to say what they thought of the matter.

"A cloak?" the taller one remarked from behind me. "In *this* weather? That poor lad's going to sweat away to nothing!"

"You know how cold the nights can get back home," I said. "He doesn't have to wear it *now.*"

"Then I can't say it makes sense for him to *get* it now, Lady Helen," the soldier ahead of us put in. "The palace women make better cloth than any of this foreign stuff. A Spartan cloak for Spartan weather, that's what *I* say."

"The palace women aren't here, and who knows what the weather's going to be like on the road home?" I pointed out. "I want Milo to be prepared." I paused at a place where two streets crossed and tapped my chin. "I wonder where the marketplace could be?"

"Everywhere, from the look of things," the shorter guardsman said.

He was right. The whole city of Delphi teemed with buyers and sellers. It didn't take us long before we found a house with piles of cloth displayed on a long bench just outside the door. The instant that I touched the first one, a fat, gap-toothed woman swooped down on me.

"Little girl, who gave you permission to— Oh!" She bit off her words the moment that she noticed how well I was dressed, to say nothing of the two guards attending me. Her expression transformed from sour to sweet with stunning speed.

"Ah, noble lady, I see that you have a keen eye for quality," she cried. You won't find better cloth anywhere in Delphi—warm in winter, light in summer, tightly woven, and proof against wind and rain. And just *look* at those colors!"

I did. They were all drab grays and browns. I held the first cloth up to the sunlight. If that was what she called a tight weave, so was a fishing net.

"I want a cloak," I told her, tossing the cloth aside. "Something long and *heavy*. It's for him." I nodded at Milo.

"Of course, just as you wish, I have exactly what you want, wait right here," she chattered. "I'll bring out the best I have, something worthy of the noble lord." She raised her hands to Milo in a gesture of reverence before ducking back into her house.

" 'The noble lord'?" the tall guard repeated, incredulous. He and his companion snickered. Milo looked miserable.

"Ignore them," I told him, speaking low. "I promise you, before today is over, you'll be the one laughing at them."

The weaver came out of her house carrying a fresh pile of cloths. These were better work, solidly woven. They were all still the color of the dusty streets, but that was what I was after. She tossed them over Milo's shoulders one after the other, to demonstrate the different lengths.

"What would the noble lord prefer?" she cooed at Milo, embarrassing him terribly. "If you're most concerned about keeping out the cold, this one's long enough to cover you from neck to heels and provide enough material to pull up over your head. But if you'd rather have something shorter . . ."

"That one will do," I declared. It was perfect, but I knew better than to let her know that. "It's not very well made, and there are snarls in the wool the size of locusts, but I have better things to do with my time than look at every scrap of cloth in Delphi." So the bargaining began.

Milo's cloak cost me the taller soldier's small bronze knife. I promised him I'd give him a new spearhead in exchange, once we returned to Sparta.

"It's an honor to serve you, Lady Helen," he said as we continued to walk through Delphi. "I don't require anything in exchange."

*We both know you don't mean that,* I thought. Aloud, I

said, "Then honor me by accepting it as a gift. I only wish there were something I could do for you now to show my thanks." I coughed as if my throat had gone dry suddenly. "Ugh, what a hard time I had, getting that woman to agree to a decent bargain! I'm ready to die of thirst. Let's find a wineshop."

"That shouldn't be too hard," the taller soldier said, sniffing the air. He was right. We came across one before we'd gone thirty steps. It was very small, little more than a storeroom with a serving table full of cups inside and a bench out on the street. I rejected it.

"I don't want to drink out in the sun," I said. "I'll only get thirsty again. Keep looking."

The next wineshop we found had a shady arbor covered with grapevines next to it, a very comfortable place for customers to take refuge from the sun. I peeked into the shop itself and then rejected this one too.

"Too few amphoras," I said. "They haven't got enough wine to sell. I want to drink wine thinned with water, not water flavored with wine!" I caught my guards exchanging a look and demanded, *"What?"*

"Oh, nothing, Lady Helen, nothing," the shorter man said, rubbing his chin. "It's just that we never expected you to be so . . . knowledgeable about wineshops."

"I want us all to share a cup of wine together," I told him. "It's to thank you for looking after me so well. I could settle for just *any* wineshop, but you deserve better than that."

"I thought you didn't want us to—" the taller man began. He was the one I'd barked at earlier.

"I was being foolish," I said sweetly. "Now that I've seen what Delphi's like, I know that I'd have been lost if I'd left the temple grounds without you. I want to apologize."

What could they say after that? They let me have my way, and soon I did find exactly the sort of wineshop I'd been seeking: dark, cavernous, crowded, and noisy. As soon as we were seated at a table, I snapped a little silver ornament off my belt and held it out to Milo.

"Bring us wine, boy," I said grandly, but instead of placing the silver into his hand, I deliberately missed and let it drop to the floor.

"I'll get it, Lady Helen!" he exclaimed, falling to his hands and knees.

I uttered a short, exasperated sound. "You'll *never* find it by yourself." With that, I ducked beneath the table as well, while my guards laughed.

Safely out of my sheepdogs' sight and hearing, I grabbed Milo's hand just as it closed over the silver ornament. "Milo, do you want to help me?" I whispered urgently.

"Yes, always," he whispered back. "Anything."

I told him my plan as quickly and quietly as I

could, then said, "I just need you to drop the cloak where I can get it and create a distraction so I can slip out. Do you think you can do it? Find some way to distract them?"

Milo smiled more happily than I'd ever seen him do before. "You'll see," he said.

I pulled myself back onto my bench while Milo scurried off to fetch the wine. The silver ornament bought more than enough for what I had in mind. Even though he drank with us, as my servant it was Milo's job to add water to each helping of wine. I drank only one cupful, which was mostly water, but he made sure that the guards drank almost pure wine.

After a while, the tall one exclaimed, "Hey, look at that! Isn't that his fourth cup?" He pointed unsteadily at Milo.

"So what?" his comrade said. "It's our fourth too."

"But he's—he's just a boy. He can't drink like that," the first man objected.

"Who says I can't?" Milo thumped his cup down loudly on the table. He sounded ferociously drunk, though he wasn't. He *had* emptied four cups, but the soldiers couldn't know that there wasn't enough wine in all of them together to equal the wine in one of theirs. "I'm from Calydon, an' in Calydon we know how to drink. Dionysus, god o' wine himself, taught us how to make the bes' wine. Song about it. Listen."

He climbed onto the bench, flung his new cloak to the floor, then leaped onto the table and began a frantic dance while singing a loud, vulgar, hilarious song that soon had my guards and every other customer in the wineshop roaring the chorus and pounding out the rhythm on the tables.

While Milo kept them all distracted, I grabbed his discarded cloak, threw it over my head so that my face was well hidden, and slipped out into the streets of Delphi.

I wanted to explore the city on my own terms, but the city decided otherwise. The crowds carried me along like a tuft of feathers caught in a gale. I was jostled up one street, down a second, straight through a third, and from one side of the road to the other. When I pulled myself out of the human current to look at the buildings, it was always in some dull little side street where there was nothing worth looking at. I had no choice but to rejoin the endless rush of people, hoping I'd be able to see something interesting the next time I got away from the crowds.

I finally got my wish when I managed to put myself behind an oxcart. It was so bulky that it cleared a wide path through the mob, and the oxen walked slowly enough for me to stroll after the cart at a pleasantly unhurried pace, looking around at my leisure. I just had to look *down* from time to time to watch where I was putting my feet, oxen being oxen.

That was how I happened to stumble across the image maker's house. It stood at the intersection of two paths near the place where the street widened into a market square. This open space was filled with even more merchants than the ordinary city streets, some selling their wares from the doors of the houses, some camped in ramshackle wooden booths, some with their merchandise spread out on a blanket, and some simply squatting in the dust with a basket full of goods.

I let the helpful oxcart go on without me as I wandered up to have a closer look at the house selling the clay images. They stood in rows on a narrow table beside the door, watched over by a dull-eyed girl who yawned with every breath she took.

"What are *you* looking at, you little grub?" she lashed out when she noticed me. "Touch any of my dad's stuff and I'll snap your dirty fingers like bean pods."

I stood as tall as I could and shrugged back my plain-looking, dusty cloak. My brothers had told me to wear my best dress that morning, hoping until the last instant that I'd change my mind and come into the temple with them. Now the gorgeous colors of the tiered skirt, the intricate embroidery patterns on the short-sleeved jacket, the gold and silver charms sewn over everything, all hit the girl with the force of a tooth-rattling slap in the face. Her jaw dropped and she stared at me.

At that moment, a bald, beaming, potbellied man came out of the house to see what was going on. When he saw me, his smile stretched so wide it seemed like the corners would meet at the back of his head. He clutched the stunned girl by the shoulders, shoved her back into the house, and gave me his full attention, apologizing for his daughter and begging me to handle as many of the figurines as I liked. He didn't need to ask twice.

Oh, they were wonderful! There were images of leaping bulls and placid sheep, goats and doves and donkeys, and many different sorts of men and women. All of them were painted with extraordinary skill and detail. I'd seen plenty of such things before—everyone took clay images to the temples as offerings for the gods—but these were works of art. I picked up one figurine shaped like a priestess of Gaia, the great mother goddess of the earth. She was holding up two snakes, creatures sacred to Gaia because their whole bodies were always pressed against the ground. The potter had painted in every detail, from the serpents' eyes to the scales covering their backs.

"I'll buy this one," I said. "What will you take for it?" I got ready for the haggling to begin.

He was about to reply when a hand slammed down on the boards between us and a brash voice proclaimed: "*There's* your price, old man!" It was a voice I knew. I looked up as Theseus of Athens lifted his hand from the table. He'd slapped down a strand of silver beads worth enough to buy every image in the shop. Rings of gold and crystal glittered on his fingers, and an enameled silver belt clasping his embroidered tunic gleamed in the sunlight. He looked so splendid that for a moment I forgot just how much I disliked him.

"Well?" he demanded. "Is it a bargain?"

The potter was overwhelmed. His hands trembled as he reached for the silver, as if he were afraid that this would all turn out to be a dream. He jabbered nonstop thanks and blessings at Theseus. Then he picked up one after another of his best figurines, offering them to his new benefactor as humbly and reverently as if he were offering them to a god.

"Give them to the lady Helen, if they please her," Theseus said. If he was trying to impress me by playing the part of the grand, noble, open-handed king, he failed. All *I* could see was a loudmouthed show-off.

"This one is enough for me, thank you," I said. "Now I have to bring it to the temple. Good-bye." I started down the street, trying to melt into the crowd.

"Not so fast, little lady." Theseus pushed and shoved his way to my side as if the other people were bales of hay. When one man protested, Theseus casually backhanded him so hard that he staggered into a wall. The great hero of Athens planted one hand on the small of my back and forced me to walk beside him. "It's a good thing I happened to find you," he said, leering like an ape. "If you want to go to the temple, you're heading the wrong way."

I gave him a haughty look. "I'm not taking this to the temple of Apollo," I said. "I'm going to a little shrine to Gaia. You wouldn't know where it is; only women can worship there." I was rattling off one lie after another, hoping Theseus wouldn't catch on, since he was also a visitor to Delphi.

"But I *do* know the place you mean," he replied so smoothly that I was willing to bet he was lying too. "And you're still heading in the wrong direction. At least let me take you there safely, even if I can't go in."

As I walked along in his unwanted company, he tried to keep up a conversation. I let him yap away, hoping he'd give up and shut up. No such luck. He was one of those people who adored the sound of his own voice.

"Ah, Lady Helen, look at you today, dressed the way you should be. It suits you. A far cry from the rags you wore when you were that insolent boy Pirithous and I met during the hunt, eh? I knew it was you. I figured it out not long after you ran away from us, waving that silly little splinter you called a sword. Where'd you get that toy, anyway? Filched it, I'll bet. No man in his right mind would give something that dangerous to a girl.

"You've got spirit, and that's all right. I like a

woman with spirit, in moderation. But what were you thinking, tagging along on a boar hunt? You could've been killed or, worse, the boar could've ruined that pretty face of yours. You'll be a beauty someday, Lady Helen, even if you are still a wild little thing. Well, a few more years and a good husband will make you settle down."

That did it. I didn't know which was worse, his lies about my looks or his gall about dictating what my future *had* to be. I stopped dead, digging in my heels the same as when I'd helped Atalanta spear the boar. Theseus tried to push me forward, but I held firm, lifted my chin, and said, "I don't know why you're blabbering silly flattery about how *pretty* I am, but you can stop now, before you make an even bigger fool of yourself. I didn't ask for your company and I don't want it. Go away and leave me alone."

He smirked and nodded at the priestess figurine cupped in my hands. "Is that any way to talk to me after I gave you such an expensive gift?"

"You bought this, not me," I said. "Take it." I thrust it at him, and if I just *happened* to drive my fist into his belly while I did it—

That was stupid. No matter how well I could handle a sword or a spear, I was still just a fourteen-year-old girl, and a blow from my fist against a grown man's well-muscled gut hurt him about as much as the flick of a hound's tail. He grabbed my wrist and twisted it until I dropped the figurine into the dirt. I cried out in pain.

"Maybe you shouldn't have to wait a few more years for a husband," he said. "Someone needs to teach you how a *good* woman behaves."

I screamed and thrashed and kicked, but he wouldn't let go of my wrist, and no one in the street made any move to help me. Who'd dare interfere with a man who was so obviously rich and strong, especially when the victim was just a girl, even if she was well dressed herself? How I wished I had my Spartan sheepdogs with me now!

"What are you doing to her? Stop at once!" The words cut through the air like the crack of a whip. Theseus's grip went slack, though he still held me. I saw the astonishment in his eyes: The voice that had just commanded him to let me go was the voice of a young woman.

## 14

# VISIONS FROM THE GODS

The young woman was standing in the street before us, flanked by two frail, white-haired men. One held a blue-fringed red sunshade over her head, the other waved an oxtail whisk to shoo away flies. She was half a head taller than I, with waist-length curls of hair so black it gleamed with blue highlights. She had the whitest skin I'd ever seen, as if it never saw the sun. Her almond-shaped face was as carefully painted as any of the old potter's images, lips and cheeks reddened with dots of carmine, emerald-green eyes outlined with a heavy black border of kohl. The flounced layers of her skirt were so elaborately decorated with gold, silver, pearls, and precious stones that walking must have been like wading through muddy water. The laurel wreath on her head was made of gold.

When Theseus didn't obey, she strode forward, eyes blazing. I know it was impossible, but I could have sworn that they grew larger, changing from green to midnight black laced with a sudden flash of crimson fire. "Son of Aegeas," she intoned. "Your father is dead, the princess who loved you is gone. How many more will you lose? Son of Poseidon, free the daughter of Zeus or lose more! Friend, mother, son, city—"

"Hear the voice of Apollo!" one of the old men cried out in his shaky voice. "Hear the Pythia!"

But Theseus didn't stay to hear any more. He dropped my wrist, held up his hands as he babbled an apology, then wheeled around and ran. The young priestess solemnly watched him go and stooped to pick up the clay figurine he'd forced out of my hand. "Oh, good, it's not broken," she said as she handed it back to me. "It's very pretty." Then she burst into giggles.

The priest who carried the fly whisk approached us. "You are the lady Helen of Sparta, yes?" he asked me politely while his companion hastened to shadow the Pythia with the fringed sunshade.

"Yes, I am," I replied. "How did you know? I'm afraid I don't remember meeting you."

He had a kind smile. "You didn't. I saw you and your brothers arrive at Apollo's shrine yesterday, that's all. I don't pretend to have *her* blessed powers." He nodded at the young woman who'd rescued me.

I drew the priest a little aside and murmured for his ears alone, "Is that *really* the Pythia?" He nodded, still smiling indulgently. "But why is she *here*, walking through the streets just like anyone else?"

"Because she has already spoken this morning to those who sought Apollo's words, including your brothers, Lady Helen. After she has prophesied, she always enjoys breathing fresh air."

I remembered what I'd heard about the Pythia's vapor-filled lair; I couldn't blame her for wanting to escape it. "I'm just surprised that she *walks*," I said. "She's the Pythia; shouldn't she be carried wherever she wants to go?"

"You can't see anything when you're being carried along in a litter," the Pythia said, coming up behind me. "I *like* walking, Lady Helen, and now I'd like to walk with *you*."

I couldn't have asked for a safer escort back to the temple precinct. When the Pythia went by, people drew back, raised their hands to their foreheads in prayer, fell silent, or spoke in whispers. I kept silent too.

"Lady Helen, what's the matter? Why won't you talk to me? Have I offended you?" The Pythia linked her arm through mine as if we were sisters.

"I—I didn't know if I should," I answered. "You're the god's voice." I hadn't believed it that morning, but after seeing firsthand evidence of her abilities, I was ready to change my mind.

She tossed her hair, making the gold leaves tinkle. "My *name* is Eunike."

"You saw my brothers today," I said.

She nodded. "They talked about lots of things while they were waiting to hear me, including you and how you were growing up to be the most stubborn woman in the world. Lord Castor told the man waiting next to him that you were lucky to be so pretty or you'd *never* find a husband."

"*Now* Castor claims I'm pretty?" I shook my head. I couldn't believe he'd said that. I knew it wasn't true. I still remembered what that Calydonian noblewoman had said about my looks. *That* I believed. "Everyone else at home *used* to say I was pretty, but when I was five he'd call me Frog-face, and even Polydeuces once called me a toad."

"What brothers say to tease their sisters has nothing to do with what they really think of them," Eunike said.

"I don't care about Castor's opinion of my chances at marriage or my looks. I'm just surprised that he chose to talk about me when he was in your presence. It's disrespectful to you and Apollo. Polydeuces must have been ready to kill him!"

"Oh, he didn't tell me himself," Eunike said. "First the priests bring the pilgrims into the sacred underground chamber and let them wait there, while they kindle the brazier and make sure that my tripod is properly positioned above the crack in the earth where the god's breath rises. I wait in another room, well aboveground, until they come to fetch me."

"Then how did you hear what Castor said about me?" I asked.

"Sound travels very well inside Apollo's house. Even when people think no one else can hear them, my priests always do, and they always make sure to tell me what they've overheard."

"Is that where your prophecies come from? From whispers and spies?" I'd really wanted to believe that there was something truly divine at the heart of Delphi, in spite of my encounters with those first two greedy priests. I narrowed my eyes at Eunike. "Why are you telling me this, about how you and the priests fool everyone?"

"I didn't say that." The Pythia's lighthearted expression became more serious. "Now *you're* interpreting my words to suit yourself, just like some of the priests do. I'm telling you about what happens in Apollo's shrine because you'd figure it out for yourself, sooner or later. You never simply accept what you're told, Lady Helen. You ask questions. You challenge things as they are."

My mouth twisted into a mocking smile. "Is that something you saw in a vision or something else your priests overheard my brother Castor say?"

"I won't lie to you: It didn't come from any vision.

The priests insist on telling me everything they hear, whether I want to know it or not," she replied.

"Well then, I hope both of my brothers paid your priests enough to buy themselves a lucky prophe—"

The words died on my lips. Eunike was staring at me. I swear I'd never met another human being with such intense eyes. They went from emerald to onyx in an instant and held an inner glow that was unnerving to see. Their vision penetrated straight to the secret places of my heart, to the dreams where I wasn't tied to a skirt or a loom or a throne or any future but the one I'd make for myself.

"What I learn from spies and whispers isn't what I prophesy," the Pythia said gravely. "The priests don't need to translate my words for the people. Some of them do try to persuade our visitors that if I say, 'It's going to rain,' it really means, 'Your wife will give you five sons,' but only the most foolish pay to hear such nonsense.

"It wasn't always like this. Some of the women who served Apollo before me needed to know as much as possible about each visitor so that, when they spoke, it would seem as though the all-seeing sun shared his infinite sight with them. But some of the Pythias were like me: I *see* things, Helen. I don't know why or how, but I do. It doesn't only happen when I breathe the god's breath. My visions come when and where they will."

"What about the things you said to Theseus?" I asked, curious to learn more. "It's no secret that his father's dead. Everyone in Lord Oeneus's palace knew that. But what about the rest? The lost princess . . . ?"

"Lady Ariadne, King Minos's daughter," Eunike said. "Visitors from Crete said she and Theseus fell in love when he made a raid on their island. They ran off together, yet when he finally came home to Athens, there was no Cretan princess on his ship."

"Do you think he—?" I didn't want to finish the awful thought. Theseus had shown me that he had no qualms about hurting people, but I couldn't imagine him as a murderer.

"His eyes fill with tears when he remembers her," Eunike said. "Whatever became of her, he mourns her memory. His hands are clean."

"Ah." Much as I despised Theseus, I felt relieved to know that. "And I'll bet Poseidon's *his* father the same way Zeus is mine," I said sarcastically.

"He's not the only man to pretend he was fathered by a god. They think it adds to their reputation as heroes. But the other things I said to him . . ." The Pythia sighed like someone carrying a heavy burden. "Those were what I *saw* waiting for him, whether or not he let you go. His mother, his son, his city, he'll lose them all." And she began to cry.

The priest with the fly whisk hurried forward to take her into his arms and murmur words of comfort in her ears. I was afraid he'd blame me for her tears, but when he looked at me it was only with kindness.

"This happens to her all the time," he murmured. "Sometimes the god's breath lingers on her lips after she leaves the temple. When she sees a truly dark future for anyone, it breaks her heart. Let's walk on. She'll be herself again soon. Won't you, child?" He gave the all-seeing Pythia a hug. I wanted to hug him myself, for his goodness to her.

Eunike recovered her cheerful manner before we reached the temple. Just as we were entering the grounds, she clutched my arm, dragged me aside, and whispered, "Do you want to know what's going to happen to *you?*"

I hesitated. It was tempting, in spite of all my protests that morning. *Maybe I* ought *to ask her for my fate,* I thought.

"Tell me," I said softly.

The Pythia clasped my hands in hers. Her eyes were shining, but they stayed green. "You're going to grow up rich and beautiful, you're going to meet a handsome man who'll change your life, and you're going to go on a long voyage with him." Then she burst out laughing. "Isn't that what every girl wants to hear?"

"Very funny." I gave her a hard look.

"If you can't take a joke, say so," she said lightly. "But really, Lady Helen, I haven't had any visions about you, so all I can tell you about your future is this: You're going to have to get back to Sparta with no one's help but your own."

"What?" The Pythia had tossed her ominous words at me as if they were a trifle. "How can you say—?"

"Helen! Thank Apollo, there you are!" Castor came sprinting out of the temple precinct gate, lifted me off my feet, and swung me around. He was so ecstatic to see me that it was as if the Pythia and her attendant priests were invisible to him. As I whirled in Castor's arms, I saw Eunike smile and move silently back through the gateway with her escorts, heading for Apollo's temple. My brother was so focused on me that he was never aware of their presence.

"What kind of a trick was that to play on Hippomenes and Arctos?" Castor demanded when he set me down again. I held his arm to steady myself. My brother's enthusiastic welcome had left me dizzy. "They went crazy when you gave them the slip. You wouldn't have been so quick to pull that stunt if you'd seen their faces when they came back here, dragging poor Milo between them. All three of them smelled like the bottom of a grape vat! None of them had any notion of where you were, but the men were convinced Milo did know and wasn't telling. I had to stop them from kicking an answer out of him."

"If they laid one finger on him—" I growled.

"Milo is fine," Castor said. "Forget Milo. Helen, listen, I've got something fantastic to tell you. Today, after Polydeuces and I saw the Pythia, we met Prince Jason of Iolkos. He's calling together a crew, even more men than Lord Oeneus summoned for the boar hunt, to make the greatest voyage anyone ever heard of, from Iolkos all the way through the Hellespont to Colchis, on the shores of the Euxine Sea, a voyage of *heroes!* Jason had gone to see the Pythia too, and she told him the names of the men he must bring if he wants his quest to succeed. Oh, Helen, you'll never guess what she said!"

"She told him he should bring you and Castor," I said dully. "I'll have to return to Sparta with no one's help but my own."

I looked toward the temple, seeking Eunike, but as I suspected, she was long gone.

That evening, my brothers took me with them to the inn where most of our guards were staying, to confer with them about the arrangements that had to be made before they could depart for Iolkos. They ordered the innkeeper to provide a lavish meal, everything from freshly caught fish, to roasted lamb, to raisin cakes laced with honey. They also sent messengers to the other inns, carrying word that similar delicacies were to be served to all of our loyal men. They were in the mood to celebrate.

"I *knew* it was a good idea to come to Delphi," Castor declared, splashing more wine into his cup. "The gods themselves wanted us to meet Jason, so they saw to it that our paths crossed. When I return from this voyage, I'll thank them with such a splendid sacrifice that all Sparta will talk about it for years after!"

"We should make an offering before we leave Delphi as well," Polydeuces said. "We can use the gods' favor on the road north to Iolkos. And it's only right that we also give something more to Apollo. The Pythia herself told us that this would happen." He was always the prudent one.

The seniormost soldier at the table spoke up. "Lord Polydeuces, before you leave Delphi, do you want to send word to Sparta, to let your royal parents know why you won't be coming back with the lady Helen?"

Before Polydeuces could say a word, Castor barged in. He'd been drinking two cups of wine to his twin's one all through the meal. "No need for that. This wonderful news should reach them only from our lovely little sister's lips. You'll tell them, won't you, Helen? Tell Father and Mother all about how we first earned glory on the hunt in Calydon and how now we're off to secure our names as heroes by bringing the Golden Fleece!"

I looked up from my plate. My brothers had

heaped it with all the finest pieces of meat, the whitest cheeses, the plumpest olives, and the best-baked breads. I'd taken two bites before I lost my appetite. "Bringing back the Golden Fleece," I repeated, mocking him. "As if it exists."

Castor frowned. "What's biting *you*? Of course it exists! We told you what Jason said. It belonged to a marvelous ram sent by the gods to rescue two royal children, Phrixus and Helle, from their murderous stepmother. A pity it wasn't a perfect rescue. Phrixus reached Colchis safely, but his sister, Helle, fell off in mid-flight and drowned. Jason says that's why the place where she plunged into the sea's called the Hellespont. If that doesn't prove the story's true, what *will* satisfy you?"

"Anyone can give a place a name," I said, rolling my eyes. "When I get home, I'll name that olive grove near our training ground Wolf Forest and see what happens. A ram with a fleece of real gold, a *flying* ram that could carry the children through the skies to Colchis, where there are dragons, oh yes, *that's* believable! *That's* worth risking your lives for on a voyage across the world! I'll bet you don't care if that story's true or not. You just want an excuse to go off chasing fame!"

Polydeuces set a honey cake on my already brimming plate. "There must be something waiting for us in Colchis, little sister," he said gently. "Maybe not the gold fleece of a flying ram, but *something*. Why would Jason go to the trouble and expense of outfitting a ship for such a long, dangerous voyage otherwise?" He smiled wistfully and added, "You mustn't worry about us. We'll come back; we'll be fine."

He was right: I was worried about what would become of my brothers on that great adventure. But more than that, I envied them with all my heart. So what if the goal of their expedition was the phantom fleece of a ram that never existed? The fascinating lands my brothers would see and the exploits they'd share would be real enough. And I'd be left behind.

*They'll see marvels I can't begin to imagine,* I thought. *Maybe they'll even see that old sailor's five-legged monster! Meanwhile, I'm going to be trundled home in an oxcart so thickly hedged around by Spartan soldiers that all I'll see during my journey will be spears. It's not fair! I can handle a sword almost as well as either of them, and I know I'm better with a bow and arrow!*

My brothers left Delphi early the next morning. They left their traveling chests behind, to be carted back to Sparta along with me. Each carried only his weapons, a waterskin, a cloak, and a small leather sack of personal possessions. We said farewell at the temple gateway, with just one of our soldiers there to witness it and attend me. Prince Jason and the other heroes he'd already recruited weren't there; Castor told me that they were waiting for my brothers to join them on the road that led north out of the city.

"This trip would be a lot easier if we had weapons bearers coming with us," he grumbled, toeing his waiting pile of belongings. He looked rumpled, red-eyed, and hurting, not much of a surprise after all he'd had to drink the previous night. "You'd think every lad in Delphi would jump at the chance to join us on a fabulous quest like this."

"We'll have weapons bearers when we reach our quest's start at Iolkos," Polydeuces told him. "Maybe before. We'll pass through many cities before we reach Iolkos. Jason hasn't completed his crew yet."

"I still don't see why we can't find any *now*," Castor persisted. "It's a fine opportunity for any boy who hopes to be a warrior someday. They can't *all* have kinsmen to teach them about the warrior's life and how to fight. We'd see to it that they learn how to use the sword and spear and shield they carry for us."

"You don't have shields," I pointed out.

"We'll get them in Iolkos!" Castor snapped, then winced and cradled his head tenderly in one hand. "Just as well I don't have a shield yet: If that scrawny boy'd had the sense to become my weapons bearer, the weight of it would've crushed him."

"*What* scrawny boy?" I asked.

"Someone with no stomach for adventure, that's

all," Polydeuces said, resting one hand on my shoulder. "Not like us, eh, Helen?"

I'd meant to be cool and dignified about our leave-taking, wanting my brothers to remember me as a young woman, not a silly little girl. My intentions shattered the instant Polydeuces touched me and I realized that this might be the last time I'd ever see him or Castor alive. I burst into tears and held on to him fiercely.

"Don't go," I whispered.

"Shhh, Helen, shhh." He stroked my back. "We'll be fine, you'll see. When we come home, I'll bring back a tuft of gold from the fleece, just for you."

"Tell the truth, little sister," Castor said, tugging a lock of my hair lightly. "You're upset not because we're going but because you're returning home." He laughed as he swept me away from Polydeuces into his own strong embrace.

I gave him a hug and a kiss before pushing him away and declaring, "If I *did* want to go running off after an imaginary dead sheep, do you think you could stop me? You remember how well *that* worked when you didn't want Glaucus to teach me how to use weapons."

"Oh, I learned my lesson there," Castor replied, feigning humility. "I know better now. If you wanted to win the Golden Fleece, I'm sure you'd find a way to reach Colchis long before we do. No one can stand in *your* way; no one would dare. Now that *that's* settled, how about one last hug to see us off? Come on, let's see if you can crack a rib or two for me, Frog-face!"

I thought I'd smother when both my brothers threw their arms around me. When they let me go and started down the street, I stood stone-faced until they were out of sight. Then, without bothering to see if my guard followed, I raced back to my room on the temple grounds and crumpled to the floor at the foot of my bed, sobbing.

I was still crying when a shadow fell across my bed. I looked up to see the Pythia, her moon-white face serene and comforting. She sat down beside me on the tiles and took my hand. "They'll be fine."

"That's what *they* said," I responded, trying to smile as I wiped away tears with my free hand. "When you say it, is it a prophecy or are you just trying to make me feel better?"

Her lips curved up. "If it were a prophecy, you'd have to make an offering to Apollo first. You know the rules." She was pleased when her joke cheered me up a little. Then she added, "When do you leave, Helen?"

"The day after tomorrow. I'm surprised you didn't know. I'm being hauled down to the port, loaded onto a ship, carried to Corinth, then piled into an oxcart and sent home."

"You make it sound like you're cargo."

"That's what I feel like." I clasped my arms around my updrawn knees and rested my chin there. "I wish you could stay with me until then, Eunike. I miss my brothers already, teasing and all, but it hurts less when I can talk to someone."

The Pythia's green eyes filled with regret. "I'd be happy to stay, Helen, but I'd be poor company. I have to be ready to answer at any time that the god calls to me. My life's not my own."

"I know what that feels like," I said.

My friend stood up and stretched. "Maybe I can't help you, but someone else can. I have to go." And, that simply, she was gone. *Everyone leaves me behind*, I thought.

Not long after, as I sat sunk in lonely misery, I heard soft footsteps behind me and a voice I knew well. "Lady Helen?" Milo stood in the doorway of my room, looking unsure of his welcome. The old priest who'd carried the fly whisk was with him.

"Go on, boy, it's all right," he said, giving Milo a gentle push forward. To me he said, "Your servant will be permitted to stay within the temple grounds, to escort and attend you wherever you choose to go during your remaining time in Delphi. Your guards and my fellow priests here have been informed of this."

"And they didn't object?" I asked. I didn't want to get my hopes up and then find out that Eunike's decision could be overruled by someone else. "No one objected, not even the other priests?"

The old man shrugged. "What would be the use of their objections? The Pythia has spoken."

I raised my hands in reverence. "Bless the Pythia," I said solemnly, holding back my joyful smile.

## 15

# THE PLOTTERS
# AND THE PLAN

The following day, my last full day in Delphi, I woke up at dawn, determined to take advantage of the precious gift that Eunike had given me. Apollo's shrine was already busy. The sun god's servants always rose to greet their divine master's first appearance in the east. Milo was up with the rest of them, having been given sleeping space with the shrine's other male servants.

"What can I do for you, Lady Helen?" he said happily. "Bring you something to eat? Clean your room? Get your things ready for tomorrow?"

"Come with me somewhere that isn't inside city walls, Milo," I said. "Delphi's amazing, but I miss seeing trees."

Milo flew to fulfill my wishes, and soon, with some helpful information from the old priest, the two

of us were sitting under an oak tree not too far beyond the gates of Delphi. A pair of our Spartan soldiers loitered in the shadow of the city walls, keeping
watch over me at a distance, but if I turned away I
could pretend they weren't there. For a time I just sat,
feeling the warm breeze on my face and listening to
the song of the leaves overhead. I'd once heard a visitor to Sparta tell about his trip to Zeus's oracle at
Dodona, where the god spoke to mortals through the
rustling branches of his sacred oak trees.

*If I really were Zeus's daughter, would he speak to me that
way?* I mused. *Would he even listen?*

It was good to be there with Milo. When had I
stopped thinking of him as merely the slave boy I'd
freed and started thinking of him as a friend? The
question was, did he think about me in the same way?
I didn't know how to tell. I'd never had many friends,
not even back home in Sparta. When I wasn't spending time with my brothers and sister, I preferred to
keep to myself or to practice the lessons Glaucus gave
me rather than share the company of the nobles'
daughters. Those girls and I had nothing to talk
about.

It was different with Atalanta and Eunike. I could
talk to them, but with Atalanta gone and Eunike so
busy, I'd have to look elsewhere for friendship. That
left Milo. He'd proved his devotion to me that day
in the wineshop, but did he distract the soldiers just

because I'd told him to or because he really wanted to help me? I glanced his way, watching the dappled shadows of the oak leaves play across his face. He saw me looking at him and smiled.

"Do you need anything, Lady Helen?" he asked. (Would he laugh if I said, "A friend"?)

"No thanks, Milo. It's just nice to be out here, lazing in the shade. There'll be no more time for it once we get on the road tomorrow. It's a long, long way back to Sparta." I sighed loudly.

Milo sat up attentively at the sound. "Why are you troubled, Lady Helen?" he asked. "Aren't you happy to be going home?"

"I am," I replied. "And I'm not. I'm sorry if that sounds like nonsense."

"Not to me," Milo said. "When Calydon was my home, I was happy to be there with my mother, but even then I wished I had the freedom to go elsewhere. The palace kept me safe, but it also kept me imprisoned." He peeled a bit of bark from the oak's root. "After my mother died, it became a cage."

"Things will be different for you when we reach Sparta," I said. "I promise."

He looked at me closely. "Except you don't want to go back there. You want to go to Iolkos and sail on to Colchis with your brothers."

"Who are you, the Pythia?" I said. "How do you know where I want to go?"

"It's where I'd go, if I could." He twirled the strip of bark idly between his fingers. "When I used to sneak away from the palace in order to bring things to the lady Atalanta, she'd thank me with tales about her travels, her exploits, all the places she'd seen. I'd repeat those stories to myself all the way back to the citadel gates, pretending I was the one who'd done those deeds and seen those sights. She talked about you too. Whenever she finished telling one of her stories, she'd always say, 'I wish Helen could have been there with me. She'd have enjoyed it! That girl's as hungry for adventure as I am.'"

"She said that about me?" I leaned toward him, eager to hear more.

Milo nodded. "She said that until she met you, she thought she was the only woman alive who'd ever wanted something more than a husband, a family, and a hearth fire. Was she wrong?"

I shook my head. "I hate it that my brothers are sending me home like a bundle of old clothes. I've had the same training from the same weapons master they did, even if they had a few extra years of lessons. I know how to handle a sword, how to use a bow, how to hunt and ride. I never used a boar spear before we went to Calydon, but I learned how. *I* should be on the road to Iolkos with them!"

"Yes, you should," Milo said in his sensible, soft-spoken way. "Lady Helen, I know what you did on the boar hunt. You were wonderful. But if you went to Prince Jason and told him how you were trained to fight just like your brothers, how you were taught to hunt and ride, if you found people to tell the prince about all your deeds during the boar hunt and showed him the trophy Atalanta gave you with the boar's blood still on it"—he took a deep breath and looked at me steadily before concluding—"what do you think he'd say?"

We both knew the answer to that, but I had to say it. "That I shouldn't bother about any fleece, golden or not, unless I was going to spin it into thread for weaving." I hit the tree trunk with my fist. "It's not fair, and there's nothing I can do about it."

"It's probably better this way," Milo said, gazing up into the tree's leafy crown. "Maybe if you were older—"

"Most of the men are taking weapons bearers with them. You can't expect *heroes* to fetch and carry and clean up after themselves. I saw those boys in my uncle's palace, before the great boar hunt. Some of them were younger than me!" I slumped against the oak and sighed again. "I could have gone with my brothers and done that kind of work for them from here to Colchis! They didn't have to leave here without even *one* weapons bearer to serve them while they chased after the fleece. Castor said that no one in Delphi wanted the opportunity that you or I would die to have."

"Why didn't they ask two of the guards to go with them?" Milo asked.

"A soldier's not a servant," I told him. "The most loyal Spartan warrior would be insulted if he was asked to be a weapons bearer, even for a prince. It looks like Castor and Polydeuces will have to take care of themselves."

Milo looked away from me. I was puzzled by this sudden shyness and tried to catch his eye, but he deliberately avoided my gaze. He reeked of guilty secrets.

"You're the one," I said. "You're the scrawn—the boy Castor asked to go with him." His silence was the same as shouting *Yes!* I knew it. "You just told me you *wanted* to join the quest for the fleece. You could have done it: Why didn't you?"

"I couldn't," he mumbled.

"Why not? Because it's safer to talk about dreams than to try making them real? What are you so afraid of?"

*"Nothing!"* He yelled so fiercely that a pair of oxen grazing in a nearby field snorted and moved farther away from us. It was the first time I ever saw fire in Milo's eyes. "I'm no coward. That's not why I wouldn't go with your brothers. I have to go with *you.*"

"Who said so? You're *free* now, Milo. Don't you know what that means? You can come and go anywhere you like. You ought to appreciate it."

"I appreciate *you*, Lady Helen!" Once Milo raised his voice, he couldn't stop. He shouted so loudly that the two oxen trotted to the far side of the pasture as fast as they could move their massive bodies. "You're the one who gave me my freedom. If I live to be fifty, I'll never be able to repay you!"

Milo's uproar attracted the attention of the two guards, but I waved them back when I saw them coming toward us. "Do you think you could be grateful *quietly?*" I asked. "This is between us, not us and all Delphi. You owe me nothing. Listen, if you leave now, you might still be able to catch up to my brothers. I'll ask the Pythia for help. There must be at least *one* of Apollo's pilgrims heading north today, one who's going on horseback. If she tells him to carry you with him, you'll overtake Prince Jason's party in no time! I'll give you whatever you'll need for the road and—"

"Then I *will* be in your debt," Milo countered. "If you say I'm free, why aren't I free to stay with you, if that's what I want?"

"Because it's *stupid!*" I forgot my own caution about keeping our voices low. I'd decided that if I couldn't win our argument with facts, I'd do it with volume. "Don't you see, Milo? This is a better opportunity than anything that's waiting for you in Sparta! What could you become if you went there? A potter, a tanner, a metalsmith, maybe a farmer's boy or a shepherd. But if you sail to Colchis with my brothers, you could be—"

"Seasick," Milo finished for me.

I raised my eyebrows. "Is *that* why you won't go? Not even if it means passing up a once-in-a-lifetime chance for adventure? For a *real* future? I'm disappointed."

Milo folded his arms. "Why don't you just *command* me not to be seasick? *Command* me to go away and leave you, while you're at it. *Command* me to join your brothers. It's not what I want, but I guess that doesn't matter after all."

I was about to launch into another list of reasons why he should rush after my brothers when his words stopped me. *Lord Oeneus was open-handed with commands, I thought. And it was worse for Milo when his hand closed into a fist. I shouldn't bully Milo into joining the quest for the fleece just because I wish I could do it myself.*

In that instant, a happy inspiration struck me with the force of one of Zeus's own thunderbolts: *Why can't I?* I found an unripe acorn lying on the ground beside me and flicked it at Milo.

"All right," I told him. "You win. You can stay with me." A look of utter relief spread across his face until I added, "But I win too. You're going to go with my brothers."

"But how can I do that if—?"

"And so am I."

Milo and I went back to Delphi, back to Apollo's shrine. While Milo waited in the portico outside my room, I dove into the baggage my brothers had left behind. It didn't take me long to find enough clothing for the trip ahead. Castor and Polydeuces were traveling light and had taken their newer garments and their best sandals, but I was still able to scrounge up a couple of tunics, a spare loinwrap, and the much-used pair of sandals that Castor had abandoned. Leaving the sandals aside, I spread a spare blanket from my own chest on the floor and on top of it laid out all the things I'd taken plus the riding garment Atalanta had given me. When the clothes were in place, I fetched the spearhead from the great boar hunt from my own chest. I placed it at one edge of the blanket, then rolled the whole thing up and tied it with leather lacings.

Before I hid this package back in my chest, on top of my sword, I had to dig out the tunic I'd worn on the boar hunt. I'd kept it at the very bottom of my traveling chest, folded inside a cloak. It still stank of blood and sweat. When would I have had the chance to get it cleaned? I was lucky that the smell hadn't gotten into the rest of my clothes. But it didn't matter now. In fact, it was a good thing, adding to the illusion I was building. I exchanged my dress for that reeking garment, clubbed back my hair, smeared my face with a dab of olive oil from the clay lamp on my table with a little dirt from the floor mixed in, then decided to add an extra touch of soot from the lamp's blackened wick. I had a passing worry that I might have overdone the whole business of hiding my face with a mask of grime, but I shrugged it off. *More's better than less,* I thought. *And safer.*

I stuck my head around the doorpost and softly whistled to get Milo's attention. "Well, what do you think?" I asked. "Am I ready to go see the Pythia?"

"Lady Helen, why did you have to change yourself like that?" Milo asked. "Why couldn't you just go to see the Pythia as you really are? It would be easier. No one would stop you."

"I don't care if I'm stopped, just if I'm recognized. I need to test this." I indicated my filthy new appearance. "If I can't reach the Pythia without someone saying, *Look at the crazy Spartan girl, running around Apollo's shrine dressed like that!* then I might as well go home."

"But if they think you're a grubby *boy* it'll be all right?" Milo asked dubiously.

I grinned at him. "Now you've got it."

He still wasn't convinced that I'd made a good plan. "Maybe I should try to bring the Pythia here to see you, Lady Helen," he said. "Even if you can pass for a boy, you look *too* grubby for anyone to believe you've got an audience with her. What if one of the priests thinks you're a beggar and throws you off the temple grounds before you find her? You might not be able to get back in, looking like that."

"You worry too much, Milo," I told him.

"Lady Helen, wait!" he called out as I turned to go. He thrust the water jug into my hands. When I gave him a questioning look, he said, "If you look like you're running an errand for your master, no one stops you. They look at you, but they don't *see*."

His inventiveness left me openmouthed with admiration. "Milo, that's *brilliant*."

He blushed at the compliment. "It's no great skill to be invisible in a palace." He folded the blanket from my bed so that he'd have something to carry as well, and we left.

Between my new appearance and Milo's ruse, we found Eunike without any of Apollo's priests or servants challenging us. She was just coming out of a room at the very back of the temple when we spied her. Milo was right, it *would* have looked suspicious if someone as dirty as I dared to approach the holy Pythia. That was why he scampered up to her and fell to his knees, holding out the blanket as if it were something she'd sent for. Eunike had a quick and clever mind. She recognized him immediately and pretended to inspect the folded cloth, giving the two of them the opportunity to exchange a few swiftly whispered words.

Abruptly, she straightened up. "You useless thing, I asked for a *brown* blanket. Bring it to my room at once and don't you *dare* to dawdle!" She turned on her heel and strode off, leaving Milo to scurry back to me.

Milo knew where Eunike's room was, thanks to the short time he'd spent among the temple servants. They didn't want to have him wandering lost, so they'd taught him how to find his way everywhere within the shrine walls. He had no trouble bringing me there. It was a small, neat chamber tucked away in an obscure corner of the temple precincts. The kitchen herb beds were within sight of her door. When we entered, the pungent fragrance of rosemary, basil, and bay leaf followed us.

I couldn't help looking around doubtfully at the undecorated walls and floor, the plain red-clay water jug and cup on the table, the patternless blanket on the bed where the Pythia now sat regarding us. Four large, painted wooden chests lined up against the walls provided just a touch of fading color. The only luxuries were a splendid bronze mirror and the alabaster pots holding the kohl and carmine to paint her lips and eyes, all sharing space with the homely cup and jug on the table. I'd expected something more extravagant, a setting worthy of the Pythia's divine gift.

Eunike seemed able to read my thoughts as well as the future. "It doesn't have to be fancy here," she said. "This is the way I like it. Now come sit down and tell me why you're dressed like that."

Milo sank to the floor at her feet, cross-legged, while I sat on the bed beside her. She caught one whiff of my clothes, wrinkled her nose, and slid as far away from me as possible. "I'm sorry about the smell, but it's part of my plan," I told her. Suddenly I was embarrassed by how badly my tunic reeked, and I had to say something to save face.

"What plan? To empty Delphi? By Apollo, Helen, I spend the best part of my life surrounded by the smoke of braziers, inhaling harsh fumes from the heart of the earth, and even *I* can barely stand to smell you!"

"And that means no one else will want to linger near me for too long either," I said. "It's all I want, at least until Milo and I are well away from this city." And I began to tell her what I had in mind.

"A weapons bearer?" Eyes wide with incredulity, the Pythia interrupted me before I was done. "You're going to try passing yourself off as a *weapons bearer* in order to reach Iolkos?"

"We *both* are," I said, indicating Milo. "Every hero

needs one, so it makes sense that my brothers would need two." I sprang up and struck a pleading pose, speaking to an imaginary traveler. "May the gods favor you, good sir, can you help us get to Iolkos? My friend and I are following our masters, Castor and Polydeuces, the Spartan princes. We were separated on the road when Milo here fell ill." Milo coughed dutifully from the floor, then looked to me for approval.

"And what if you happen to meet your brothers *before* any of you reach Iolkos?" Eunike asked. "Would you like me to breathe the god's breath and tell you how pleased they'll be, or can you guess?"

"Oh, I already thought of that," I replied breezily. "We'll be careful enough to let Castor and Polydeuces stay well ahead of us on the road. My brothers can't be the only heroes who've joined the fleece quest without weapons bearers of their own. Once we get to Iolkos, we'll surely be able to find at least two men looking to hire servants. They'll be glad to have us."

"Probably gladder than you know."

"What do you mean?" I asked.

The Pythia pressed her palms together and tapped her fingertips to her lips in thought. "Helen, what if your disguise fails? What if someone finds out you're a girl?"

I went over to her table and picked up the bronze mirror. It was smaller than the one Mother owned but in better condition. I could see my reflection perfectly.

In spite of what Theseus had said about "that pretty face of yours," all that met *my* eyes was angles and awkwardness. My over-eager application of olive oil and dirt was already making the skin erupt into angry red bumps. I couldn't see anything feminine about me at all.

I set the mirror back down. "Unless someone demands that I grow a beard on command, I'll be safe enough, Eunike. And I do have a sword and know how to use it."

"That's not what I mean," she said. "I'm talking about women's matters."

"Women's—"

"And the moon. What I mean is the time each month when—"

"I know, I know!" I exclaimed, stopping her before she could say any more. My cheeks burned. "My nurse, Ione, told my sister and me all about that when we were ten years old. Mother repeated all of it right before my sister left Sparta to marry. They both told us that this *isn't* something for men to hear." I nodded at Milo. He looked disappointed.

"Men know more about women than you think," Eunike said. "But since you're already so knowledgeable, how *are* you going to manage to hide it when you're on the road and you—"

"I won't," I said sharply. "It hasn't happened to me yet. I don't know why. My sister, my *twin*, she's been a woman for at least two years. I'm still a girl." I hated recalling how Clytemnestra had lorded it over me when she'd changed and I'd stayed the same. Worse, every month after that she made it a point to ask me whether "it" had happened to me yet, and every month I had to say no. Ione told me not to fret, that every woman walked the same path eventually, that it would come to me before I knew it. I was still waiting.

"Hmmm." The Pythia was silent for a time, then said, "This may be a blessing for you, Helen. It might even be an omen, a sign from the gods to let you know they want you to succeed."

"Do you really think so?" I asked eagerly. *About time my monthly humiliation did me some good!* I thought.

"It's a shame I can't tell you if it's a blessing that will last," Eunike continued. "The gods might whisk away their favor at any time if you offend them. Even if you don't, they might simply change their minds one day. You'd better give some thought to what you'll do then."

"Don't worry. I'll come up with something." I spoke with a nonchalance I didn't really feel. *I'll come up with something* was what I'd told myself when I first began to lay my plans for joining the quest for the Golden Fleece. I'd only thought matters through as far as getting Milo and me to Iolkos and on board Prince Jason's ship. But how big would that ship be? Would

Milo and I be able to keep ourselves out of my brothers' sight and still manage to serve our new masters? What would happen if our luck ran dry and Castor and Polydeuces recognized us when we were too far out to sea for turning back? I hadn't thought that far ahead. I didn't want to. No matter. *I'll come up with something.*

"Well, at least you're confident," Eunike said. "Even if you are insane." She giggled.

"This is a perfectly reasonable plan of action," I told her, sitting back down on the bed. "We're going to have a magnificent adventure, and I'll pledge a fine sacrifice to all-seeing Apollo when I return."

"But before you go, you want something *from* him, don't you?" Eunike smiled knowingly.

"How did you guess?" I mirrored her smile.

"I never guess," Eunike said with mock seriousness. "*I'm* the Pythia." She squeezed my hand. "And I like you. You've set your heart on this exploit. I doubt I can persuade you to change your mind. I think it would be an insult for me to even try. So instead, I promise to help you. What do you need?"

"Nothing much," I said. "Just Apollo's blessing. What can the all-seeing sun do to give us a successful departure from Delphi?"

"Isn't that the whole purpose of your disguise?" Eunike waved her hand at my overall shabbiness.

"This is to hide my identity once we're on the

road," I replied. "I could escape the temple precincts and the city in my own clothes, if that were all I wanted to do. Simply getting out of Delphi doesn't have me worried half as much as what might happen here *after* I go. I don't want anyone who's left behind to suffer on account of what I've done."

"Who'd suffer?"

"My guards, first of all," I said. "Castor and Polydeuces gave them their orders in detail before they went off with Prince Jason. They're supposed to bring me back to Sparta tomorrow morning, shielding me by sea and land. They'll come here at dawn and send the gatekeeper to fetch Milo and me. What do you think will happen when he comes back to tell them that we're gone? They'll pull this place apart stone by stone, searching."

"You're exaggerating. They wouldn't dare touch Apollo's shrine," Eunike said.

"Maybe not the buildings, but they'll have no qualms about touching the people. If no one can tell them where I've gone, they'll keep knocking innocent people's heads together until they find out or run out of heads! Panic makes people go mad."

"Panic? That's not a word I've heard applied to trained, experienced Spartan soldiers," Eunike remarked. "Are they guards or geese in a thunderstorm?"

"Guards; the guards who'll be punished for my

sake," I replied. "If Father doesn't have them fined or beaten or banished for losing me, they'll still have to live with the shame of having failed him. They're good, loyal men, and I can't ask them to bring my parents word of the tragedy in Calydon *and* that my brothers have gone off to the world's end *and* that I vanished while in their care! I need to *know* they won't be blamed. Please, Eunike, can Apollo let you *see* that future for them?"

"My prophecies come to me according to Apollo's will." The Pythia sighed. "I'm sorry, Helen, but no matter how rich an offering you bring, it's not like ordering a potter to make you a jar that's just the size and shape you want it to be."

"I know." My shoulders slumped. "I was only hoping that just this once . . . Oh, Eunike, I have to find a way around this! I don't want my men to harm your servants or be punished for my disappearance, and above all, I don't want my parents to suffer for one moment on my account."

"You're asking for a lot, Helen," Eunike said gently. "Are you begging me for a prophecy because you're worried about all of those people, or is it something else? Are you having second thoughts about this quest of yours?"

"I *want* to go to Iolkos," I repeated with passion. "To Iolkos, and from there to Colchis, and wherever Prince Jason's ship sails! I want it more than I've ever wanted anything. This may be the last time in my life that I'll have the chance to see the world, to decide to take this road and not that one, to choose whether I walk, or go lumbering along in an oxcart, or ride, or even *fly!* I know it's going to be dangerous, but so is having babies, and everyone expects me to do *that* someday. But if there's no way for me to reach Iolkos except by hurting my parents and the rest, then I—I won't go."

Before Eunike could respond, Milo sprang up, eyes wide with apprehension. "Someone's coming! Lady Helen, quickly!" He grabbed my hand and pulled me down to kneel beside him at the Pythia's feet. "Keep your head bowed," he muttered. "Whoever comes, don't look him in the eye."

I did what Milo told me, fixing my eyes on the tiles. I heard footsteps come shuffling closer and a piping, aged voice calling to the Pythia, asking for permission to enter. She gave it, and the footsteps grew louder. I glimpsed the embroidered hem of a priest's robe out of the corner of my eye.

"Holy Pythia, an embassy from the king of Thebes is here to see you," the priest said. I recognized his voice: He was the good-natured old man who'd carried Eunike's fly whisk. "Will it please you to greet them now?"

"Have them wait for me at the main altar," Eunike said. "I'll see them as soon as I've finished with these two." I saw her point one foot at Milo and me. "They'll be fetching me some things from the town, and you know how it is with boys: They don't pay attention. I have to repeat everything at least four times before it sticks to the straw between their ears."

The old priest chuckled. "Ah, just like I was at their age. The world was filled with so many captivating things, each one *much* more interesting than my responsibilities. Isn't that so, lad?"

I watched in horror as his brown wrinkled hand reached down and cupped my chin, forcing me to meet his gaze. His eyes were bright and clear, with none of the clouding that sometimes blurs the vision of the old. I had nowhere to hide. I could only look up and shiver as I saw how drastically his expression changed the longer he looked at me. The friendly smile dwindled, rapidly replaced by a look of shock and disbelief. *He's recognized me,* I thought. *Farewell, Iolkos! I'm doomed.*

"By Zeus, that *face!*" He gasped and jerked his hand away, wiping it briskly on his robe. "Don't you boys *ever* wash? I swear by the all-seeing sun, if I catch you looking half this filthy the next time you serve the holy Pythia, I'll drag you down to the shore, throw you in the sea, and scrub your skin off with my own two hands."

I ducked my head, muttering a breakneck string of apologies, but he left before I was done. Even the nicest of Apollo's priests had more important things to do than listen to a servant. I heard his steps retreat and fade to silence while I was still speaking.

I raised my head, elated. "Did you see *that*?" I crowed at Milo and Eunike. "He looked right at me, and all he saw was a servant—a servant *boy*!" My heart danced with glee.

"That was all he expected to see," Eunike said. "Haven't you noticed that people don't really *look* at ordinary things? If I told you, 'Look at this apple,' I doubt you'd even *think* of biting it to make sure it wasn't painted clay. Most folk are too busy looking after themselves to ask too many questions; they accept what they're told, as long as it's not something that will make their own lives harder to bear."

I grew thoughtful. "And if they're told something that they believe will make their lives *easier*?"

"Oh, they'll swallow *that* whole and swear it was soaked in honey," Eunike replied. She raised one eyebrow. "Helen, why are you smiling like that? You look even happier than when you were mistaken for a boy. What are you thinking?"

"I'm thinking that the road to Iolkos just laid itself down at my feet."

# 16

# THE PYTHIA HAS SPOKEN

That night, with a fat, nearly full moon dying in the western sky, I stole across the temple grounds to the Pythia's room. I crept along barefoot, my dress tucked up high, my ears alert for the smallest sound. Once, I thought I heard a dog bark. I threw myself into the shadow of a building and held my breath, wildly wondering if the servants who patrolled the temple grounds at night kept dogs with them on their rounds. A good hound would smell me out in an instant. Then the bark came a second time, too weak to have come from nearby, and I could breathe again.

The herb garden outside Eunike's room was thick with fragrance. I stepped on a mint plant and released a fresh burst of scent into the night. Peering through the open doorway, I saw a small oil lamp burning on the table and two figures waiting for me inside. Milo and the Pythia were standing together, deep in urgent discussion, when I joined them. Eunike glanced my way, then went back to arguing with Milo.

"Why *won't* you take this?" she said, holding out her hands. The flickering light of the oil lamp danced over a dagger almost as long as my sword. A pattern of golden leopards and grapevines glimmered down the center of the blackened blade. "You'll need it for the road ahead. You can't go defenseless."

Milo stared at the wonderful weapon. I could see how he longed to accept it, but what he said was: "I told you, I *can't* take it. It's too fine for me to have, even for a little while. If my masters ever found me with something as costly as this, I'd be beaten for stealing."

"Milo, you *have* no masters anymore," I said softly. "And it's a gift, freely given. Do you know how to use it?" He nodded. "Well then, take it. Who ever heard of weapons bearers who didn't have at least one weapon of their own?"

Eunike put the dagger into Milo's hands. He gazed at the blade, fascinated and a little apprehensive. "Holy Pythia, this blade isn't—it isn't an offering someone made? It doesn't belong to the god, does it?"

"It belonged to my father," Eunike replied. "He was a cousin of the king of Corinth and the first to recognize my visions for what they were. He brought me here, to serve Apollo, and left this with me."

"To remember him by?" Milo asked. "Holy Pythia, if that's so, you should keep it."

"I was ten when he left me. If he wanted me to remember him, he could have come back to visit or sent a message in the six years since then." She shrugged, though her eyes were sad. "I know my visions can make people fear me, but I thought my father was braver than that. The dagger's mine to give, Milo. You *will* be glad to have it."

"This is a noble's dagger," Milo said. "It's not for me." He turned his face to me. "But I'll carry it if it will please you, Lady Helen."

Milo's declaration made Eunike cover her mouth and do a bad job of smothering a snicker. I didn't mind so much. I was glad to see her cheerful again.

"Instead of wasting time making fun of me, why don't we get started?" I said. "It'll be dawn before you know it."

"Not before *I* know it," said Eunike. We all laughed at that. Then she went to one of the four large chests and motioned for me to help her lift the lid. Milo dashed ahead of me, removed the heavy lid, and set it silently on the floor all by himself. He might look scrawny, but his life of slavery had given his skinny arms and legs hidden strength. I was impressed.

Eunike rummaged around in the chest and finally pulled out the most splendid, colorful, magnificent gown I'd ever seen, even among all of my parents' royal finery. The flounced skirt must have had at least fifteen tiers, each one vibrant with patterns of red, blue, orange, white, and green, all of them decorated with twinkling gold and silver charms. The tight green bodice was so thickly embroidered with wild roses that it could have fooled a swarm of honeybees.

"Wait outside, Milo," Eunike said before helping me take off my own dress and put on that fantastic garment. The weight was staggering, but she cinched in my waist so tightly with a wide enameled belt that I *had* to stand straight as a spear shaft or I'd snap in two. Once the gown was on, she began adding to my burden with earrings, necklaces, and finally a diadem of beaten gold for my hair.

"Am I ready?" I asked. I yearned to pick up Eunike's mirror and see what I looked like, but she wasn't yet satisfied with what she'd done to me.

"I'll let you know when you're ready," she said, reaching for the pot of kohl on her table. I had to stand perfectly still, not even daring to sneeze and *definitely* not daring to blink while she painted my eyes, then traded kohl for carmine and painted my lips. Last of all, she dug a third jar out of the open chest and told me to put out my hands, palms up. "Henna," she said, tinting my fingertips a deep, rich red, then working the colorful dust through my hair.

She stepped back and considered the results for a while, then nodded. "Yes, that will do; that will do *very* well, I think." She glanced out the open doorway. "And just in time too. Dawn is almost here."

I never did get to see what I looked like in my borrowed glory. Eunike insisted that there wasn't enough time for that. She herded Milo and me out of her room and across the grounds to Apollo's temple. We were climbing the steps when a young priest came out to bar our way.

"Halt! Where do you think you're going?" he demanded. Then he realized whom he was confronting. "Holy Pythia, forgive me, I didn't know you were—" His words froze. He'd seen me. His hands seemed to rise on their own in a gesture of reverence. "Lady, how may I serve you?" he asked in a voice so worshipful it frightened me.

"Summon the others," Eunike snapped at him, yanking his attention away from me. "The god has spoken concerning the lady Helen of Sparta. Tell the gatekeeper to let no visitors enter the sacred ground until I have revealed what I know to you all. The only exception will be the lady Helen's guards, when they come for her. Bring them into the temple the instant that they're here. Go!"

The priest bolted down the temple stairs, and the three of us went up as fast as we could. Eunike hurried

Milo and me into the same small room at the back of the temple where we'd found her yesterday and shut the door behind us. The room had a window set high on one wall. It let in enough of the predawn light for us to be able to see one another's faces dimly.

"I'd ask you to sit down and rest until it's time," Eunike said, waving at the lone chair that was the only piece of furniture in that room. "But I've worn that dress and I know you *can't* sit down in it. You can't even have a sip of water; you'll smear your lip paint."

"I can wait to rest and drink," I said. "How soon do you think everyone will arrive?"

"Soon enough. You know what you're supposed to do?"

"Stand there and look pretty," I said archly. "I ought to know: It's my plan, after all. What about you? Do you know what *you've* got to do?"

"Stand there and speak for the god," Eunike replied just as playfully. Her expression turned suddenly earnest. "But I won't lie, Helen. Remember that. I like you and I want to help you, but I won't, I *can't* dishonor Apollo with lies."

"I wouldn't want you to," I replied.

"Holy Pythia?" Milo ventured. "You would never lie, I know it, but . . . well, just now, when you told the priest you'd had a vision about the lady Helen—"

"I never said I'd had a vision about her," Eunike replied. "I said that the god has spoken concerning her. I didn't say which god or what form his words took or that he'd spoken to *me*. The gods are always speaking to us. Some people are just better listeners."

"It sounds to me as if you've been listening to Hermes the trickster as well as Apollo," I told her fondly.

"And why not? Hermes was an infant when he stole Apollo's cattle and forced them to walk backward into a cave. The backward hoofprints fooled Apollo into thinking that they'd come *out* of that cave and gone who knows where. He finally did catch Hermes at his tricks, but the new god bought Apollo's pardon with the gift of a lyre, an instrument Hermes had created himself from a tortoise's shell. All this on the very day that he was born! Apollo will pardon me too, as long as I don't lie outright."

"May Apollo and Hermes both help you, Lady Helen, and bring you everything you want today," Milo said gravely.

I felt someone give my hand a brief, reassuring touch in the small, dark room. *Milo? No, impossible.* I wouldn't mind if it were him, but I couldn't imagine him finding the courage to do that. *It must have been Eunike*, I thought.

A faint clamor sounded from outside. The Pythia cocked her head, listening as the sound got louder. "They're coming," she said. "We must be waiting for them." She opened the door, directed Milo to take a hiding place behind a pillar in the darkest corner of the temple, and led me forward to stand beside her before Apollo's altar.

The god received his sacrifices on a painted stone slab at the top of three shallow steps. Standing there, I had a wonderful view looking east out of the temple door. The dawn sky was streaked with peach and pink, purple and gold, as the priests brought my Spartan guardsmen into the temple. My men looked extraordinarily ill at ease, as if they were being led into a mountain pass where an enemy army lurked in ambush. They murmured among themselves and darted suspicious glances into every angle, every shadow, every face, including mine.

I met their wary, unhappy looks calmly. In my mind, I pictured the statue of Aphrodite that stood in the rooftop shrine at home, the one I'd loved from childhood. I also thought of the smaller figure of the goddess, the one that the old sailor had carved from a monster's tooth and given to me. I tried to hold myself as coolly and elegantly as those images.

Eunike stepped forward and raised her arms to the dawn. "Hear me, servants of Apollo, men of Sparta!" she cried.

"Silence for Apollo's chosen!" one of the priests called out. "Hear the Pythia!" The murmurs stopped. Somewhere in Delphi, a rooster crowed.

"It has been revealed to me that the lady Helen will not leave Delphi this day," Eunike declared. "She will not go back to Sparta until it pleases Apollo to bless her return. This is how it must be." She lowered her arms. "Men of Sparta, who is your leader?"

The same soldier who'd witnessed my brothers' leave-taking stepped forward. "I am, holy Pythia."

"Hear me, then. You will lead your men home and tell the lady Helen's royal parents what I have told you, that she will not come back to them until it is the will of the gods."

The man bowed his head. "Yes, holy Pythia, I'll do as you say, except . . ." He took a deep breath. "Great lady, *when* will they see the lady Helen's return?"

One of the priests glared at the man. "You question the Pythia?"

My guard returned the priest's scowl redoubled. "I have a daughter, and I know how I'd feel if she were taken from me. I've served Lord Tyndareus and his queen long enough to have seen how dearly they love their children. I ask this for their sake. If that's an offense, let me be the only one to suffer for it."

"Spartan, you are a faithful man; you commit no offense in questioning me," Eunike said. "Tell the lady Helen's parents this as well: that although it will be a year or more before they can hope to see their daughter, they will have frequent word from Delphi to comfort them. Let them be content with that."

With that, Eunike turned her back on the crowd and faced me, holding her hands above my head. "May the all-seeing sun bless you in all your paths, Lady Helen, and bring you safely home."

Later that morning, Eunike, Milo, and I stood in the gateway of Apollo's shrine, watching my guards march away. They raised their spears to me in one last salute as they passed, and though some still looked a little dubious about the whole matter of leaving me behind, most of them were smiling. They believed that the gods had spoken. I was not supposed to be going with them, and that was that. They accepted this unconditionally.

When the last of the Spartans were out of sight, Milo murmured a few words to Eunike and darted back into the temple grounds. "Who lit a fire under him?" I asked.

"He has things to do." She linked her arm in mine and drew me aside far enough to keep our conversation private from the gatekeeper. "He's got to be ready for when you leave tomorrow."

"Thanks to you," I said, squeezing her arm. "Eunike, you were wonderful. Now there's no way that my parents can blame those men for coming home without me. The Pythia foretold it."

"I never foretold a thing," Eunike reminded me. "Can I help it if people expect everything I say to be a prophecy?"

"Not even when you said it was *revealed* to you that I wouldn't be leaving Delphi today?"

"So it was, just not by the gods. *You* told me you'd need one more day to prepare for your journey." She winked at me. She was right. There wasn't a single thing she'd said in the temple that morning that couldn't be interpreted two ways. I *wouldn't* be going home until at least a year had passed. My parents *would* have frequent news from Delphi; it just wasn't going to come from me. And as for *why* I wasn't going back to Sparta with my men, when the Pythia said, *This is how it must be,* no one demanded a more specific reason, because those words came from her lips. My friend controlled an awesome power. She'd used it to help me, but I thanked all the gods that she was too honorable to abuse it for herself.

"Eunike, you should serve Apollo *and* Hermes," I told her. "How can I ever thank you for—?" I clapped my hands to my mouth: A sudden flash of revelation struck me. "The priests!" I exclaimed. "What about the priests? How can I leave for Iolkos tomorrow if they're expecting to see me here, in Apollo's temple, for at least a year to come?"

"Helen, I doubt your father has the power to

punish Apollo's priests for misplacing you," Eunike said calmly.

"And who'll have the power to comfort him and my mother once they find out that *no one* knows where I am?" I countered.

"Well, you can't change your mind about going to Iolkos now—"

"I'm not doing that!" I cried.

"—even if you wanted to," Eunike concluded. "It would make me look like a liar, even when both of us know I'm not. Apollo would *not* be pleased." She planted her hands on my shoulders and steered me back through the temple gates. "Don't worry about it. Prepare for your journey and leave the priests and their expectations to me."

I'd seen how clever Eunike was; I decided to put my confidence in her. She *would* come up with a way for me to leave for Iolkos and stay in Delphi at the same time. I simply couldn't imagine *how* she'd manage it.

That night, I dreamed I was standing beside her at the sun god's altar once more. The temple filled with sparkling golden light, and Apollo himself appeared to us. *I have heard your prayers, my Pythia,* he said to Eunike. His divine voice shook me down to my bones. *I will answer them.*

He touched my head with a branch of laurel, and suddenly there were two Helens standing before the altar. My other self turned to face me, but before I could say anything she grabbed my arms and shook me violently, shouting in my face, *You're not Lady Helen! You never wanted to be Lady Helen! I'm Lady Helen! Say it! Say my name! Lady Helen! Lady Helen!* I tried to ask her, *Then who am I?* but my tongue wouldn't move. And still my other self shook me, crying out, *Lady Helen! Lady Helen!* until I realized that I was awake and Milo was standing over my bed, calling my name.

"Lady Helen, hurry, it's almost dawn, it's time!"

I sent him out of my room while I put on one of my brothers' tunics. It wasn't the foul-smelling one from the hunt; I'd decided to keep that in reserve for only the most dire emergency. I didn't want to draw anyone's attention on the road to Iolkos, and I'd realized that being *too* filthy might have just the opposite effect. I bound back my hair, tied on my sword, draped Castor's old sandals around my neck, picked up my bundle of belongings, and was out the door.

We didn't leave the temple precinct by the front gateway. Because Milo knew the grounds, I let him lead me to a place where the wall was low and a broken gardener's wagon gave us just the bit of extra help we needed to scale it. Once over the wall, Milo guided me carefully through the dark, silent streets until we were clear of the city.

The road we took away from Delphi was easier than the road we'd scaled to reach Apollo's sacred city. Our feet picked up speed on that downward slope. I smelled pine needles, which was nothing remarkable, but I also breathed in the scent of the sea. The longer we walked, the stronger it grew. That shouldn't be: The sea lay *south* of Delphi, and to march to Iolkos I knew we had to take the northern road.

"Milo, are you sure we're going in the right direction?" I asked.

"This is the way we need to go, Lady Helen," he replied, looking back over one shoulder. "She's waiting for us by the shore. She sent for me last night, after the two of you said your good-byes, and told me to bring you to her here this morning."

I didn't have to ask who *she* was. "Why?"

Milo shrugged. "I don't know. I've told you what she told me, Lady Helen."

"Milo, we're going to be traveling together," I said. "Don't call me Lady Helen anymore."

"It would be disrespectful if I only called you Helen, my lady," he said.

"It would be *ridiculous* if you called me Helen. I'm supposed to be a boy, remember? Call me Glaucus."

"Yes, Lady—*Glaucus*," he muttered. I could tell he wasn't happy about it.

*Happy or not, you'd better get used to it, Milo,* I thought. *We've got a long way to go, and this isn't the road that's going to take us there. What's Eunike up to, I wonder?*

She was waiting for us by the sea, standing beside

the smoking embers of a driftwood fire. She was wrapped in a rumpled cape that looked like she'd slept in it. She must have sneaked out of the temple as soon as Milo left her and spent the night on the beach in order to meet us here at this hour. While we'd made the downhill trek from Delphi, the new day had come.

Eunike wasn't waiting alone. A stocky, middle-aged man wearing only a loincloth stood on her left, his skin the same deep brown as his hair. On her right stood—

"Lady Helen," Milo breathed, staring at the girl with Eunike.

At first glance, she did look like me as far as height, weight, and the color of her eyes and hair. She was dressed in the same elaborate gown I'd worn to Apollo's temple, adorned with the same jewelry, her face painted with the same carmine and kohl. But if you didn't allow yourself to be distracted by details, if you really *looked* at her, studied her closely, you could tell she wasn't me.

"Who are these people, Eunike?" I asked, bewildered.

The Pythia beamed. "This good fisherman came to Apollo's shrine years ago, to hear if his daughter here would recover from a fever. The god allowed me to give him good news. Since then, he's felt that he's in my debt, no matter what I say. He and his daughter come to honor Apollo every day, when he's not out at sea, and never empty-handed. While you were in your room yesterday morning, preparing for your journey, I saw them in the temple and realized how closely this girl resembles you. It was as if Apollo himself was giving you the way to stay in Delphi and still seek a *hundred* Golden Fleeces!"

The fisherman stepped forward and raised his hands to me. "The holy Pythia told us what you need, great lady. I've sworn to keep your secret safe, and so has my girl. May Apollo destroy us both if we betray you."

"You can't do this," I told him earnestly. "You can't let your daughter masquerade as me. Think of what could happen to her if she's discovered!"

The fisherman smiled awkwardly, avoiding my eyes. "Great lady, my girl's all I've got, since her mother died birthing her. I don't know what I'd've done if I'd lost her too, when that fever hit. When I serve the Pythia, I serve the god who gave her back to me, and the Pythia says she wants us to help you. Let us."

"I won't let anything happen to this girl, Helen," Eunike said, stepping between the fisherman and me. "Not even if she's found out."

"What do you mean, *if*?" I said. "She might fool someone for a moment, but to pass as me for a year or more? One good look at her—"

"Who'll bother doing that?" Eunike replied smoothly. "How often did Apollo's priests pay any attention to you when you passed them on the temple grounds, let alone *look* at you? Even the servants never really *saw* you. You could be any girl at all to them, as long as that girl dressed like a princess."

"And what if one of them has to *speak* with me?" I demanded. I turned to the fisherman. "Do you think your daughter can *talk* like a princess too?"

"Oh yes, great lady, yes, certainly." He bobbed his head eagerly. "My Alkyone's *very* bossy, when she wants to be."

I saw that I wouldn't be able to talk anyone out of this scheme. The fisherman saw it as the best opportunity he'd ever get to repay Apollo for his daughter's life. His daughter saw it as a dream come true, the chance to live like a princess. They trusted Eunike to save them in case the plan failed, but you could tell by looking at their faces, radiant with confidence, that they refused to believe anything *could* go wrong.

If I wanted to go to Iolkos and then on to Colchis and the Golden Fleece, I'd have to borrow some of that wholehearted faith. I bowed my head and raised my hands to the fisherman's daughter. "Lady Helen, do I have your permission to go?" I asked.

She stood tall and looked down her nose at me, but her lips curved up in a graceful smile. "Go with the blessing of the gods," she said. Her voice was only a little lower than mine. "And with Poseidon's blessing above all." She gestured at the little boat rocking on the waves not far from where we stood on shore.

"No road for you, Helen," Eunike said gaily. "Not yet. This man has promised me to take you as far as Corinth." She patted the fisherman's shoulder. He looked ready to die of joy at receiving such a sign of favor from Apollo's chosen one.

"I'll do better than that!" he declared. "I'll take you all the way to Iolkos, if the gods let me."

We said our farewells and the three of us waded out to his boat. Milo looked as if he were going to his own funeral. Considering what a sorry sailor he was, he might have been right. Once we climbed aboard, he sank down on the deck and buried his head in his hands.

"What's wrong with him?" the fisherman asked me as he prepared to set sail.

"He gets seasick," I told him. "*Badly* seasick."

Our new friend pursed his lips, then went toward the back of the boat and returned carrying a small, sealed clay flask. "Have a swig of this," he said, forcing it into Milo's hands. "It's mostly mint and ginger; settles the stomach. Back that up with a proper sacrifice to Poseidon, and I guarantee you'll think we're sailing over glass."

While Milo sniffed the neck of the flask warily,

then drank, a favorable wind sprang up. The fisherman made haste to set the sail. The painted cloth belled out and we were under way. I waved good-bye to Eunike until a curve of the coast hid her from my sight, then I went to see if there was anything I could do to help the fisherman.

"Help? Bless your kind heart, no," he told me. "I'm used to sailing this sweet girl on my own. You look after your friend and see to it that you don't forget to make that offering to Poseidon, like I said. The gods are watching."

I went back to Milo, but he'd stretched himself out on the boards and had fallen asleep. Maybe there was something stronger than ginger and mint in that little flask, but as long as he wasn't being sick again, I was happy. I left him in peace and walked forward, to the small vessel's prow.

With Milo napping and the fisherman busy, I'd have to come up with an offering to Poseidon on my own. I opened the soft leather pouch at my belt and fished around inside. It was packed with beads of gold, silver, and precious stones. As part of my preparations for this trip, I'd taken apart several of my necklaces, intending to trade them, bead by bead, for supplies on the road.

"Lord Poseidon of the seas, earth shaker, horse tamer, guide my hand," I prayed. "Choose your sacrifice." My fingers closed on what I thought was just another bead, but when I pulled it out into the light, I saw that it was the monster's tooth that the old sailor had carved into the shape of Aphrodite riding a dolphin. Poseidon had made his choice.

I held the little image to my heart. Out of so many possibilities, why had the god chosen this for his sacrifice? Did it mean something? I wished that Eunike were still with me. She was used to understanding divine messages. Aphrodite was born from the ocean's foam and I was giving her back to the sea. Was that a sign that I'd return safely to the place where I'd been born or a warning that the ocean would swallow me up too?

*If I'd never left home, I wouldn't have to tangle my brain over omens,* I thought. *I wouldn't need to worry about my fate, or Milo's, or what will happen if I—if I don't come home at all.* I filled my lungs with briny air and let out my breath slowly. *A rock at the bottom of a well is safe from worries too.*

We were sailing east, into the sun. I raised my arms and called out, "Lord Zeus, ruler of gods and men, even though I'm not your daughter, give me a father's blessing. All-seeing Apollo, give me your light; Athena, lend me your wisdom. Beloved Aphrodite, let Milo and me find only kindness on this journey. Lord Poseidon, grant us a safe voyage and accept this sacrifice!"

I threw the carving of my goddess as high and far

as I could, into the sky above the waves, and watched its arcing path through the air. As it fell, I saw a golden shape come diving toward the plummeting image, a huge eagle that seized the monster's tooth in his talons. The feathers on his breast skimmed the sea before he soared back into the sky and flew away.

"Did you see that, La—Glaucus?" Milo's voice sounded in my ear. He'd woken from his nap and come up behind me unexpectedly. I almost jumped overboard with surprise. "It's a good sign, isn't it? Or is it predicting that something's waiting to snatch *us* away? If that's so, I swear I won't let it touch you. But *is* it a good sign after all? Ah, what does it mean?"

"You worry too much, Milo," I said as if I had no such worries of my own. "If every hero stopped to think about all the what-ifs in his path, none of us would ever take one step beyond our own doorways."

"But you saw what it did," Milo protested. "The eagle is Lord Zeus's bird. We can't just ignore it. Ah, what does it *mean?*"

"What it *means*," I said, smiling, "is that you and I have just seen either the world's most unmistakable omen or the world's most nearsighted eagle." *May the gods stand by us,* I thought as I laughed and Milo stared at me in dismay. *May they favor and guide us, but may they never hold us hostage through our fears.*

"Don't look at me like that," I told him, wiping

sea spray from my eyes. "I haven't said anything wrong. I love the gods and honor them, but I'm not their slave. Neither are you. From now on we're going to make our own omens." I took his hand, and when he pulled it away, I took it again. This time he let me.

We were free.

Don't miss the sequel to

# NOBODY'S PRINCESS

Sailing into bookstores in April 2008

# SOMETHING
# ABOUT HELEN

People have always loved stories. We love them, and when we find one about the adventures of a truly fascinating character, we hate to see it end. For every storyteller who concludes his tale with "And they lived happily ever after," there's always someone in the audience who says, "Great, and *then* what happened?"

Sometimes there *is* nothing more to tell. The dragon is slain, the war is won, the world has been saved from Evil, the main character has fallen off a cliff and *died*, for heaven's sake! After all that, how can there possibly be a "*then* what happened?"

Never underestimate the power of an eager audience, or the desire of a storyteller to keep that audience happy. There can always be another dragon to slay, another war to fight, another world to save, and as for those characters who died at the end of the first story . . . well, it was all a dream, or a trick, or a case of mistaken identity. The sequel will go on!

But what about when the climax of the original story is so awesome that the sequel falls flat because "and *then* what happened?" is a letdown by comparison? Sometimes it's better to have no sequel instead of a lame one. (Though you can always try telling the story of one of the original tale's supporting characters. Spin-offs have been around since long before TV sitcoms, but I don't know if Homer would have liked to think of the *Odyssey* as a spin-off of the *Iliad.*)

Never mind, all's not lost. When a favorite character reaches the unmistakable end of his or her adventures and there's honestly zero chance for coming up with further exploits that are believable and interesting, there's something left to tell: "Well then, what happened *before* that?" Which is just what I asked myself before I began to write about Helen of Troy.

I wanted to tell more of Helen's story than the best-known version, the one that's come down to us in the *Iliad.* Did she *know* that everyone agreed that she was the most beautiful woman in the world? Did knowing that make her feel proud, or smug, or embarrassed, or bored with all the never-ending compliments? ("Yes, yes, I know I'm gorgeous, but what I *asked* you to do was please pass the olives!") Did she *like* being thought of as nothing more than The Beautiful

One? Did she worry about who she'd be when she got old and her beauty faded away? Was she just another (spectacularly) pretty face, or was there more to her than that? Who *was* Helen?

Daughter of the king of Sparta, she was so beautiful that it was said she couldn't possibly be an ordinary woman and that her *real* father was Zeus, king of the Greek gods. What did a story like that imply about her father *or* her mother? Did Helen mind hearing her real parents whispered about in that way?

The Trojan prince Paris fell in love with her at first sight, stole her from her husband, Menelaus, and carried her off to his father's walled city. Was it true love, or was it the work of the gods? Did she go with him willingly, or was she kidnapped? If she didn't want to leave Sparta, did she ever try to get away from her kidnapper? Did she even believe she had the chance of succeeding if she tried to rescue herself?

Menelaus's brother, King Agamemnon of Mykenae, rallied an army led by the greatest kings and heroes in Greece and fought for ten years to reclaim her. Countless men died in battle, the great city of Troy was destroyed and its people slaughtered or enslaved, all because of one beautiful woman. When it was over, Paris was dead and Helen was given back to her husband. The end of her story makes her sound like nothing more than a pretty prize to be awarded to the winner of the Trojan War. Was she heartbroken, furious, frightened, relieved, or did she feel anything at all?

And so she went home to Sparta with Menelaus, which is more or less where Helen's story ends, as far as the Greek writers were concerned. ("Hey, Helen! You just caused a ten-year war and the destruction of one of the world's mightiest cities! What are you going to do *now*?" "I'm going to Disney World!")

Helen's "and *then* what happened?" was pretty well sewn up, but her "well, what happened *before* that?" was wide open. Plenty of her story remained untold, and I wanted to tell it. The only traditional tales about young Helen concern her birth as Zeus's daughter and her abduction by the Athenian hero Theseus when she was still just a girl but already incredibly beautiful. There's no mention of her being at the Calydonian boar hunt, though her brothers, Castor and Polydeuces, were. There's certainly nothing in the old tales about her knowing how to use weapons or hunt or ride. Exploits like these make a good story, but did I have any sound reason for letting her do them?

Oddly enough, though Helen herself is mythological, much of what I've written about her in this book is based on ancient Greek history. Many people used to believe that myth and history had nothing to do with each other. They thought that Troy itself was an imaginary place, like the lost city of Atlantis. Then in 1876, the German amateur archaeologist Heinrich Schliemann was so deeply inspired by the *Iliad* that he decided to search for Troy. He was only a merchant, but a merchant with vision, passion, and an abiding love for a good story. He, too, must have believed that there was more to the tale of the Trojan War than what the *Iliad* had to tell—maybe not "and *then* what happened?" or "what happened *before* that?" but "did it really happen at all?" Using information from that ancient epic, he astonished the world when he uncovered the ruins of a great city on the very spot Homer's poem described. There was even evidence that the city had been destroyed by violence and been burned, just like Helen's Troy.

Since Schliemann's success, we no longer look at myths and legends in the same way. Fantastic stories may contain hidden grains of truth that archaeologists and historians can use to guide them in putting together a more complete picture of the past. Even the sinking of Atlantis might be based on a real event, the volcanic explosion that destroyed most of the Mediterranean island of Thera.

Myths take place in the past, but some of them can be assigned to a *specific* part of the past rather than a vague "once upon a time." Helen's story takes place during the Bronze Age, almost 2,500 years ago. We know this for various reasons, including the fact that the great kingdom of Mykenae, where Agamemnon ruled, flourished during this era. Therefore, the weapons, clothing, food, transportation, royal palaces, and such that appear in this book belong to Bronze Age Greece. Most of what is known about this time comes from archaeological finds, including jewelry, statues, wall paintings, pottery, and sites of major ruins. In addition, some of Homer's descriptions of life in Helen's day make the archaeological evidence come alive.

Helen's era was quite different from what most people think of when they hear the words *ancient Greece.* The Parthenon, the graceful statues, the works of Sophocles, Euripides, Socrates, Aristotle, and Plato, all came nearly a thousand years after Helen's time, during the classical era. In the Bronze Age, no one yet knew how to make brittle iron flexible enough to use for tools and weapons. Art, especially sculpture of the human form, was stiffer and more stylized. Few people could read or write. Instead of signing important papers, you would use a stone seal to leave an impression on clay tablets. The design on the seal would be as unique as a signature. There *was* a kind of writing in Bronze Age Greece, but it was mostly used to keep track of financial matters, such as royal tax records. Messages, poems, songs, and stories were not written down but were memorized and passed along by word of mouth. Inevitably, they'd change when someone with a poor memory or a rich imagination retold them. Money hadn't been invented yet. The first coins were centuries in the future, so Helen lived in a barter economy, with lots of haggling, negotiating, and trading goods for goods instead of paying for them outright.

Though markedly different from Helen's time, there were some aspects of life in classical Greece that influenced me while writing this book. Chiefly, these things concerned the Spartans, who lived a thousand years after Helen. Today we use *Spartan* as an adjective meaning "plain," "austere," "strict," even "harsh." Spartans of classical times were famous for being all of these, as well as being known for their warcraft. At birth, all infants were brought before the elders, who decided whether a child would be allowed to live or be left in the mountains to die from exposure. This decision was based entirely on whether the child looked strong enough to survive. It's hard to think of anything harsher than that. The Spartans' whole way of life seemed to center on physical perfection, endurance, and skill in handling weapons. Most significant was the fact that, unlike other Greeks, they trained their daughters as well as their sons in athletics. The girls ran, wrestled, practiced throwing the javelin or spear, and, like the boys, they exercised unclothed, to strengthen their bodies. Spartan men were frequently away from home for long periods of time, fighting wars. This left Spartan women in charge on the home front. As a result, they were much more independent than other Greek women.

In spite of the centuries separating them, I like to think that the classical Spartans' attitude toward women might have had its roots in Helen's time. There is archaeological evidence that Bronze Age women were powerful and respected, holding important positions in their society. One image, taken from a seal, shows a huntress armed with bow and arrows.

No doubt Greek females could also be independent. Mythology is full of stories about such women, but unfortunately they usually end with some great disaster caused by the woman's independent behavior. Was this the original ending of the story, or was it changed over the course of the centuries and turned into a "lesson" against women's freedom by those who feared it?

I like to think that the part of Helen's story I've told is about not fearing freedom. Freedom wasn't something to take for granted in Helen's time, nor is it now. Slavery was very much a reality of the Bronze Age, classical Greece, and even some parts of the world today. Other kinds of oppression are even more widespread. Little by little, we're challenging and overcoming the attitude that people are *things*. It's not easy work, and accomplishing it means that sometimes we have to become warriors, even when we're told that it's not the path we're expected to follow in life. We do it anyway, because it's the right path.

Helen would approve.

# ABOUT THE
# AUTHOR

Nebula Award winner Esther Friesner is the author of 31 novels and over 150 short stories, including "Thunderbolt" in Random House's *Young Warriors* anthology, which led to the creation of *Nobody's Princess*. She is also the editor of seven popular anthologies. Her works have been published in the United States, the United Kingdom, Japan, Germany, Russia, France, Poland, and Italy. She is also a published poet, a produced playwright, and a onetime advice columnist. Her articles on fiction writing have appeared in *Writer's Market* and Writer's Digest Books.

Besides winning two Nebula Awards in succession for Best Short Story (1995 and 1996), she was a Nebula finalist three times and a Hugo finalist once.

She received the Skylark Award from NESFA and the award for Most Promising New Fantasy Writer of 1986 from *Romantic Times*.

Ms. Friesner's latest publications include *Tempting Fate*; a short story collection, *Death and the Librarian and Other Stories*; and *Turn the Other Chick*, fifth in the popular Chicks in Chainmail series that she created and edits. She is currently working on the sequel to *Nobody's Princess*, titled *Nobody's Prize*.

Educated at Vassar College, receiving a B.A. degree in both Spanish and drama, she went on to receive her M.A. and Ph.D. in Spanish from Yale University, where she taught for a number of years. She is married, the mother of two, harbors cats, and lives in Connecticut.

Ms. Friesner's proudest public-appearance moment came while serving as toastmaster for the 2001 World Science Fiction Convention in Philadelphia, when she took the stage as Rapmaster Toast and, yes, *rapped* before an audience of thousands. And at her age, too. She has promised her children not to do that again.

Maybe.